Pretty Chrysanthemum
and Other Stories

Nancy Lane

OPEN BOOKS

Published by Open Books

Copyright © 2020 by Nancy Lane

Interior design by Siva Ram Maganti

Cover image © momo sama shutterstock.com/g/momosama

ISBN-13: 978-1948598316

*For my husband, Don Lane, who believes in me and likes to
tell everyone what a good writer his wife is.*

Some of the stories in *Pretty Chrysanthemum and Other Stories* first appeared in online publications. "Looking for the Blue Man," "The Bird on Silver Strand," "Mr. Williams' School Bus," "Riley, Redeployed," and "Michael Rourke, The Ladies' Man" appeared in *Fiction on the Web*. "The Fourth Friday in November" appeared in *Mid-American Fiction and Photography*. "The Accidental Life Coach" appeared in *Chantwood Magazine*. "Sycamore Leaves" appeared in *Scarlet Leaf Review*. "The Bird on Silver Strand" was also included in the print anthology, *The Best of Fiction on the Web*.

Contents

Pretty Chrysanthemum

"Where we love is home—home that our feet may leave, but not our hearts."—Oliver Wendell Holmes, Sr.

San Francisco, California – 1923

MAH JING INCHED THROUGH the crowd to find standing room along the street and catch a glimpse of the dancing dragon as it passed, its red, yellow, green, gold, and silver body whirling from side to side to the delight of shrieking children. The boys, in bright-colored shirts, impressed the girls, in red dresses, by taunting the gigantic, undulating dragon. *"Gung hay fat choy!"* the crowd yelled over the sounds of drums and cymbals. Firecrackers lit up the night sky, and thunderous booms tricked old men into ducking, hands covering their heads, until the laughter of the young merrymakers brought them back to Gold Mountain, back from their memories of bandits and warlords in South China.

Jing pulled candies and a red envelope from his pocket. A keen-eyed boy in a yellow shirt darted across the street to accept the candies and the envelope, which contained *lai see*, lucky money. The boy bowed with gratitude and ran after the dragon. When the tall, round man in a Buddha mask, leading the dragon, waved his arms to signal the stroke of midnight, the crowd cheered and blew whistles and horns. The old men covered their ears to the deafening sounds but nodded and smiled toothless grins.

Jing, who had cooked for Chinese and Americans alike during a twenty-hour shift in the run up to New Year's Eve, began the Year of the Pig by dragging himself back to his quarters in a storeroom on the second floor of a wooden building on Washington Street, just above his uncle's restaurant. Before climbing the stairs, he entered through the kitchen's back door to fetch a bamboo bowl of *fu yung dan* he had prepared before going to watch the dragon dance.

He ascended to the storeroom, set the food bowl on his bedside table, and lit a candle. Celebrations on the street continued. Lights popped in the sky behind a sackcloth curtain across the window above Jing's bed, but he thought only of eating and sleeping until he heard a rustling sound, unlike the pops and cheers and horns and whistles from the street, and close at hand, within the storeroom. He heard a scrape, something pushed across a surface. He grabbed a stick, picked up his candle, and looked around the storeroom, listening for more sounds and lifting the candle to illuminate corners from where he had previously chased out cats, rats, and raccoons.

No more sounds, but when he crept behind a row of broken chairs to a cabinet holding drums of cooking oil, he saw the door ajar. Aha, the scrape had been the sound of an oil drum disturbed from its place, not a sound that could be made by the usual varmints. He set the candle on a chair in front of the cabinet and flung the door open, stick held high and ready for any New Year's beast unlucky enough to hide in a confined space. Nothing moved.

By the dim candlelight, Jing discerned dark clothing behind the drums and a child hiding, face pressed against the cabinet back. He dropped his stick, pushed oil drums out of the way, and pulled the child out. The child, with hair chopped short and uneven, wore boy's clothing, all black and too large, and stood rigid and silent, eyes cast down. Jing had never seen him before.

"What are you doing here? Where are you from?" No answer. Jing's eyes darted around the storeroom. He looked for anything to account for the errant intruder but spied only the specter of Trouble. What should he do? He sat the boy upon a broken-back chair and decided to leave a note in the restaurant for his uncle to come to the storeroom on his return from the festivities.

When Jing returned from the restaurant, he found his bowl of *fu yung dan* overturned on the floor, the food gone, not spilled but missing, and chopsticks still on the table, clean and unused. He sprang to the chair where he had left the child. He looked through the cabinet, under the bed, through stacks of linen, in cupboards, behind boxes. He searched throughout the kitchen and restaurant.

Up and down the street, he dashed around celebrants, scanning the small figures still out with their families.

"Jing, I found your note. What is wrong?" Mah Gwan, Jing's uncle, called from a doorway down the street. Jing ran to meet him.

"Uncle, I found a child hiding in the storeroom. He did not speak. When I came down to leave you a note, he ran away. We should find his family."

"Did the child have poorly cut hair," the uncle gestured toward the side of his head, "and black clothing?"

"Yes, Uncle."

Mah Gwan bent close to Jing and whispered, "The girl belongs to the madam of Spofford Alley. The tong looks for her. Do not tell others you saw her."

The tong looks for her—Jing shuddered. Only the bandits and warlords back home rivaled the Chinatown tongs for brutality. Gwan must have heard of the missing girl when he paid the New Year's Eve extortion money to Wu Lung, the tong collector.

Jing wrestled dragons all night in his bed beneath the window, where a shaft of moonlight fell across his blanket. In dreams, he raised the shaft from the bed, wielded it like a sword, and overpowered every fire-spewing beast plunging from the ceiling or springing from the floor. In dreams, he rescued the girl with uneven hair.

Jing worked the noon trade, took an afternoon break, and then worked the supper and after-theatre trades. He often found time before closing to slip into the dining room and chat with frequent last hour guests, including San Francisco residents, Jackson and Sylvia Hopewell.

"You outdo yourself, Jing, every time we stop in," Sylvia said, "or is it just that we've become addicted to your specialties?"

"Making good food is how I show friendship."

"And so you do," Jackson said. He helped Sylvia with her shawl and donned his hat.

After the Hopewells bid goodnight, Jing went back to the kitchen to put away food and utensils. He planned to take a plate of leftover egg rolls upstairs but couldn't find them, nor could he find the bowl of rice soup he had poured from the iron kettle. The plate and bowl had disappeared.

Footsteps—the kitchen door opened. Gwan stepped in, looked

around, and closed the door behind him.

"Is anyone else here?"

"No, Uncle, I am alone."

"Wu Lung asked about the girl from Spofford Alley."

"I have not seen her again."

"If you see her, we must tell Wu Lung."

Jing had not seen her but suspected her presence nearby. After Gwan left, he grabbed boiled eggs from the icebox and carrots from the vegetable bin. He placed half of them on the kitchen counter and took the remainder upstairs.

The Hopewells returned the next evening at their usual late hour. Both artists, he a sculptor and she a portrait painter, Jackson and Sylvia enjoyed citywide recognition as freethinkers and well-connected advocates for social change.

"Jing, what do you think of the Chinatown Squad?" Jackson said. "Sergeant Jack Manion has put the tong on the run. Don't you agree?"

Jing pulled up a chair at the Hopewells' table. "We are getting more business. Maybe Americans feel safer at night in Chinatown than before, but crimes against merchants go on, and the sergeant has not closed down the madams. Do you know Sergeant Manion?"

"He runs in our circles," Sylvia said, "along with a few politicians and judges and patrons of the arts. I predict influential leaders will grant Chinese merchants property rights and freedom to live in other parts of the city."

Jackson frowned. "Let's not get Sylvia started on politics. She brought you a present." Sylvia pulled a book from her handbag and handed it to Jing.

"*The Autocrat at the Breakfast Table,*" Jing read the title. The Hopewells had made it their mission to teach Jing English. In less than a year, he had become proficient in spoken and written English.

"It's by Oliver Wendell Holmes," Sylvia said. "He was a poet, physician, and professor. You'll find Holmes's perspectives interesting. You have come so far, not only in English but in Western ideas."

The book weighed like gold in his hands, a treasure he wanted to deserve. He bowed to both. "Thank you."

Each night, Jing waited for all other workers to leave. He warmed pork and rice, or beef and vegetable, or chow mein. He left a bowl of food on a counter in the kitchen, chopsticks alongside, and took a second bowl upstairs. Each morning, he washed the emptied bowls before others arrived. One morning he found a smooth, flat pebble, the size of a thumbnail, on the counter beside the empty bowl. After that, he found a pebble "payment" each morning.

One night before sleeping, Jing sat in bed, reading by candlelight. When moonlight shone through his window, he pushed aside the sackcloth curtain to better illuminate Holmes's words: "Talking is like playing on the harp; there is as much in laying the hand on the strings to stop their vibrations . . ." He stopped reading. The skin on his arms and the back of his neck prickled. He looked up. A small figure stood at the end of his bed. Jing did not move. The apparition stepped back and melted into deep shadows. He heard no sounds of exit from the storeroom. He checked all corners and inside the oil drums cabinet and found no one. A fitful sleep consumed the remainder of his night.

Produce vendors rolled carts along the street and shouted morning greetings to one another. Their din woke Jing, whose sleepy eyes sprang wide open at the sight of the missing girl, matted hair and dirt-caked clothes, sleeping on the floor. The din roused her, too. She lifted her head, turned toward Jing, and rose to a crouching stance. Her eyes, like those of a cornered alley cat, darted around the room.

Jing unfolded the blanket on his bed and spread it out to drape down to the floor on each side and over the foot of the bed. "Hide under here," Jing whispered. "I will not hurt you, but you must not be seen."

He backed out of the storeroom and returned in minutes with bread and honey. Had anyone seen her near the building? Would Wu Lung come for her? He peeked under the bed. She shrank away from him. He could think of nothing but to keep her hidden.

He worked his shifts and told no one about the girl. She remained hidden but crawled out from under the bed and sat on the floor when they shared food. They also shared a bucket toilet, which Jing emptied into the restaurant flush toilet. He dared not take her to the public bath house, even on a Tuesday morning, restricted to female bathing. She slept in the bed. He slept in a corner on a pile of goatskins he found in a storeroom box.

She spoke in Cantonese but at a level below her years. Jing guessed her to be ten or eleven, but she spoke as a five-year-old.

"Where are you from?" he said.

She shook her head.

"What is your name?"

"Not know."

"How old are you?"

"Not know."

When Jing took his afternoon breaks between shifts, he sat on the bed with the girl and wrote in a bound journal with wooden covers, given to him by another immigrant held at Angel Island. He wrote his hopes for a good life in Gold Mountain. The girl watched him ink the characters. He also wrote of his fear of Wu Lung taking her and his fear of immigration officials deporting him and Gwan because they had lied about being related to one another. He read to her in a whisper as he wrote about his hopes, but when he wrote about his fears, he made up other words to whisper, good words to create a magical story for a little girl.

He wanted her to watch a butterfly emerge from a cocoon, breathe the fragrance of joss sticks outside the joss houses, catch raindrops on her tongue, and sing the songs he learned as a child. But she had to remain unseen and unheard. He watched raindrops on his window roll down and join other raindrops. He remembered torrential rains sweeping his village. The girl's presence opened a floodgate of memories, ones he could not whisper to her because of their violence and pain.

He needed someone to talk to.

The Hopewells, just back from gallery showings in Los Angeles, lingered over their dessert of *laopo bing*, wife cake. Sylvia waved to Jing when he poked his head out from the kitchen. He joined them.

"Commerce and culture flee to Los Angeles," Jackson said. "The City of Angels will someday overshadow San Francisco as the West Coast beacon."

Jackson's words sounded like a jumble. Jing simply nodded.

"You seem distracted," Sylvia said. "Does something trouble you?"

Yes, but which of the hissing dragons in his mind should he expose first? Not about the girl, not yet.

"I have thought about my family, Sylvia. I never told you about my coming to America."

"You didn't seem to want to talk about it, and we didn't want to pry."

Jing looked around the restaurant. The last customers had left. They were alone. He leaned toward the Hopewells and whispered,

"Bandits killed my family. They burned our huts and stole our pigs and chickens." Jing paused to swallow the boulder in his throat. "I lay flat in a rice field. They did not see me. I walked to the next village, where I became the slave of a landowner. I was twelve years old. When I turned seventeen, the landowner sold me to Mah Gwan."

"He sold you to your uncle?" Jackson said.

"Mah Gwan is not my uncle. He is my *paper uncle*. The landowner told me what to say to officials on Angel Island. I told lies to become Mah Jing, Gwan's *paper nephew*. He paid the landowner, and I paid him back double by working for him."

"Mah Gwan and his wife could face deportation for fraud," Jackson said, "and you, too."

"Friends, I am in worse trouble," Jing said. "I have interfered with the tong. Gwan does not know it yet. When he finds out, he may sacrifice me to the tong *and* the immigration officials."

"But wouldn't he get in trouble, too?" Sylvia said.

The dish washer and cashier stepped into the dining room, said goodnight to the trio at the table, and left. Jing waited to hear the door close before he answered.

"If he confesses and pays the right people, he may slip from peril. But I did not tell you all. I fear the tong because I hide a girl who escaped from a madam."

"What will you do with her?" Jackson said.

"I must keep her out of sight. I cannot take her away without someone seeing."

"Can we help you?" Sylvia said.

"I need clothing for her. Hers is dirty and too large. The girl is maybe this high." He threw his hand out about four feet from the floor.

The next day Sylvia brought Jing a leather bag. He took it, along with poultry scissors, pails, towels, soap, and water to the storeroom. The girl watched him draw out the bag contents: a pastel pink dress with white sailor collar, high waistline, and pleated skirt; two pairs of underpants; two pairs of white knee socks; and a pair of pink slippers.

"What for?" she said.

"For you to wear, but first we will fix your hair." Her uneven hair had grown to her shoulders in places and stuck out oddly elsewhere.

She giggled while he washed and towel dried her hair but gasped when he held up the poultry scissors, with their serrated edges. Perhaps she thought of a dragon's teeth, but he had no smooth scissors. She closed her eyes, scrunched her nose, and held her arms across her chest as he snipped. She opened her eyes when he stopped. He leaned back and admired his work. He had tamed her mane, making it all one length, just below her ears. When he left for work, he instructed her to wash herself and put on the new clothes.

The next day, when Jing took his afternoon break between shifts, he sat on the bed with the girl and wrote in his journal. She watched every ink stroke. He stopped writing and read to her about the girl in the pink dress. She held out her collar and patted the skirt pleats.

Bang! The storeroom door burst open. Gwan rushed in and screamed, "Traitor!" A vein stuck out on his forehead. He twitched up and down on his toes. "Dak-Jin saw the girl asleep on the bed when she looked for table decorations. I have to tell Wu Lung. We must say we found her today."

"No, Uncle, I will stand up to him."

"You will be deported and lose the girl anyway."

"Uncle, you will be deported also."

Gwan scowled. Jing stepped back and wished his words could return unsaid. "Please, Uncle, it is best for us to hide her." He waited while Gwan thought. Sweat beaded on his forehead.

Gwan shook his head. "Wu Lung does not know yet, but in time he will come looking for her. Hide her better. I will think of a plan." He glared at the girl.

After Gwan left, the girl turned to Jing, her eyes wide as an owl's. She trembled and sobbed. Jing brushed her hair away from her wet eyes. "Do not shed tears on your new dress. You look so pretty."

"No, no," she screamed. Jing put two fingers to his mouth. She whispered, "I must not be pretty. Men ask for pretty girl."

He held her and rocked back and forth until it was time again for her to hide and him to go downstairs and cook.

The after-theatre crowd, more boisterous than usual, lingered and laughed and ordered more desserts. The waiters darted like hummingbirds. The cooks clanked utensils and filled plates just cleaned, rinsed, and dried by the dish washers.

After closing time, Jing brought a bowl of vegetable soup upstairs to share. He lit a candle in the dark storeroom and clicked his tongue. He clicked again and again. He crouched and reached under the bed. He felt something sticky. In the dim light he saw blood on his fingers. He pulled the girl out, the white sailor collar of her pink dress mottled in red and in her hand, his poultry scissors, the serrated blades smeared with blood. Congealed blood formed around a jagged line down her left cheek from just below her eye to the corner of her mouth. Blood pulsed from the line, spilling across her face onto the floor.

Jing lifted her into his arms and carried her out the door and down the stairs to the soundless street. He crossed to the corner of Waverly Place. A streetlamp illuminated rats scurrying from his footfalls and the footfalls of someone following him. He did not look back but ran a half block to the dark herb shop. Choi Zan, the old herbal doctor, occupied the apartment above the shop with Old Wife, who had stitched many wounds.

Choi Zan motioned toward a table onto which Jing lowered the girl. Old Wife mixed powder and liquid in a cup and coaxed the girl to take a few sips. She held a needle over a candle flame and threaded the needle while the old man washed the girl's wound.

"Go. Do not watch." Old Wife shooed Jing outside.

In the cold darkness in front of the herbal shop, Jing discovered his pursuer. He felt the breath on his ear and heard Gwan's voice. "The street will talk. By afternoon, Wu Lung will come for her."

Jing fell asleep in the stairway and woke to morning light and the clack-clack-clack of carts on the street. He knocked on the apartment door. Choi Zan ushered him inside. Sitting in a chair, her wound laced up, face swollen, eyes open, and gaze unfixed, the girl wore a different dress, clean but tattered.

Jing bent before her and took her hands in his. How delicate her fingers, how slight her wrists—he couldn't reconcile them with her stitched and swollen face, nor could he reconcile her innocence and fragility with the fear and pain she had suffered.

"Who is she?" Choi Zan said.

"I do not know her name or how old she is."

"Old Wife bathed her. She says the girl is thirteen or fourteen. Leave with her now."

Jing peeked out the window to the street below, which still slept except for a few shopkeepers opening doors. Jing wrapped the girl in a sheet and carried her back to the storeroom. He brought her tea and rice soup from the kitchen and propped her up with pillows on the bed.

"Not pretty." She traced the stitches on her face with her finger. "No one will marry me."

He raised her chin in his hand. "I will marry you, but not until you are ready."

"Will you give me your name?"

"Yes, of course. You will be Mah, like me."

"You are Jing. Who am I?"

He thought of the beauty he had seen in Guangdong Province, beauty even in the unyielding lands and ghostly ruins of ransacked villages. A vivid image, one that inspired festivals and celebrations in his homeland, blossomed in his mind's eye. He took her hands in his and whispered in her ear, "Your name is, 'Lai-Guk.'"

Lai-Guk, *Pretty Chrysanthemum*, the flower people wait for. He would wait for his flower to blossom and then marry her. She smiled, whispered the name, and then said it aloud. She giggled at the sound of her name. The little boy beside her giggled, too.

Wu Lung would come soon. Jing knew, but the girl did not. He waited while other cooks prepared the supper dishes. He could not leave her alone. He watched the sky through the storeroom window. Fog grew thick and masked the sun as it descended. He lit his bedside candle.

Jing jumped when Gwan entered the storeroom. "He is coming. I saw him on the street." Gwan bent toward Lai-Guk. She sat up straight and turned her disfigured left cheek toward him. He winced.

He turned to Jing. "She is worthless now. He will slice us with a thousand swords and feed us to sharks in the bay." The color drained from his face. "We must think of something." Poised to say more, Gwan stopped at the sound of boots on the stairs.

Wu Lung kicked the door in. Flickering light from the candle reflected off his shiny, bald head. He glared through eyes as black as deep wells. "Mah Gwan, you make a fool of me. You hid the girl from me."

"No, no" Gwan said. He shook his head and jerked his hands in the air like a puppet on strings. "We just found her. She came last night with a cut. My nephew took her to Choi Zan to heal her face." His head bobbled.

Wu Lung stepped toward Lai-Guk. She shrieked and shrank back from him. He stared at the ragged line on her swollen face and spat on the floor. "No good, no good at all. We will settle this." He grabbed Gwan by the collar and pushed him out the door, following behind. Thumps and thuds reverberated all the way down the stairs.

Jing held Lai-Guk. He wanted her to feel safe although he knew she wasn't. All had changed. He waited, but for what? What would happen next? The silence following the sounds on the stairs melted into the usual sounds from the restaurant and the sounds of customers arriving. He waited.

An hour had passed when Gwan returned to the storeroom alone, his shirt and coat ripped. He sank into a chair. "Jing, you must pay for the girl. Give me all the money you have saved since you finished your debt to me. I will give the money to Wu Lung to pay off the madam."

Jing nodded.

"You must also pay monthly. I will take your wages, let you keep a few coins, and give Wu Lung his due to keep the tong from having the girl deported."

The rest of the evening, Jing sat with Lai-Guk, wrote in his journal, and read to her. When he left for the after-theatre shift, he did not tell her to hide or stay quiet. Chinatown harbored no secrets. He knew by then everyone gossiped about the scar-faced girl in the storeroom above the restaurant.

The Hopewells swept in with other post-midnight diners. Sylvia hugged Jing before he pulled up a chair.

"I worry for you, Jing," she said, "and for the girl, too."

"As long as I pay Wu Lung, we will know no harm."

"Does Wu Lung still collect for the tong?" Jackson said. "The police have gotten the upper hand. I heard many merchants stopped paying extortion money, and some madams have taken their fortunes back to China. Are you certain Wu Lung is not just putting the money in his own pocket?"

"Paying the tong or Wu Lung himself, either way, I protect the girl from being deported."

Jing's and Lai-Guk's new freedom, with daily outside explorations, replaced their days of hiding in the storeroom. On the street with bag in hand, Jing stretched out his arm. Lai-Guk looked in the bag. She giggled and pulled out bits of bread. She waited for Jing to show her something. He took bread pieces in his hand and threw them high. Squawking gulls swarmed above him and caught the prizes in flight. Lai-Guk threw. Bits of bread dropped to the ground, enticing some gulls to sweep low and look, but not risk landing so close to humans. Jing pulled her away to give the gulls space. They swooped, landed, fought, and carried the bread away. Jing and Lai-Guk took turns throwing bread skyward. They laughed, made funny faces, and imitated gull squawks. When the afternoon sun softened, Jing looked at the clock tower on the ferry building. Fog swept in from the bay. They turned and walked back to the restaurant.

Each day as they strolled through Chinatown, passers-by stared at Lai-Guk, but neither she nor Jing reacted to their stares. An acquaintance of Jing's, a worker in the shirt factory on Stockton Street, asked Jing about the girl. Jing introduced her as his sister, as he would introduce her to anyone who asked, although anyone who asked already knew the truth.

In the mornings, before his shift for the lunch trade, Jing taught Lai-Guk. He showed her how to write Cantonese characters, recite numbers, and add and subtract. He told stories about China and sang songs with her. He translated for her words written by Oliver Wendell Holmes, to which she laughed because those words reflected a Western way of life unknown to her.

Jing and Lai-Guk needed little beyond their food and shelter, for which Jing didn't have to pay. Jing discovered his luck at Fan-Tan. He wagered his few coins at the gambling houses above the general merchandise stores on Grant Avenue. If he won big, he bought something bright and new for Lai-Guk.

Jing took care of Lai-Guk and paid for her freedom. He would not become a rich man as some immigrants had, nor even save enough money to book passage back to China as others had. But he and Lai-Guk found treasure in each other. He, orphaned at age twelve, and she, with no family she could remember, became each other's family, and not a *paper family*, but a family of the heart, two birds together in the eye of the storm.

On April 8, 1927, Lai-Guk and Jing stood in the San Francisco City Hall Rotunda, before Judge Franklin Petty and in the presence of

Jackson; Sylvia; Sylvia's sister, Gloria; Gwan; and Gwan's wife, Dak-Jin. Lai-Guk wore a white dress with butterfly embroidery across the bodice. Sylvia had helped her select it and gave it to her as a wedding gift. Jing wore a navy blue suit and vest given to him by Jackson and tailored for Jing's smaller frame. Lai-Guk had picked out a veil, but Jing asked her not to wear it. He wanted to see her pretty face throughout the ceremony.

The night of March 15, 1928, Old Wife and Dak-Jin flanked Lai-Guk on either side of the bed.

"Man is no help now. Go." Old Wife shooed Jing. Her hands flapped toward his face like the wings of a mad hen. Dak-Jin took note and started flapping, too. Jing bent to peek at Lai-Guk, her forehead wet and mouth drawn in pain. Old Wife blocked him, so he went outside and joined Choi Zan downstairs in the doorway of the pawn shop next door.

"What will you name your son?" Choi Zan said.

"Do you know it is a boy?"

"A woman who gets prettier is carrying a boy. Did she get prettier?"

"Yes, so much," Jing said, and his tears flowed at the thought of a son.

After many hours of labor, Lai-Guk gave birth to a son, and Jing named him, "Wendell," in honor of Oliver Wendell Holmes, from whose writings he had learned so much.

Wendell toddled through a bifurcated world. Jing spoke to him in English and explained the ways of Americans and America. He infrequently spoke of far away China. Lai-Guk spoke only Cantonese and sometimes struggled to understand her little boy, whose developing utterances mixed words of both languages and his own neologisms. Lai-Guk delighted in teaching him Chinese customs, especially those centered on New Year's Eve celebrations and his role in taunting the dancing dragon.

Mornings, before Jing went to work, Wendell sat on Jing's lap and watched him ink characters into his journal. Wendell ran his fingers across the wooden journal cover, with its raised, red, Cantonese characters. He fingered the leather cords which held together the covers and the pages inside. He pored over the pages' intricate ink strokes. Jing read to him from the journal, translating into English as he read. He frequently returned to the two pages on which he recounted Wendell's birth and the reason for Wendell's name. He told his son he wanted him to grow up to become a poet, physician, or professor.

Jing brought Wendell with him, starting from age seven, to watch the men gamble at the Fan-Tan parlor. When Jing left with winnings, they stopped on the way home at the confectionery for a treat.

One afternoon, Jing heard footsteps behind them as they left the confectionery. Jing grabbed Wendell's arm. A man stepped beside them.

"Wu Lung watches you," the man whispered.

Jing opened his mouth to question, but the man hurried away. Jing held Wendell's arm more tightly. After leaving Wendell upstairs with Lai-Guk, he confronted Gwan in his apartment behind the restaurant.

"I tell you," Gwan shouted, "Wu Lung comes around like a mad dog, and I throw him his meat." His face reddened. "Twelve years we pay him, and still he is mad and he growls. Do not worry. A growling dog does not bite, he just makes noise. I can handle Wu Lung."

Weeks passed with no more talk of Wu Lung.

"Daddy, Fan-Tan, I want to go."

Jing had not gone to the Fan-Tan parlor in weeks, weeks beset with nightmares—dragons gnashing their teeth, bellowing smoke, hissing, growling, and biting Jing's sword until he woke with his pillow drenched in sweat.

"Take him," Lai-Guk said. "His joy will take your mind from the night monsters."

Jing helped Wendell put on his coat. Wendell ran to the door.

"Wait, son, first say good-bye to your mother."

"Oh, yes, good-bye, Mama."

She hugged and kissed him. "I love you, my son." He squirmed from her embrace.

Jing kissed La-Guk. The boy tugged on his sleeve, grabbed his hand, and pulled him out the door.

Jing most often wagered on number four, but that afternoon he placed all his coins on the number three side of the square.

"Daddy, why three?"

"Son, I think of you and your mother and me. We are three."

Wendell smiled and watched with others as the *tan kun* lifted the inverted bowl repeatedly and removed four buttons at a time from the pile. Wendell stepped from one foot to the other and then jumped up and down when the final batch revealed three buttons.

Jing won more than ever before, enough for treats at the confectionery and a necklace for Lai-Guk.

Wendell picked out candy for them both. He danced out of the store while Jing paid. They walked to a jewelry store where Lai-Guk had admired a long, double-strand, pearl necklace in the storefront window. Father and son emerged from the jewelry store hand-in-hand, with Lai-Guk's prize wrapped in tissue paper and tucked in Jing's inside coat pocket. They hurried back and ascended the stairs.

Jing felt a chill as he opened the door. Wendell skipped into the room ahead of him and stopped. Something was wrong—a pillow from the bed on the floor, the bedside table overturned, no Lai-Guk. Jing called out to her, looked for her, panicked. He told Wendell to sit on the bed and not move.

He ran to Gwan's apartment, but Dak-Jin didn't know where Gwan was. He ran up and down the streets looking for Lai-Guk, Wu Lung, or Gwan. By midnight Gwan had returned home. "Uncle, where is she? What has Wu Lung done?"

Gwan put a hand on Jing's shoulder. "Be calm. They hide her outside of town. We will receive a demand in one week. We will pay for her then."

"But why, Uncle, we pay every month?"

Dak-Jin, standing behind Gwan, shook her head.

"Uncle, you greedy swine! You took my money, but you did not pay Wu Lung."

"No, Jing, I did not know what he would do. I tested him so you might keep your wage."

"Liar, you tested him so *you* might keep my wage!"

Jing could not bear a week waiting. He could not stand a minute without her, but he could only wait. Other cooks filled in for Jing. He would no longer work for his lying uncle. He spent his days consoling Wendell, pulling threads of hope from the air to offer his son. He barely slept or ate. He hid his fears and heartache because a seven-year-old boy missing his mother should not watch his father disintegrate. Five days passed.

At midnight, Jing pulled a blanket up around his sleeping son and slipped outside and down the stairs. He found the Hopewells' Chevrolet Master among the automobiles parked on Washington Street. When they returned to their car after dining, he told them about Lai-Guk's abduction.

"Are you certain Wu Lung will make a deal?" Jackson said. "Do you trust what your uncle says?"

He didn't trust Gwan. He needed the truth and the help of his friends. Sylvia wrote their home address on the back of an art gallery brochure.

"Is my uncle still in the restaurant?"

"Yes," Sylvia said.

"Good, Dak-Jin is alone. I will ask her for the truth."

Dak-Jin came to the door weeping when Jing knocked. "Lai-Guk is on a ship to China," she said. "Two men took her to the Angel Island ferry while you were at Fan-Tan." His wife, his life, his son's mother—in the five days he had waited, she had been taken from Chinatown, subjected to deportation processing, and forced upon a China-bound ship.

When Gwan arrived home, Jing demanded money for passage to China. Gwan took money from a hiding place and gave it to Jing without saying a word.

Jing ducked away from streetlamps as he scurried toward nearby Russian Hill. He feared the police might stop him, a Chinaman outside Chinatown at night. He feared American hooligans more, boys who might delight in beating him for amusement. Fog, as a friend, concealed him, as a foe, conspired with those who might ambush him. He turned up the collar of his dark coat to cover his neck and ears. He hid his hands in the pockets.

At the Hopewell home, Sylvia made tea and Jackson ushered Jing to a breakfast nook.

"I must hurry to China," Jing said. "Lai-Guk will not know what to do. She does not know her family name, her village. She has no money. Someone may enslave her and take her to work in fields far from the port in Canton. I must book passage on the next ship. I may never find her if I get there too late." Those last words crushed him as he spoke them. Jing bowed his head on the table and sobbed.

"Will Wendell go with you?" Sylvia said.

"I want him to grow up in America. If he goes with me, he may not be allowed back. I will be turned away because I lied the first time. The officials may block him because of me and Lai-Guk."

"Yes," Sylvia said, "and the US may at some point block travel to and from China for fear of Communist influence."

"If I leave him here, I may never see him again."

Sylvia nodded. "Jing, we will leave you alone to think what to do." She patted Jackson's arm, and they left the breakfast nook.

Seek Lai-Guk in China, yes, but take Wendell to China or leave him in America? When the Hopewells returned to the breakfast nook, Jing told them, "I will go to China, but I must somehow leave Wendell to grow up in America."

"Jing," Sylvia said, "Jackson and I talked. We will take Wendell into our home if you will allow us to."

"We can raise your son," Jackson said, "and send him to the best schools."

Jing returned to Chinatown from Russian Hill before dawn broke. He ran through the dark streets, burdened with the mission of telling his son the decision he had to make.

Wendell, awake when Jing arrived, sat on the bed and smiled. "Daddy, did you find Mama?" He looked toward the door as if his mother would enter.

"Son, I must go to China to find your mother. You must stay here and live with the Hopewells."

"When will you be back?"

"I may not come back, Wendell."

"Then how will I get to see you and Mama?"

"You may not see us again, son. It is better for you to stay in America."

"No, no, no, Daddy! No, I will go with you. Do not leave me. I will help you find Mama." He slapped his fist on the bed. "Then we will all come back here."

Wendell sobbed. Jing sobbed. They held each other as Lai-Guk and Jing had held each other in times before, like two little birds in the eye of the storm.

The next China-bound ship would leave four days later, one week after the last ship had carried Lai-Guk away. Jackson drove, and Jing sat up front. Sylvia and Wendell sat in back. Jing watched the clock tower in the ferry building as it loomed closer.

Wendell clutched a sackcloth bag in which Jing had packed his possessions to take to his new home in Russian Hill. Jackson pulled up near the ferry building. He and Jing got out. Jing also clutched a sackcloth bag, with his possessions to take to China, the one prize still in his inside coat pocket, Lai-Guk's necklace. Wendell had kissed it good-bye. He also kissed his favorite wooden dragon, the one painted green and yellow, with red eyes. He threw it into his father's sack for him to give to his mother.

Sylvia got out and stood by Jackson. Jing handed her his journal to keep. He kissed Sylvia's cheek and shook Jackson's hand. He leaned into the back seat and kissed Wendell good-bye.

That day in San Francisco in 1935, Mah Jing turned toward the dock and walked away.

Berkeley, California – 1956

Wendell quickens his pace, and the footsteps behind him speed up to match. In his walks between Dwinelle Hall and the Doe Memorial Library, he frequently hears taunts, such as, "Hey, Chink," or "Commie, go back to China." Many assume him to be a Chinese national. Some believe all Chinese to be communists. He has never been to China, and the only person in his life with communist leanings is Sylvia. When Sylvia spoke with him about literature, the arts, economics, or philosophy, she never tried to influence his social or political thinking, but because he had attended only exclusive, private schools through twelfth grade, she warned him about bigots and bullies he would encounter at the University of California.

He takes the library steps two at a time. At the main entrance to the library, he turns to glimpse his menace. Not a menace does he see, but a girl wearing a blue sweater and gray skirt, blonde hair tied back in a ponytail. He has seen her before, in one of the library's reading rooms.

"Sir, please stop. You dropped something." She continues up the steps, stands in front of him, and offers a bundle of folded pages tied together with a string.

He looks down at his leather briefcase, a side pocket hanging open, zipper unzipped. He blanches at the sight of the treasure nearly lost on the sidewalk. He accepts the bundle from the girl and stands still as stone, distracted by the near tragedy of his loss and unable to think of anything to say.

"Hi, I'm Jenny Palinski. I'm a graduate student from the University of Nebraska."

Her smile refocuses his thoughts. "I'm Dr. Mah, Associate Professor, China History. University of Nebraska? Does that make you a

Cornhusker?" He knows it does.

"Yes, but actually a former Cornhusker," she says. "I'm enrolled here now for graduate studies."

"Welcome, Jenny, and thank you. You don't know how much you helped me. Are you going into the library?"

"No, Dr. Mah, I'm headed to Wheeler Hall. I'll probably see you again sometime at the library."

"Wendell"—he should have asked her to call him that. He should delay her long enough to think of somewhere to invite her. But she half turns, waves, and descends the library steps.

He navigates the silent bookshelf aisles and finds his favorite spot at his favorite table in his favorite reading room, perfect light through the tall, west-facing window and only a few other readers in the usually crowded room—his lucky day. He sits with the briefcase beside his chair and pulls over a newspaper discarded on the table, something to pretend to read. He places the tied bundle atop the newspaper and runs his fingers along the string. He will read the five letters in the bundle without untying the string or unfolding the pages. As an undergraduate, and later as a graduate student, the future China History professor often retreated to this same reading room to reconnect with his own history in the pages his father sent from China. He knows their words by heart.

He and Sylvia had sat on the breakfast nook bench. He kicked his legs back and forth and watched Sylvia open the envelope of the first letter she received from his father. She read silently and then read to him:

> I followed false leads. One said he saw a woman with a scar in a village thirty kilometers from the port. I went and found an old woman with a red birthmark. Another told me of someone with a knife mark. I traveled fifty kilometers and found nothing.

At the time, he couldn't understand why his father didn't find his mother. If only his father had let him go with him to China, he would have helped his father look harder. When Sylvia received his father's second letter just four months after the first, he turned his back to Sylvia while she read silently. She grabbed his shoulder and turned him around. "Wend, my dear, he found her! Your father found your mother!"

He pictured his mother and father returning home, and he

convulsed. His tears raced toward a spinning floor. He barely heard Sylvia as she read his father's words aloud:

I am reunited with my wife. I found Lai-Guk in a village seventy kilometers from Canton. Her health is not good. She fell in waters when floods broke the levees. She was brought to the main building with others sick from exposure. I take her place in the fields, work double, and we both remain.

Wendell squints at the newspaper as other readers take places at the table. Good, no one sits next to him on either side or directly across from him. He swallows hard, takes a deep breath, and focuses on the string holding the letters. He always pauses before recalling the words of the third letter Sylvia received:

I have more sadness than the oceans and the heavens can hold. Lai-Guk has died. She sank from me each day in the past six months. I held her when she took her last breath. I returned to Canton to work and save money for passage back to America, back to my son. Some say the US will allow more Chinese immigration because we fight against Japan. My future is uncertain because I may be forced into the military.

Wendell gazes out the tall window in the reading room. Eucalyptus trees surrender their branches to the wind and sway.

His mother swayed beneath the window in the storeroom when she sang the songs his father taught her. He danced with his mother. The last time she would ever embrace him was on the night he insisted on going to the Fan-Tan parlor.

His hopes rested on a vision of his father returning on a ship and bursting through the front door in Russian Hill, but the vision shattered the day Sylvia received an envelope from the postmaster of Guangdong Province. The envelope contained a note addressed to Mrs. Jackson Hopewell and a letter addressed to Mr. Mah Wendell. Sylvia cried and told him his father died at the hands of Japanese fighters in June 1943. She handed him the letter the postmaster said Mah Jing had written in January 1943 and asked for it to be sent to his son in the event his death.

The wind diminishes. The eucalyptus branches still. Wendell recalls his father's last words to him:

Son, live with honor and perseverance and you will find love. Love is the master key that opens the gates of happiness. You will take a wife someday. Remember to protect her above all else. I chose to find my wife in China and leave you, my son, in America. When you are married, you will understand. I hope you never face the same dilemma.

At age fifteen, he didn't understand how his father could leave him.

A heavyset boy bumps the back of Wendell's chair with his book bag as he leaves the table behind where Wendell sits. "Sorry, Chink," he whispers. Wendell ignores the boy. At age twenty-eight, he still does not understand how his father could leave him.

Repetition numbs pain. In his bedroom in the Jackson home in Russian Hill, he read the fifth letter so many times, the paper grew thin, and the folds tore in places. The letter, written by his mother and translated into English by his father, became lost in Canton and somehow arrived years after both parents had passed on. His memory of his mother had faded. He parsed the words in the letter to recreate her essence—her voice, style, expressions, tone, touch, scent, heartbeat.

The wind returns. The eucalyptus branches sway. Wendell can feel his mother's embrace when he recalls her words:

My sweet boy, you are my joy in America and my lost hope in China. I cry for you each day. Your father translates words from my heart. You are always with me. I am always in you when you become a man. You will be like your father and find a wife. Your father found me hiding. We did not know on that day the life and love we know forever. You will not know it on the day your forever comes. Think of me and you will know your heart.

He moves the tied bundle and raises the newspaper in front of his face. "I cry for you each day," his mother said. "Think of me." Each day he thinks of Pretty Chrysanthemum.

The Fourth
Friday in November

In Southern Illinois in 1958, Jim Callahan learned he could take over one of many abandoned houses in the county just by paying the property tax for the year. He drove throughout the county, viewing dilapidated shacks on bare dirt lots.

"There's only one worth getting," Jim told his wife, Lorraine. Their one bedroom apartment had been adequate for Jim and Lorraine and baby Joy on the way. After Joy arrived, Mary came along. They needed a larger home.

"Tell me about it, Jim, please. I'm so excited about moving to a house."

"It needs a lot of work, but nothing I can't handle."

"Can we get it?"

"We've got it. I paid Claude Tilden, the county clerk. He prorated the tax because it'll come due again in November. I gave him thirty-six dollars."

"So it's ours? That's all we have to pay?"

"No, Lorraine, we have to pay the property tax every year. Claude told me how it's supposed to be paid—in person, in Claude's office by two o'clock on the fourth Friday in November."

"Why so complicated?"

"Claude says the county officials want to be fair and give others a crack at a place if the current occupants don't jump through the hoops."

"So, what if you're late?"

"He said after two o'clock, other people can waltz in with the tax money and get your place right out from under you. He puts a notice on your door saying you have sixty days to vacate."

In the next years, Jim labored mornings to replace roof shingles, unstop pipes, unblock the chimney flue, patch dry wall, repair floors, install fans and a baseboard heater, build kitchen cabinets, paint inside and out, plant trees and shrubs, and straighten porch rails. Afternoons, evenings, and weekends, Jim sold encyclopedias door-to-door and used his access to family men to also pitch life insurance.

Jim gave Lorraine grocery money every week. She never asked for more. Spaghetti, tuna casserole, shoe string potatoes, powdered milk, tomato soup. If ground beef went on sale, she baked stuffed bell peppers. Lorraine's frugality helped Jim afford building materials. On the fourth Friday in November in 1958 through 1962, Jim paid the property tax on the best maintained house on the county pay-taxes-only register.

On the third Friday in November 1963, Jim worried his brother-in-law's sudden death, requiring a road trip from his home in Southern Illinois to attend the funeral in Albuquerque, New Mexico, might make him late paying his property tax. Jim's sole sibling, Faye, telephoned from the hospital in Albuquerque, where Alan had died of a heart attack. Jim decided his family, then including third child, Connie, could drive to Albuquerque, console Faye, attend the Tuesday afternoon funeral, and return to Illinois in time for tax day.

The Callahans had been to Albuquerque before, but always in summer. In 1962, on the last visit, Judy showed her cousins the frogs in her friend's yard, and Alan Junior showed them the cat skeleton he had unearthed by the garage. Alan drove the two families to the countryside. They strolled down a hillside to an abandoned coal mining town, with its rows of dead houses. Faye wore a colorful dress Lorraine bought for her through the mail order catalog. Jim snapped pictures of the happy explorers that sunny day.

Late Sunday afternoon, sixteen months after that summer visit, Jim pulled his car into the gravel driveway next to Faye's and Alan's house. Faye, at the front door, held Judy and Alan Junior each by the hand and stared at the darkening sky. Lorraine, carrying two-year-old Connie, ran to Faye. Jim, with eight-year-old Joy and six-year-old Mary, grabbed belongings from the car and trudged up the walk.

Faye released her children's hands and hugged Lorraine. Then she clung to her brother. All went inside. Jim's usually vibrant younger sister resembled a rag doll as she sat with Lorraine in a big, stuffed chair. Jim sat in Alan's recliner. The five children lined up on the sofa.

"The funeral's been moved to Wednesday morning," Faye said.

"Why? What was wrong with Tuesday afternoon?" Jim said.

"Alan's brother, Payton, can't get here before Tuesday night, something about fixing the electrical on the Airstream trailer."

"Faye, I don't know about staying for the funeral if it's on Wednesday," Jim said. "We must get back."

Faye leaned forward in the chair. "I know you have to, Jim. I understand though I wish it were otherwise."

Lorraine sprang up from beside Faye and pulled Jim into the hallway. "Faye needs us to be at the funeral. Payton will be no comfort to her, and his wife won't help with the kids. Jim, you made good time getting here, even with the motel stay in Oklahoma City. We can leave by Wednesday noon." Lorraine paused to calculate. "That gives us fifty hours, gobs of time to get back, no worries."

Lorraine's abiding Pollyanna demeanor annoyed Jim more than raccoon footprints on a freshly-painted porch. How did Lorraine not realize mid-November weather could turn nasty going back? Lorraine's "no worries" vexed Jim, who attributed her optimism to her lack of responsibility. He was the one who had to drive their 1960 Corvair fourteen hundred miles each way because Lorraine hadn't learned to drive a stick shift. The drive home would challenge Jim's skills and stamina while Lorraine would need only to lead the girls in singing "Moon River" and "Sugartime." At times Jim felt he and his wife were not evenly yoked.

"The consequences if we don't get home in time will be devastating," Jim said. "Do you understand, Lorraine?"

"Yes, Jim, we could get evicted. I know that, but it's not going to happen." Lorraine gave Jim what he thought of as her Mother Earth smile—mouth closed and turned up at each end, eyelids fluttering as if telegraphing Morse code to a celestial orb to confirm nothing bad ever happens. Bad things happen and usually on Fridays, Jim thought.

"We'll stay through the funeral, Sis," Jim said on re-entering the living room. "But we absolutely have to leave right after."

Faye bounced up and hugged him. "You're a godsend. This is tough for me, Jim. I need you. You can't know how much it means to me and the kids to have you and Lorraine here." She buried her face in his chest.

Lorraine sent Joy to the car for her "dinner bag," a paper sack with a package of wide egg noodles and cans of tuna and cream of mushroom soup. Twelve-year-old Judy helped Lorraine fix supper. Joy and Mary sat on the floor with seven-year-old Alan Junior and taught him how to play Old Maid. Jim sat with Faye in the big chair, Connie straddling the two of them. After dinner, Lorraine started a load of wash for Faye. Joy and Judy did the dishes and later helped Lorraine hang up the wet clothes in the back porch. Throughout Monday and Tuesday, Lorraine took over meal preparation and cleaning. She used Alan's car, with its automatic transmission, to pick up groceries to fill Faye's refrigerator and pantry.

"Jim," Faye said, "my boy's having a rough time. Your girls helped by playing cards with him. But other than that, he's been curled up in a ball."

"I know what to do," Jim said. He grabbed up Alan Junior and carried him over his shoulder to the car. The motionless boy felt like a dead weight. Jim lowered him into the front passenger seat. The impromptu outing seemed less of a good idea when Alan Junior folded his arms across his chest and bowed his head. Jim didn't know what to say to the silent boy during the ten minute drive to the go-cart track. Jim, Alan, and Alan Junior had rollicked at the track during a hot summer afternoon the year before. Sixteen months later, clouds grayed the sky, a breeze chilled the air, and Alan Junior stood next to Jim at the track entrance, fatherless for the rest of his life. Jim, who had thought he knew what to do, didn't.

Jim ushered Alan Junior to the concession area. "What do you want to eat, son?"

Alan Junior shrugged his shoulders and watched the ground.

Jim bought two corn dogs and two sodas and picked out a table and bench. He ate his corn dog while Alan Junior stared at his. Jim tried to put himself into the mind of a seven-year-old. Did he worry about what life would be like without a father? What could he do to help? He had to try something.

"Son, maybe this coming June your mother could put you on the train and send you up to spend the whole summer with me and Aunt Lorraine and the girls."

Alan Junior looked up. He sniffled, wiped his nose on the cuff of his sleeve, and picked up the corn dog. "I never rode on a real train, Uncle Jim."

"I've only done it once, but it was a lot of fun. It's a long ride from here to Illinois, but I know you'll be able to handle it." Jim, encouraged because the boy had spoken, raked his mind for another good idea. He noticed Alan Junior's eyes sticking to a red go-cart roaring around the track oval. "Once you get to our house, son, you can help me put a go-cart together. I've been thinking about buying one of those kits, but I need a buddy to help me with it. You know, to help me plan it all out, manage the tools for me, help me paint it. Do you want to be that buddy?"

Alan Junior took an exaggerated bite from the corn dog and bobbed his head. He blinked his eyes while chewing and swallowing until he could answer. "I'll be your buddy, Uncle Jim. We can make the best go-cart ever. Then we can ride it all summer long." He took a swig of soda and ran a finger around in an oval on the table.

Something to look forward to, a plan for future happiness—hope—that's what the fatherless boy needed. After three hours, Jim returned with a smiling boy.

"Uncle Jim took me to the go-cart track at Five Points," Alan Junior told his mother. "We ate corn dogs and drank sodas and I rode with Uncle Jim in a red go-cart. Next summer we're gonna build our own go-cart."

Faye's tears spilled. She shook her head. "Brother, you can't know how much I appreciate what you've done for him."

At the funeral Wednesday morning, Faye, dressed in a black suit and black hat with a veil over her eyes, went limp as Jim and Payton helped her to the gravesite. Rain dripped. Mourners clutched black umbrellas placed by cemetery staff beside the green canopy shelter covering the gravesite and row of folding chairs next to it. The pastor delivered his message of comfort and peace and a prayer for Faye, Judy, and Alan Junior to heal softly, holding one another within the eye of the storm.

After the service, Jim escorted Faye from the gravesite. Lorraine took Judy and Alan Junior by their hands, and the Callahan children followed. Lorraine drove the girls back to the house in Alan's car. Jim drove Faye and Alan Junior in his car. By half past eleven, Jim had packed the car for the trip back to Illinois.

"Will you be okay?" Lorraine asked Faye, who had wilted into the bulges of the big chair.

"Yes," Faye said. "I know you have to hurry back. We'll be fine. Payton and Joanne are staying on a couple more days. Thank you for everything."

The whir of the Corvair's rear-mounted engine, along with the monotony of highway scenery, lulled the girls to sleep. Past Amarillo, Texas, Jim pulled over to the highway shoulder for a rest. Lorraine had packed food for their stops. They each ate a sandwich and drank from one of the milk bottles Lorraine had rinsed out and filled with water. Jim pushed his seat back and slept, waking up when the girls finally stirred.

"The weather's holding fine," Lorraine said. "We're getting down the road quickly, no worries."

"No, Lorraine, we're still in the Great Plains. Worries, please! Through cross timbers in Oklahoma and into Missouri we still may run into downed trees and flooding. You can't possibly think we're out of the woods yet."

Lorraine smiled. "Okay, but we still have plenty of time."

"Not if something bad happens."

Near three in the morning Thursday, road weary Jim rolled into the same motel lot where the Callahans had stopped on Saturday night. A gas station and a hamburger drive-in flanked the two-story motel, where a flashing neon sign confirmed a vacancy.

Hours later, a shaft of sunlight peeked between the drawn drape panels in the dimly illuminated motel room. Lorraine pushed the door open with her hip, entering the motel room, hands laden with bags of cheeseburgers, fries, and orange sodas. "Not our usual breakfast, but they do only one menu seven o'clock to midnight."

Jim sprang up in the bed and squinted, fumbling for his watch on the nightstand. Nine twenty. "Gee, Lorraine, why didn't you wake me sooner? We should've been on the road by now."

"You needed the sleep, Jim. No worries, the children are ready to go. Get dressed. We can take the food and sodas with us."

Jim expected to get gas and roll onto the highway before ten o'clock, but he heard only a click when he turned the key in the ignition. He tried again and again, but the engine did not crank. He slapped his hand down on the steering wheel.

"Son of a beehive! The battery's not working. Foo-ey!" Jim always tempered his cursing in front of the girls.

"Good thing we are next to the gas station, Jim. The mechanic can charge the battery and have us on our way."

Six hours later, with a new battery brought in from Amarillo, the Callahans left Oklahoma City. Past Tulsa the road changed: more curves, higher elevation, oak trees here and there, and a view of rolling hills in the distance. Jim, a native of rural Illinois, always felt uneasy crossing the Great Plains, as if exposed by the open expanse, like a black spider on a white wall. He had grown up hugged by hills and woods and tethered to the Mississippi River. If Faye hadn't moved to New Mexico with Alan, Jim would never have ventured beyond Missouri.

When Jim read the highway sign aloud, "Welcome to Missouri," and blew a raspberry in celebration, the girls doubled up in giggles. He checked his watch, 8:20 p.m. Good, he thought, home by three in the morning Friday. Rain sprinkled the windshield. A few miles further, the road ahead made a sweeping curve around a wooded hill. Jim pressed the brake pedal hard when he came upon a line of cars and trucks at a standstill.

The headlights of a lone car came westbound, a state patrol officer, stopping along his way to give the eastbound drivers a report of the trouble ahead: a head-on crash, chain reaction collisions, and a fatality. The highway would remain shut down for hours. He suggested drivers make a U-turn and stay the night in a motel, more comfortable than waiting in your car for the highway to reopen.

"Officer, is there another route to get around the closure?" Jim said.

"There's an old dirt road, a left turn as you go back. That'll take you south about two miles. It turns east and then bears north. It'll put you on the highway about five miles ahead, past the pileup. But it's a rough road, not maintained. You have to drive slowly."

"Jim, I don't think we should drive a dirt road," Lorraine said. "What if the rain picks up? Might be better just to wait for the cars to start moving."

"Look, it's only a short way and then back on the highway. I'd rather go forward than stop or go backward. We can't waste time, Lorraine."

Along the dirt road, the rain splashed in heavy drops into potholes illuminated by the Corvair headlights. Jim swerved back and forth and slowed near stopping where potholes couldn't be avoided. He worried for the tires and the time. The detour could cost more than two hours. Connie whimpered in the backseat. Lorraine turned around and pulled her over the seat and into her lap.

"What's wrong with her?" Jim said.

"She's scared."

Jim felt scared, too, in the dense woods, away from any houses or lights. He could see only where the headlights shined. As the rain pelted harder and louder, water pooled deep in the potholes.

The headlight beams fell upon a sharp left turn in the road. As Jim steered, the Corvair bumped through a deep pothole, making the car shake side-to-side and up-and-down at once.

"Daddy, go back," Mary screamed. "I'm afraid."

"Please, Daddy," Joy said. "The road is getting worse. We could turn around and go back."

"Girls," Jim said. "We'll be okay, only a little bit further."

Jim gripped the steering wheel and hunched forward, trying to see past the water cascading across the windshield. The wipers running at high speed couldn't clear his view. Leaves swirled past and over the car. Jim slowed even more because the potholes, covered by water and leaves, were indistinguishable from the even road. The Corvair, driven at crawl speed, dipped and shook until the headlight beams fell upon an obstacle. Jim braked and peered between the rivulets running down the windshield. A fallen tree blocked the road.

"Can we move it or get around it?" Lorraine said.

"I'll have to get out and look." Jim pulled the hood of his parka over his head. He pushed on the fallen tree trunk and then splashed from one side of the road to the other to assess the tree length. With his coat and boots wet, Jim swung back into the car.

"It's a huge tree. We can't budge it. It would take three or more men to move it, and no way around it. We have to go back the way we came." Jim checked his watch, almost midnight.

"Jim, we can't turn around. You can't see behind us. We'll have to wait for the rain to stop, maybe even until we have light at dawn."

He knew she was right. He couldn't risk backing into a low spot. If they got stuck, there'd be no one to help. He shut off the car headlights and motor. They waited in the dark. Lorraine led the children in "Moon River" until they fell asleep. Jim and Lorraine then dozed.

Jim awoke to silence, no more rain pita pat. No sunrise yet, but dawn afforded enough light to see the road. He shook Lorraine and whispered, "I think we can go now."

Lorraine stretched and looked over the seat at three motionless mounds covered in car coats. Jim backed the car to a safe turn-around and maneuvered around potholes to the northward turn.

When they reached the highway at sunrise, vehicles sped by in both directions. The road had re-opened, but tax day, November 22, bedeviled Jim, with only seven hours left to make his payment. Jim guessed he had six hours more driving, unless delayed by weather or by traffic around Springfield or St. Louis. The more he thought, the more he worried. He tried to tune out as Lorraine and the girls sang "Sugartime." They sang in unison for each verse, "Be my little sugar/and love me all the time." If only the Corvair radio worked, he could tune in something else and make them stop singing. He hated that song and couldn't bear listening to it any longer.

"Stop, Lorraine. That's driving me nuts. I can't stand it."

Lorraine, Joy, and Mary fell silent as soon as Jim spoke, but little Connie wound down like a top, wobbling her words to verse end.

"What's wrong, Jim? You can't just spoil their fun."

"What about *my* fun?" Jim said.

"What are you talking about, Jim?"

"I'm worried about keeping our house, and you seem oblivious, Lorraine. You've held me back all the way, making us stay another day for the funeral, not waking me up at the motel, and, worst of all, not helping me drive. We'll miss the tax deadline and it's your fault." Jim's neck glowed red, and his facial muscles twitched.

"We both know it was right to stay for the funeral. Faye needed us." Lorraine paused, but Jim expected more.

"We got to the motel at three in the morning. How short a stay did you want? Besides, we got stuck waiting for a battery, not my fault."

Jim glanced back to see the girls holding hands, their heads down. He stared back at the road, fearing he would disintegrate if he made eye contact with Lorraine.

"Your detour delayed us. I told you we shouldn't go on the dirt road. You didn't listen to me then or a year ago when the transmission went out on the Studebaker Lark and we considered the Ford Falcon or the Corvair—same year, same price, but the Falcon had automatic transmission. You picked the Corvair. Last summer, I wanted you to teach me to drive it, but you said you were too busy."

She was right. He knew it. He felt embarrassed by his own

complaints, vacuous as she proved them to be. Was it only Callahan men or all Midwestern men who couldn't end an argument with their wives by apologizing? He had learned from his father what to do next.

"The weather's looking better. So, Lorraine, will we get home in time?"

"Yes," Lorraine said without hesitation. "We'll get home in time." One more thing he needed to say.

"This afternoon, when I get back from Claude's office, I'm going to hang that shelf you want in the closet." He remembered after an argument between his parents, his father's peace pipe had been a row of planted iris bulbs along the front walkway.

The miles rolled by, the car engine whirred, and the Callahans remained silent. Lorraine looked in the backseat and then touched Jim's arm. He knew she wanted to discuss something. She would check if the girls were really asleep.

"Jim, look. There's a mama bear in the road. She has three of the cutest cubs. One looks just like Connie." Lorraine looked back again. No stirring. They were really asleep.

"You're pregnant, aren't you?" Jim said.

"How did you know?"

"When you turn to the backseat, I can see a little bump. Also, you and Faye did a lot of whispering on the back porch."

"She's delighted for us."

"This time it's a boy, right?"

"It's too soon to tell. The rabbit test only tells us we're having a baby. Later Dr. Haller will guess based on how I'm carrying the baby. He says it's fifty-fifty, boy or girl."

"Then it's a boy for sure. We have three girls. We're overdue for a boy."

"No, it's fifty-fifty each time. Doesn't matter what came before."

"It's my turn to pick the name—James of course."

"What if it's a girl?"

"It's gonna be a boy."

"Please, pick out a girl name just in case."

"Okay, after we get home I'll figure out a girl name."

Lorraine and Jim couldn't stop smiling and laughing all the way to, through, and past Springfield. On to St. Louis, Jim thought, with four children in the car, one of them his son. Lorraine had said they would get home in time, beautiful Lorraine who had been a great comfort to his sister. He didn't want to argue with her. She was the right person in his life. They were not evenly yoked, he thought. Lorraine was the better half. He felt fortunate being her husband.

The Callahans rolled past familiar St. Louis landmarks. Five past one, Jim steered the Corvair to the turn leading to the lineup of cars at the toll booth on the Missouri end of the Veterans Bridge. A longer line than usual, thought Jim, but then he most often crossed the Mississippi River on other days of the week, seldom on Friday afternoon.

"We'll get across by one-fifteen, then thirty minutes at most to get to the house," Jim said. "Listen, Lorraine, we won't spend time unloading. I'll hurry inside and get the tax money while you get the girls into the house. We'll unload everything when I get back from Claude's office. Okay?"

"Sure, Jim, where did you put the tax money?"

"In the cookie jar, on top of the refrigerator."

Ten past one, the cars ahead moved, and Jim handed the toll to the woman in the booth. She appeared to Jim as if she had been crying. He dismissed the thought as none of his business. The traffic spread out once on the bridge and past the toll booth bottleneck. Jim smiled to see the "Welcome to Illinois, Land of Lincoln" sign at the east end of the bridge.

"Jim, did you notice the flags?" Lorraine said.

"No, I noticed the Illinois sign and now I see the old grain elevator. What about the flags?"

"Men were lowering the flags to half mast, the state flag and the US flag. Somebody must have died."

"Must be somebody important, a state or US official," Jim said. "Too bad the car radio is on the fritz. I think the toll booth lady had one of those little transistor radios."

"Tonight we'll watch the TV news," Lorraine said. "Maybe they'll say who died."

"It's one-forty and we're two miles from home, everybody," Jim said. "There's nothing that can stop me from paying Claude on time." Lorraine gave Jim her Mother Earth smile. The girls cheered.

Lorraine shuffled the girls to the porch as Jim sprang out the front door, the tax money bulging in his coat pocket. He kissed Lorraine on the forehead and sprinted to the car while checking his watch, one-forty-five.

One-fifty-one, Jim turned onto Burnt Oak Road and saw the American flag flying at half mast in front of the county building. He parked and bounded up the stairs and down the hallway to Claude's office, where he found the door locked and a note on it.

Ten past two, Jim stepped through the front door at home. He pulled Lorraine into his arms. "Lorraine, I have bad news."

Lorraine patted the money bulge still in Jim's coat pocket. "What happened?"

"The President is dead, Lorraine. He was shot in Dallas and he died. President Kennedy is dead."

Lorraine cried. Jim blinked back tears. Together they went into their daughters' bedroom and explained to them what had happened. All three girls sat on the bottom bunk with Lorraine. Jim plopped down into Connie's daybed. Minutes passed before anyone spoke.

Jim stood up and waved his hands. "C'mon, let's go sit on the couch. I'll turn on the TV. There'll be news on every channel."

They learned President Kennedy had been shot at half past noon and pronounced dead at one o'clock. Later that night, Jim remembered to tell Lorraine about the property tax. When Claude had found out about the President, he closed the county office and moved tax day to Tuesday.

The Callahans and the rest of the nation mourned throughout the weekend and on into Monday.

"I've made my decision," Jim said on Tuesday, when he got back from Claude's office. "If we have a girl, I know what her name should be."

"Well, what?" Lorraine said, with a half smile and furrowed brow.

"Hope."

Lorraine's smile blossomed. "I really like that, Jim, but how did you decide on Hope?"

"I was thinking last night how much Mrs. Kennedy looked like Faye, I mean at the funerals. We saw Mrs. Kennedy with her daughter and young son on TV. She wore the black suit and hat with the veil, same as Faye."

Lorraine nodded.

"You know, Faye has to move on," Jim said, "and Mrs. Kennedy will have to also. The country, we're all grief stricken, but we have to go forward. To me that means we must have hope. We must hope for a better day. Don't you agree?"

In 1964, Jim and Lorraine welcomed baby Hope Caroline Callahan in May, and Alan Junior spent his summer vacation with the Callahans. In 1965, Jim and Lorraine welcomed their fifth child, James Kennedy Callahan, born on the fourth Friday in November.

The Widow in the Tide Pool

"[...] all things are one thing and that one thing is all things—plankton, a shimmering phosphorescence on the sea and the spinning planets and an expanding universe, all bound together by the elastic string of time. It is advisable to look from the tide pool to the stars and then back to the tide pool again."—John Steinbeck

Portland, Oregon

MY MOUTH HURT—TOO many nights clenching my jaw and grinding my teeth. My swollen eyes stung. I watched flurries of pink and white tree blossoms dance with the April wind behind Peter Duke's head. A huge, west-facing window dominated the grief counselor's fourth floor office. I wished to be there, with the blossoms, outside and away. I ached to cry and convulse in the solitude of my car and shake the parking garage off its foundation and wallow in the rubble.

"Have you been writing in your journal? Exercising?"

I nodded.

"Good, Valerie. Often when dealing with grief, people resist forming new habits. You do well to embrace both, develop new habits and cherish old routines."

The timer bell buzzed. Peter reached over and tapped it silent.

"Unfortunately, this is the last session covered by your insurance for the year," he said. He withdrew a pamphlet from his desk drawer. "This is a guide to the seven stages of grief. We've talked about the stages, but this also gives you a list of services and hotlines. Do you have any questions?"

I should ask him something. "Yes, Peter, which stage am I in now?" I expected his answer would be, "Stage Three, Anger."

"Valerie, only the person experiencing grief can assess their current stage. That said, it's still not easy. Emotions can swing widely throughout a day, and you won't necessarily experience all seven stages. You are intelligent and resourceful. I'm confident you'll work through the stages and reach acceptance and hope."

I took the pamphlet, shook his hand, shut the office door behind me, and bounded down the hall toward the exit sign. I banged on the elevator button until the door opened. The elevator car whirred and jolted to a stop at the orange parking level, where I exited and dropped Peter's pamphlet into the nearest trash receptacle.

Journal entry—April tenth

WOTD: resist, as in, "People resist forming new habits." I resist the pastor's suggestion I sit up front in the widows' pew instead of back where Ray and I always sat. I resist Jake's suggestions: get out, meet new people, go to classes. Jake, with his wife and his life in Atlanta, checks in with Mom every few weeks. I resist what others tell me to do. I'm alone. Nothing I do will change that.

I didn't tell the pastor about my decision to leave Portland and move to the Oregon coast. When I told Jake, he started to say something, but Judy, obviously listening on the phone speaker, whispered to him. He whispered something back and then asked me if I needed his help.

"No, you can stay put in Atlanta. I've arranged everything, moving tomorrow morning."

"Wait, Mom. Did you sell the house? Did you buy another one?"

"I've listed the house for sale. Tomorrow movers will take my boxes and some furniture. An estate sale company will sell the rest, but I'll be gone when they do, seven hours away in a mobile home in Scenic Shores Estates."

"A trailer?"

"No, Jake, a mobile home in a senior community at the coast."

"Where exactly?"

"Medley Beach."

"Never heard of it."

"It's an unincorporated community founded in the seventies. It's way south, almost to California. Dad and I drove through it many times on vacations to San Francisco. We mused about moving there someday."

A pause, more whispers.

"You have to watch your finances now." I could imagine Judy nodding with Jake. "Shouldn't I take a look at the paperwork, make sure you're not getting scammed?"

I had to remind myself boys grow into men and feel protective, which can come across as being chauvinistic. Jake had always been a good son, and Judy, always sweet and supportive. They helped, as I needed them to, with the funeral details, but now, recovered from the initial shock and disbelief of Ray's death, I didn't need them looking over my shoulder.

"Son, it's done. I can manage my own affairs, thank you."

Journal entry—May thirteenth

*WOTD: daughter, as in, "A daughter is a daughter all of her life."
The poem is right. Jake took his wife, so I don't have him the way
I would have had a daughter. Ray and I grieved together over
the miscarriage, Jake's little sister who was not to be. Probably
why I felt emotionally engaged with the girls I taught at school.
They seemed like daughters. When they had problems, I wanted
to help. I'd love to have a granddaughter, but Jake and Judy seem
in no hurry to have kids.*

The next day, my home in chaos with packed boxes everywhere and green stickers on furniture bound for the moving truck, I sat at the kitchen table and watched a red-headed sapsucker through a panel of the casement window. He hopped out along a branch of the giant fir tree, Ray's favorite tree. I preferred the young magnolia tree Ray planted the day after his retirement party. Four years my junior, Ray retired at age sixty and died at sixty-five. He stood next to this same table, spilled his coffee, put the mug down, touched his head, and collapsed. He felt no symptoms until the aneurism ruptured.

An EMT, a man so young the bones in his face seemed not to have fully formed yet, turned to me, turned ashen, and then turned my world into a flatland, devoid of substance or shape, having no reason or purpose, no answers or questions. The young man hugged me with one arm and mumbled, "I'm so sorry," and then he and his partner wheeled my life out the door.

I left a few items unboxed, things to use on move day morning and take with me in the car, including the coffee maker, coffee, filters and two mugs, "V" on one and "R" on the other. Since the funeral, I had indulged in a charade of having coffee with my husband as each dawn whispered Ray's voice. I didn't pour Ray's coffee, just placed the R mug on the table, sipped my coffee, and watched robins, chickadees, jays, woodpeckers, and the occasional kestrel.

I placed the house key under the doormat for the movers and drove down the long, maple-lined driveway. I counted the trees from side-to-side to avoid looking in the rearview mirror—eighteen, nineteen, twenty, mailbox number 12702. I taught myself the game as a child. Think of numbers to block thoughts. Twenty maple trees. How many at the funeral patted my hand and said, "You're stronger than you think?" Forty-three years married, four months a widow.

Medley Beach, Oregon

A knock, I had to answer. The lady looked right at me through a side window panel in the door as I unpacked one of many boxes in the living room. She smiled and waved. I opened the door.

"I'm Gladys. I always bake a batch of cookies on Fridays, sugar cookies today." The woman stood, waiting, holding a dinner plate full of cookies, plastic wrap across the top.

I stared at the plate.

"I live two coaches down. Betty, next door, wants to meet you, too, but she's in a wheelchair, and you don't have a ramp. I can take you over there."

"I've a lot to do right now," I said. "Perhaps I can meet her another day. Oh, the cookies, thanks. I'll transfer them so you can keep your plate." I stepped back from the door.

"No, dear, you can give it to me later."

"Here we go," I said. I slid the cookies and plastic into the closest unpacked object, a casserole dish, and handed Gladys her plate.

Gladys's smile wilted. "Maybe this is a bad time. Stop in if you need anything, Valerie." She left.

Perhaps I had been rude. Perhaps she had been. She knew my name even though I hadn't introduced myself. A senior community full of busybodies—I imagined watchful eyes and wagging tongues. Someone told her my name. Who in the park knew what about me?

The next morning I bought a "DO NOT DISTURB SIGN" at Jerry's Hardware in the Medley Beach Plaza, a strip mall on the east side of Highway 101. On the corner, a highway sign pointed to Maybeck, a city nine miles north. Maybe in Maybeck I would find window coverings for the glass panels in my front door.

Before I had signed papers to purchase my coach, I stayed at the Golden Surf Motel and explored the rocks at the beach. I discovered starfish, some bright orange and others, deep purple. Gulls screamed and glided above tangles of seaweed and driftwood. Waves crashed on jumbles of boulders, some big as a bus. Water roared over the sand and when it pulled out, tinkled over thousands of shells and smooth pebbles on the shore and sounded like coins rattling through a coin counter.

Water shoes—I almost gave them to Goodwill when Ray and I tired of kayaking and took up mountain biking. I looked at my feet. How many holes in the mesh of each shoe to let the water out? How many sharp mussel shells on top of the biggest boulder? I smiled at my feet. The rubber soles and cushiony sock liners would out muscle the mussels. "You're stronger than you think," people had told me. How could they have known what I thought?

An old stainless steel thermos with a bright red serving cup/lid teamed up with the water shoes and a lime green tote from the Maybeck Market King store as accessories for a new daily routine. Each morning at seven, I checked a tide schedule some thoughtful soul laminated and tacked weekly on a pole along a footpath leading to the public beach walkway. The heads-up set my expectations: low tide promised tide pool exploring; otherwise, I'd listen to the mighty ocean from a rock seat well back from the surf. I heard Ray's booming voice in the incoming waves and my reply in the rush of receding water. I sipped coffee and kept separate counts of the waves and the sea gulls.

One morning I identified the tide schedule keeper. The Scenic Shores Estates manager, Randy Gillespie, stapled the weekly schedule to a post and turned to me. "News you can use every day, Valerie. I wish more of our Estates mates enjoyed the beach as much as you do."

"I'm sure the residents have other interests." I waited for him to move out of my way. He didn't.

"Sure," he said, "they bake cookies, rearrange garden gnomes, and wonder why the lady put a sign on her door and covered the glass panels."

Aha, there it was, wagging tongues. I had bought a home in a fish bowl, no privacy. I said nothing and stepped off the path to go around him.

Journal entry—June twelfth

WOTD: solace, as in, "The beach will be my solace, my neighbors I will just have to ignore." Nosey RG knows my habit, and, because of his job, he knows much more from the new resident form I had to fill out. He annoys me, with his salt and pepper hair just a tad too long and always cut-off jeans and t-shirt showing muscled arms.

By mid-June, along with the seagulls and crabs and people beach-combing or walking their dogs, the beach took on an additional life form—children. Some came with parents, seeking shells and skipping stones when the surf stilled momentarily. Two came, un-accompanied by parents and separate, but together.

I missed low tide and sat on my favorite rock and watched the water lick the sand a few yards from me. The surf roared, and I didn't hear the boy approach. I twitched when he stepped in front of me.

"Sorry, lady, I didn't mean to scare you." Skinny kid with freckles on his face and arms, his red hair swirled to a point, like ice cream atop a cone. Overabundant teeth crowded his big smile.

"You didn't scare me," I said, "just startled me because I didn't hear you come up. Are you here on vacation?"

He looked puzzled. "Well, uh, it's summer vacation from school. My school is over there." He pointed east, up the hill.

"Oh, you live nearby. I've never seen you here."

"I come every day after school, but in summer I come any time. Did you come to the beach before?"

"I come every day, too, but always in the morning. That's why we haven't met before."

He extended a sandy hand. "I'm Augie. I'm eleven almost."

I shook his hand. "I'm Valerie. I'm seventy almost."

His mouth formed an "O," which he covered with his hand, perhaps to conceal shock at meeting such an old person. He looked past me and waved to someone. I turned. A girl waved to Augie and then turned away and stared at the sand verbena plants along the beach walkway ramp.

"Is she your sister?"

"No, that's China. She's in my class at school. She won't come over while I'm talking to you."

China, with blonde, matted hair, wore a red sweater over a yellow dress, hem hanging at the back.

"Is she shy?"

"She just doesn't like to talk, but she talks to her grandma and me and her baby brother."

"What about her mother and father?"

"Her father died. China lives with her grandma. She takes care of her brother 'cause her grandma is old and sick."

"Where's her mother?"

"Her mother left. China says she's coming back. She hangs out with me 'cause I don't make fun of her."

The girl retreated up the walkway ramp and disappeared over the rise to the highway.

"I'd like to meet her, Augie. Please ask her to come and say hello sometime."

In the next days, I sipped coffee and waited for midmorning low tides. I knew where starfish clung to wet rocks and pools of trapped water offered community to green sea anemones and tiny fish. I eyed the snail shells and tried to guess—empty, inhabited by a snail, or ready to sprout the legs of a hermit crab and disappear among mussels and seaweed? As much as I avoided the company of my neighbors, my inner child ached for playmates to delight with me in the tide pool discoveries.

I stood astride two boulders as a wave engulfed my water shoes and seaweed wrapped around one ankle. I looked across the sand for Augie. He wasn't there, but I glimpsed China bent over my green tote bag next to my favorite rock seat. I waved, but she didn't look my way.

The next morning, the beach quarreled with the forces against it. Walls of water pounded the shore, dumped fresh loads of driftwood and seaweed, and scrambled the rocks, even good-sized ones. The sea foam riding the edge of the surf etched a wavy line far closer to my favorite rock seat than ever before. I moved my tote behind me and pulled my rain jacket hood up as wind blew my hair in all directions. I faintly heard the shout beside me.

"Okay for me to sit here?" Randy Gillespie plopped on the sand five feet from me. "I came to warn you about sneaker waves," he said.

"I've lived in Oregon most of my life. I know about sneaker waves."

He pointed to homes on the cliff to the north. "Dr. Chet Blankenship lives up there, marine biologist, retired. Later in the summer he'll give his talk at the high school auditorium. *Tide Pools 101*, don't miss it."

"I'll watch for it."

"What do you do in the afternoons?"

"I read a lot." I anticipated his next question. "I reread the classics—John Steinbeck, Ernest Hemingway, William Faulkner, Jack London." I didn't mention the half-dozen, dog-eared coping-with-grief books I'd read cover-to-cover.

"Do you like history?"

I nodded. I had hoped to sit alone and nibble the cheese and crackers in my tote. Maybe the whipping wind and cold sea spray would chase him away soon.

"Did you know Medley Beach was almost named, 'Bricolage Beach' or 'Chaos Beach'?"

"I never heard that." I should have said, "Yes."

He smiled and pushed his tousled hair from his eyes. "Well, the two guys that founded this place thought about the jumble of rocks and driftwood on the beach and how the pounding surf reshaped it again and again. They narrowed the names down to 'Medley Beach,' 'Bricolage Beach,' and 'Chaos Beach.' One of them told a reporter they decided on the name with the most positive connotation—the water, rocks, driftwood, and life forms—a mixture of things working together, as in a medley."

I'd look up, "bricolage," later rather than ask.

Two feet of water rolled toward us. I grabbed my tote and stood on the rock to keep all but my feet and ankles dry. Randy jumped up and retreated a few yards in the sand. "Are you going back now?" he shouted, his hands cupped around his mouth.

I shook my head.

He waved, turned, and ran up and over the rise to the highway.

A couple walked on the beach, leaving a double trail of footprints. I dug into my tote for my cheese and crackers. I looked up, no couple on the beach. Of course not, the beach had been deluged. They could not have been where I had seen them. Yet there remained a single set of footprints on the sand, a lone person I hadn't seen. I turned, counted to three, and looked again. No sand, no footprints, only water everywhere.

At home I drank tea and ate the cheese and crackers. Dull sunlight filtered through the curtains on my front door glass panels—more tea, more cheese, a cookie, the pit-pat of raindrops, a ticking clock. China had stolen cookies from my tote the day before. I would ask why if I ever got close to her. When evening faded, memories and regrets rushed in.

Seven stages of grief—where was I? "There's looping in the stages," Peter had said, "going back to previous stages and multiple stages at once. It's not just a straight line."

"Then how can anyone have hope?" I said. "You make it seem like a roller coaster."

"Valerie, it's better to think of your emotions like a stock market performance line. Peaks represent good days, valleys represent bad days. But the ups and downs generally reach higher points toward the right, that is, over time. There's the hope."

Then I asked about stock market plunges.

"Valleys are one thing, Valerie. Ride them out. But if you plunge, call a hotline or go to a crisis help center immediately."

Maybe I should have kept Peter's pamphlet, but I could probably find hotline phone numbers on my phone. I picked up my phone to look just as it rang the Jake ringtone. If I didn't answer, he'd call again. I tried to sound cheery.

"Mom, you sound terrible. Is something wrong?"

"I may have caught a cold, Jake. I strolled on the beach, and it was so windy."

"Judy and I can't imagine why you moved to such a remote, harsh place. You can probably still sell your trailer and move back to town."

"It's not remote. I'm near Highway 101, lots of stores and eating places."

"I bet you haven't even met people, made friends."

"No, Jake. In fact, I have to get off the phone right now. I see my friends Gladys and Betty at my door. We're going to the clubhouse to play cards. I'll talk to you another time, dear."

I put the phone down and sobbed, not because I lied to Jake, but because I had lied to myself, had told myself moving away would take my pain away.

Journal entry—July tenth

WOTD: bricolage, as in, "Bricolage is something constructed or created from a diverse range of available things." Life with Ray was a medley. I'm trying to cobble together the rest of my life. Some days it's bricolage. Tonight it's chaos.

I went to bed at 12:15 a.m. and watched my bedside clock for hours. Should I listen to Jake? What if I moved back to Portland? What good would that do? Should I call a hotline? No, I'm stronger than I think, or so I'd been told. I counted to five hundred, then backward from five hundred, then forward by sevens.

Ray sat beside me at our kitchen table and lifted the lid off the old shoebox, the one holding dozens of cartoons he had doodled. I felt his warmth, smelled his scent. Our collaboration—he drew and I captioned. He took paper and pencil from the box and drew a two-faced man, one face looking right and the other looking left. I wrote, "Mr. Undecided, go ask your wife."

He whispered, "I always ask my wife, dear, even when I know what she will say." His laughter rolled, deep and loud like thunder. We doodled and wrote, laughed and loved the hours away.

My fingertips felt crust on my eyelids, "eye glue," like an infant gets after a deep sleep. Light poked between the slats of my bedroom window blinds. I heard tap-tap, tap-tap-tap. I threw on my robe, stepped to the front door, and peeked behind the curtain covering one of the glass panels. I thought it was Augie standing on my porch, costumed like a garden gnome, pointed red cap and blue robe, until the figure raised a wrinkled arm from the robe sleeve and tapped again. I had seen the short neighbor woman but had never spoken to her. I opened the door.

"Valerie, I'm Agnes. Folks call me, 'Shorty.' Just checking, like we all do, but you don't have to. Roy and Dorothy on the other side watch out for me."

"Is something wrong?" I said.

"No, I just didn't see you go to the beach at seven like you always do. I waited, but then I decided I'd better check."

"I'm okay, Shorty, no worries." I closed the door. Imagine, we were all supposed to watch out for one another. Sounded good, except that gave everybody license to watch.

I opened the kitchen window blinds. The storm had passed, and white clouds rode a gentle breeze. I drove out of the park at eleven in the morning, heading to Peggy's Hair Salon in Medley Beach Plaza for an overdue cut and color.

I had explored the Medley Beach community in my first days living there. On the west side of Highway 101, mansions perched on the cliffs and vacation rentals huddled below at the end of gated driveways. On the east side, away from the ocean, residents lived modestly. I had driven the streets behind the plaza. Apartment complexes shared dead end streets with small cottages. Children of all ages played in the cul-de-sacs.

I knew Augie and China lived somewhere behind the plaza but didn't know Augie's mother owned the hair salon. Augie spun around in a salon chair when I walked in, an overstuffed duffel bag on the floor beside him. "I'm going to Petaluma for the summer. Grandpa has a chicken farm." He flashed his toothy grin. "I'm waiting for him to pick me up."

Peggy, as freckled and red-haired as her son, offered me coffee and cookies and continued cutting hair for a young woman in her chair. Peggy's father, a wiry, white-haired man, arrived and chatted with us before tossing Augie's duffel bag over his shoulder and ushering his grandson to his truck.

"How long will Augie be away?" I asked Peggy.

"He'll come back after Labor Day. I'll close the salon the last week in August, visit my folks, and bring Augie back for the start of school."

"Have you seen China lately?"

"No, Augie told me he thinks she's staying in her house because she got in trouble at the grocery store for shoplifting."

In the next weeks, I brought extra snacks in case China looked in my tote while I examined tide pools. I left a note saying it was okay for her to take the snacks, but I didn't see her. The snacks and note remained. I thought perhaps her family had moved.

In the late afternoon on August twenty-eighth, Shorty came to my door.

"Valerie, I need a ride to Dr. Chet's talk," she said. "Everybody's going, but the carpools are full. You should go. I can show you how to get to the high school auditorium."

I planned to go to the *Tide Pools 101* presentation anyway. Why not take Shorty?

She barely saw over the dash as she pointed out the turns and prattled incessantly. We took seats in one of the rows of folding chairs. Neighbors greeted Shorty and waved at me. Young people, perhaps vacationers or residents of the east side of town, also came. The room hushed when Dr. Chet Blankenship stepped behind the lectern.

He threw his arms out in a welcoming gesture, introduced himself, and began:

> *Where sea meets land, wave action causes constant change: some destructive, like rocks wearing down; and some constructive, like nutrients flooding in to enrich the habitats of animals adapted to survive in the ever present churn of water. Waves bring in and take out—a pretty impressive process of renewal. In over thirty years as a marine biologist, I found nothing more fascinating than coastal tide pools.*

He clicked a remote to dim the overhead lights and project images of tide pool life forms as he described the appearance, activities, and partnerships of purple sea urchins, green sea anemones, hermit crabs, black turban snails, mussels, and starfish, which he called the rock stars of the tide pools. I caught Shorty watching me. I patted her hand. The corners of her smile raised her plump cheeks toward her red hat so high her sparkling blue eyes disappeared into slits.

A wave crashed over rocks in the next projected image. Dr. Chet continued:

> *I've explained how tide pool life forms work together to survive in their challenging, ever changing environment. It's called, "mutualism"—the way in which two organisms share a relationship*

which benefits both and harms neither. Why are tide pools worth studying? It's because tide pools model our communities. In the best of communities, the members are mutualistic.

On the drive back, Shorty chatted about Dr. Chet, the presentation, the audience, how Roy and Dorothy were able to drive Betty because of their van's wheelchair lift, which Dorothy's late mother had used. Shorty talked about her eighty-ninth birthday coming up and something about leaving her shed unlocked. Then she told me something I listened to.

"You're not the only widow in the park, just the most recent one, and that will change in time." She had removed her hat. Her eyes seemed focused somewhere beyond me.

"When did your husband die, Shorty?"

"Seven years, five months, and three days ago." She flicked a tear from her cheek.

Journal entry—August twenty-eighth

WOTD: subtlety, as in, "Shorty put me in my place with such subtlety I just now realize what she meant." Perhaps nearly half the women in this park are widows. Another widow will move here, or some married woman in the park will lose her husband. I'm one of many adapting to grief.

The beach-going population spiked in the days leading up to Labor Day. Families spread beach towels and blankets and positioned folding chairs and umbrellas. On the Monday holiday, pedestrians streamed back and forth across Highway 101 between the beach access ramp and Bill's Grocery and Deli. A wad of people rose along the ramp to the highway. Among the tanned legs and arms and brightly-colored swim trunks, bathing suits, hats, and towels, a splash of red over yellow crested the rise and disappeared.

I hurried up the ramp and waited with other pedestrians for cars to stop. I saw China run around the corner of the grocery store. When I reached the street behind the plaza, I scanned the apartment driveways and balconies and the yards and porches in front of houses. No China.

Child advocacy—a large part of my mindset early on as a teacher and later as a school administrator—I couldn't shake my need to check on China, especially since hearing the shoplifting rumor. The next morning, I checked again behind the plaza. Adults and children came and went, but no China. I asked a few people. No one I asked knew where she lived.

"Are you Bill?" I asked the man behind the counter at the grocery store. He had waited on me many times, but I didn't know if he was the owner.

"Yes, I am Amalraj. Not all Americans can pronounce my name. So, they call me 'Bill.'"

I introduced myself and asked if he knew China. He did. I asked about the shoplifting.

"Her grandmother, Alma Clay, always buys on credit. China brings me a check for the balance every month. The last check bounced. I told China to tell her grandmother to buy with cash until she paid the bill."

"Did you speak with the grandmother?"

"No, Mrs. Clay used to come in, but I guess she's bedridden now. China came in mid-August. She left while I waited on customers, and several sandwiches went missing from the deli case. After that, I watched her. I can see to the back aisle in this mirror beside the register. She came again and just loitered. When I got busy, she went to the back, grabbed up baby food and diapers, and ran. The next time she came, I ordered her out."

I offered to pay Alma Clay's bill so China could again buy what they needed on credit.

Amalraj smiled and shook my hand. "You are a kind lady. If China comes in I will explain what you did. If you want, I can show you the returned check with Mrs. Clay's address."

I found the gray house with chipped paint, weeds instead of a lawn, and torn shades in the front windows. I knocked, called out for Mrs. Clay, then for China. No one came. I left a note on the door explaining that China could shop again at the store.

When the tourists disappeared and kids returned to school, the beach belonged solely to me at sunrise. I wanted to talk to Augie, but he would not be at the beach or his mother's salon until late afternoon. I checked my favorite tide pools, counted the starfish, and watched crabs scurry for cover in the mussel beds.

Back at home by ten o'clock, I scanned my bookshelf. My eyes fell upon *The Log from The Sea of Cortez* by John Steinbeck. I had read it long ago, but now, having explored tide pools and learned about them from Dr. Chet, I relished diving back into its pages. I stopped reading for a lunch break and later in the day for tea and cookies. Back on the couch, I read until I fell asleep.

I woke to a dark room. It was too late to find Augie at the beach, so I drove to the hair salon.

"Hi, Valerie," Peggy said, "haircut tonight? I'm finishing with Gladys. Myra is up next."

"No, Peggy, I just wanted to welcome you and Augie back."

My neighbor, Gladys, in the salon chair, nodded and then introduced Myra, who waited in a chair with a cane beside her. I had seen the elderly woman before, sitting on a front porch down the street from my coach.

"Augie's at home doing homework," Peggy said. "He had a great time in Petaluma."

"Did he see China today?"

"No, he said she wasn't at school."

Not at school? I wondered why not. I left the salon to walk to China's house, but I spotted her in the plaza. Face hidden in her hands, she sat on the walkway curb outside of Bill's Grocery and Deli. When I spoke to her, she lifted her head. Tear lines streaked her dirty face.

"China, dear, did you get my note? It's okay for you to shop at Bill's."

She pushed greasy hair back from her forehead, lifted a gaunt arm, and pointed to a sign on the door of the dimly lit grocery store: "STORE CLOSED—FAMILY EMERGENCY—COME BACK LATER."

"I need everything on Grandma's list," she said. She pulled a folded, worn paper from a pocket and handed it to me.

Lines, written in pencil in large, cursive scrawls, bore evidence of erased and re-written check marks. I guessed Grandma reused the list, checking the items when needed—lunch meats, mayo, bread, cookies, cereal, milk, fruits and vegetables, bacon, grilled chicken, soap, shampoo, toothpaste, paper towels, toilet paper, baby food, disposable diapers and wipes, protein drinks, and hamster food.

"Don't worry, China. I'll get everything on your list. I'll drive to Maybeck and then meet you at your house."

"No you won't."

I spun around. I had heard someone step up behind me. Gladys reached out for the list.

"You won't make it to Market King in time," she said. "They close at nine."

Eight-fifty by my watch—she was right. "China, I'll go to Maybeck early tomorrow."

"I can't wait. I have to change Mason's diaper. He's all dirty. He won't stop crying." She sighed and took a deep breath. "I ran out of baby food two days ago. And Grandma can't eat. She needs her liquid food. The water got shut off. We need bottles of water." She looked from me to Gladys. "Mighty Joe, my hamster, is out of food, too."

"How old is your brother?" Gladys said.

"Not one year, about ten months."

Gladys turned to me. "I'll get everything on the list if you just wait for Myra and drive her home. I'll have everything by your door before you return."

"How can you get everything?"

Gladys pulled out her phone. "I'll use the call tree. Baby food, diapers, wipes? At least a dozen neighbors stay supplied for grandchildren visits. Hamster food? Bob Santos, the retired judge, has a hamster. Protein drinks? We all have them. I'll add bottled water to the list. Valerie, among us we can do it all."

Within an hour I arrived at China's house with four bags full of groceries. China reached to me for a hug, and I knelt to her. "Thank you, thank you," she said. Her voice broke, her body shuddered. "I can't do this by myself. I can't."

I understood the desperation in her voice. China had been trying to solve problems a little girl cannot solve by herself.

"No worries, China, I'll help you. Is your grandma in the bedroom?"

"I'll see if she's awake." China disappeared into another room.

I surveyed the groceries. Gladys had put all the items needing refrigeration into one bag. Nice touch!

I reeled back and gagged when I opened the refrigerator and found rotting food: gray lunch meat, decomposed vegetables of some kind, half a cantaloupe with a crown of mold. I opened a milk carton and sniffed the sour remnants. Light on and dial set near high, but no cooling—a dead refrigerator. I'd clean it out later and talk to Alma about getting it repaired.

China returned with Mason in her arms. He fussed as I took him. "Grandma's still sleeping," she said.

I laid the stinky child onto a couch cushion. China searched the grocery bags for what I needed while I peeled off Mason's filthy t-shirt and diaper. She brought me diapers, wipes, and a jar of baby food. Then she brought the bottle of water and paper towels I asked for.

I gave Mason a sponge bath while China went for a spoon and sippy cup. The pink skin on his chest and back radiated heat, but his splotchy hands and feet felt cold, a sure sign of dehydration. He needed immediate medical attention.

"China, watch Mason while I look in on your grandma." I wanted Alma's okay to call an ambulance for Mason.

Alma Clay, in a pink flowered nightgown, lay motionless on her bed, sheets wadded around her ankles. I spoke. No response. I picked up her limp hand and patted her shoulder. She did not move, but the bodice of her nightgown rose and fell. I watched to confirm her breathing and returned to China and Mason.

China watched as I dialed my phone.

"9-1-1, what's your emergency?"

"I need an ambulance. There's an elderly woman here, breathing but non-responsive. Her grandson is dehydrated."

"Did the woman take a new medication or perhaps mix up dosages?"

China could hear the operator on my cell phone speaker. She stared blankly at me and twisted her fingers.

"I don't know," I said.

"Are you a relative or neighbor?"

"No, I just know they need help. Please send paramedics right away."

"Ma'am, calm down. Is there someone else there who knows the family?"

Questions, delay, precious time wasted.

I heard a car door outside, footsteps on the porch, and a knock. China jumped up to answer. Randy Gillespie entered.

"Ma'am, are you still there? Ma'am?"

I looked to Randy. "I'm trying to get an ambulance for the baby and grandmother, but the operator keeps questioning me. They need help right away."

He took the phone from my hand. "Who's this? Travis, Coach Gillespie here. Send paramedics to 503 Agate Court, ASAP." He handed the phone back to me.

"You know the operator?"

"Yep, I coached Travis and a lot of other Medley High Mavericks. I taught them history, too."

"Why did you come here, Randy?"

"Gladys said you'd be here. I thought maybe you could use some help."

Randy distracted China with questions about school, teachers, and games on the playground until flashing lights outside illuminated the torn window shades and cast swirling red and white patterns on the living room walls. Two paramedics, a man and a woman, attended Alma and Mason separately and then took Alma out on a stretcher. The woman came back, took Mason in her arms, and motioned me into the kitchen.

"Even if the grandmother recovers, she won't be able to take care of herself, let alone grandchildren. I'll notify the sheriff to contact Child Protective Services. Would you tell the girl she should ride with her grandmother to the hospital?"

"Will the children go to foster homes?"

"The sheriff needs to find the mother. Beyond that, I don't know."

I walked China to the ambulance and helped her step up into the front seat. She held onto my arm and whispered, "Please take care of Mighty Joe."

"I will. I promise."

After the ambulance left, Randy helped me clean out Alma's conked out refrigerator. He also offered to take the donated bags of groceries to the homeless shelter in Maybeck.

"Have you ever met China's mother?" I said.

"I know Krissy. She was one of my students, nice then but she turned irresponsible."

"Where do you suppose she is?"

"She disappeared before," he said, "but only for a few weeks that time. She took Alma's bank card and helped herself to cash when she needed it. She's probably doing the same now. I'll keep you posted on what happens to the family."

"How will you know?"

He smiled. "A lot of former Medley High Mavericks work county jobs in Maybeck. I'll find out from them."

Randy walked me back to my car in front of the hair salon.

Highway 101 slept at one in the morning, no traffic in either direction. A raccoon loped across the driveway leading into the mobile home park and disappeared into the privet hedge beneath the *Scenic Shores Estates* sign. I left the headlights on to get out of my car in the dark carport and open my front door. After switching on the outdoor lights, I went back and turned off the car headlights and retrieved the caged hamster and bag of hamster food from the back seat.

I removed four screws and the "DO NOT DISTURB SIGN" they had held at eye level on my front door. Four little holes begged for a dollop of white paint. I glanced over at Shorty's place, inside lights on and outside lights off. I remembered her telling me when I wasn't listening she left her shed unlocked so neighbors could borrow utility items as needed at any hour and that she kept paint and brushes on the middle shelf. Amazing how the mind can recall prattle and reshape it into useful information. I stepped around foot-high garden gnomes illuminated in my flashlight beam and opened Shorty's shed.

Swish. A window opened. "Which lame ass is out there?" Shorty yelled.

"Lame Ass Valerie," I shouted toward the silhouette in the window. "I'm getting paint and a brush."

"Do you need me to help?"

"No thank you, Shorty, just taking down my door sign."

"About time," she shouted. "Come over later for strudel?"

"Okay."

Too keyed up to sleep, I painted over the screw holes, made coffee, and wrote in my journal.

Journal entry—September ninth

WOTD: bound, as in, "We are all bound together by the elastic string of time." Widows, long time, recent, and future, are bound together by a timeline, with peaks and valleys, and a mutual need to adapt to ongoing churn. But other life forms are bound with us: a little girl, her baby brother, her grandmother, a hair salon owner and her son, a storekeeper dealing with a family emergency, paramedics, county workers, and a former coach/history teacher. This morning another life form shares my world—a brown and white hamster named, "Mighty Joe."

Peter had encouraged me to embrace new habits. By October, I switched to beach-going in the late afternoon so I could tag up with Augie. His school day reports transported me back to my days working with kids. My mornings I left open in case Shorty felt like sharing coffee and strudel. Some Friday mornings, Gladys joined us with a plate of cookies.

One morning, Randy came to my door carrying a roll of rubber.

"What brings you here, Randy?"

"It's time for your front porch to reflect who you are now." He unfurled a rubber mat with a grinning cartoon gnome and "WEL-COME" on it. "It took us nearly six months to wear you down, but we turned you into one of us—like the body snatchers in the movie!" He chuckled at his own joke.

I thanked him.

"And I can tell you about China and her family," he said.

"What is it?"

"China and Mason now live in Colorado with their other grandma, their deceased father's mother. Alma lives in assisted living in Maybeck."

"What about China's mother?"

"Krissy is back. She's going through a court ordered program. So, I guess all's well."

Randy held out his arms and I hugged him.

Jake and Judy flew in for Thanksgiving. Judy and I picked up the dinner items at Market King. I invited Shorty and Judge Santos to join us because they didn't have other plans for the holiday. Jake and the judge watched football, and Shorty, Judy, and I cooked dinner.

Judge Santos had brought two bottles of wine. I poured a glass for each of us, but Judy moved her glass over to Jake. "Mom, I'll just have water tonight," she said and smiled.

I stared at her. She gave me a little nod. I could hardly wait then for Shorty and the judge to leave, enjoyable as they had been. When they left, I turned to Jake and Judy.

"Mom, we're having a baby," Judy said. Jake put Judy and me inside a bear hug.

Journal entry—November twenty-seventh

WOTD: undecided, as in, "Mrs. Undecided, go ask your husband." My darling Ray, do we move or stay? We talked for years about moving to Medley Beach, and we finally did, but maybe we need to be near our son and daughter and our grandchild. I'll sit beside you tomorrow at the beach at high tide, when the ocean roars. Whisper to me then, dear, so I can hear my heart.

Looking for the Blue Man

ON MY FIRST DAY in the Pico-Union district, blocks west of downtown Los Angeles and a six-hour drive from my home in Phoenix, Arizona, I captured a cell phone image of the mural painted on the side of a two-story apartment house at West Twelfth Street and South Union Avenue. I had read how the original mural from 1971 had been painted out by mistake and later restored, but never why the muralist painted Steve McQueen blue, or why the blue-eyed actor graced this Hispanic neighborhood. The museum-worthy portrait shared space with an occupied residence where tenants shot hoops in the adjacent parking lot and bought ice cream from push-cart vendors along the sidewalk.

I rented a furnished apartment on West Eleventh Place and, with help from the landlord's grandchildren, transferred a few boxes of housewares, bedding, and "have you seen" posters and fliers from my car to what would serve as my search center. The blue Steve McQueen marked the trailhead of my search for my son, Kris. I would begin in the exact spot where the psychic had told me to start.

By the second night in the apartment, sirens became part of the evening din, along with the whir of car tires on the asphalt driveway and loud voices permeating apartment walls. From dusk until after midnight, music blared—polkas rattling on, with words unintelligible to me except for the frequent *mi corazon* shouted over horns and accordions.

I remembered a few words from high school Spanish class, beautiful words with lots of vowels, but too few words to stitch together a sentence to speak or unravel one spoken to me. In the neighborhood of the blue Steve McQueen, few adults spoke English, but the children did. I showed a flier to my landlord, Mr. Damaso, and his grandchildren, Mario and Andrea. I had made my posters and fliers bilingual, finding the needed Spanish words by using a translation app on my cell phone.

Mr. Damaso spoke in Spanish. Andrea translated. "Why is your son missing?"

"He drove into the desert near Phoenix and crashed into a giant saguaro," I said. "He may have been injured. No one knows. He just left his car and disappeared."

The children looked confused. "What is a giant . . . whatever you said?" Mario said.

"Saguaro, it's a cactus, like a tree that grows in the desert."

Mario spoke to Mr. Damaso, raising his hand high when he said, "*árbol gigante.*"

"How old is your son?" Andrea said after Mr. Damaso spoke.

"Twenty-five."

"*Veinticinco,*" she told him.

He asked and Andrea translated, "Why do you look here instead of in the Phoenix desert?"

"Everyone searched around Phoenix for more than six months. Tips came in he had been seen at a truck stop." When I paused, Andrea translated.

"He could be anywhere," I said, "but a psychic told me to start at the blue Steve McQueen." Andrea hesitated. "A psychic is like a fortune teller," I told her.

She nodded and then explained my words to her grandfather, who smiled when she said, "*Señor Steve McQueen.*"

"*Si, el hombre azul,*" he said. He spoke to the children. Andrea told me they would help me after school.

My young translators helped me affix posters to telephone poles along Union Avenue and then along Pico Boulevard where, Mr. Damaso told them, a missing Anglo man would more likely be seen. "Is he like a homeless man with a beard?" Andrea said, staring at Kris's clean shaven appearance in the picture.

"He may be," I said. "If he suffered a concussion in the crash, he may have amnesia. He may be wandering around without knowing his name or where he came from. I expect to find him among homeless people." My own words pierced me, and I turned away from Andrea. My sweet little boy, now a grown man, and I described him as homeless. My pocket Kleenex always ready, I dabbed and sniffled while Andrea clicked the heavy-duty stapler to affix the next poster. What's worse: homeless, dead, captive, or estranged? I chose to look for a homeless man suffering from amnesia instead of, as Phoenix police suggested, an estranged man suffering from depression.

That night my next door neighbor brought me a plate of chile rellenos poblanos for dinner. Her daughter, Pilar, translated. Mrs. Garza welcomed me to the apartment building and said to come to her door if I needed anything. I smiled and thanked them both. Mrs. Garza spoke and Pilar wished me luck in finding my son. Pilar said Señor Damaso had told them my story. I stretched my arms to hug each, and each hugged me back. When they left I grabbed my cell phone to translate *dama triste*, which I had heard Mrs. Garza say to Pilar. *Sad lady*—yes, so I was. Alone, away from home, and fearing I might be looking in the wrong place, I wept for my son, for me, and, while I was at it, for the whole world. Tears splashed onto my plate of chile rellenos. I ate the food, it was good. I listened to the polka music and lay awake even after it ended.

Pilar knocked on my door before leaving for school and asked for one of my fliers. Her father managed the barbershop on Pico Boulevard and offered to put the flier in the shop window.

"He said to tell you about a place where homeless go for meals," Pilar said. "Go to Olympic Boulevard and turn right, then a few more blocks to Hope Street. It's called Sunrise Café. Ask for Sister Soledad. She can help you."

At the Sunrise Café, people, homeless I assumed, waited within the doorway while others ate at the filled tables. What if Kris were here? I looked at the men standing and those seated—no Kris. "Are you looking for someone?" the young, Hispanic hostess asked.

"I'm looking for my son. Someone told me to speak with Sister Soledad. Is she here?"

"Yes, she's in," she said. "I'm Gabriella. Call me Gabby. Is that a flier about your son?"

"Yes, Gabby. I'm Gail Kramer, and my son is Kris." I handed her a flier.

"Blue eyes and blond hair, he is handsome. But I have not seen him. I'll ask the guests if they have."

Gabby led me to a back office where she introduced me to Sister

Soledad. I was struck by the woman's beauty. Fiftyish, maybe five-four, Sister Soledad had large brown eyes and dark, shoulder-length hair. She wore a flowing, emerald green dress and a necklace with turquoise clusters and matching earrings.

She smiled. "Gail, I surprise you. You were expecting a nun, which I am not. 'Sister Soledad' is a nickname from my TV days. I'm Soledad Reynosa. Call me, 'Soledad.'"

Papers cluttered her small desk. Wall hangings spoke of accomplishments: a university diploma denoting a degree in Languages and Linguistics, certificates of outstanding performance from the State Department, plaques of recognition from the city and county.

"I was a local celebrity with a popular TV show. People came with problems, and I solved them on-air. When the show ended, I started Sunrise Café to feed homeless people."

"What did you do before the Café and the TV show?"

"For twenty years I translated at the State Department. I spoke Spanish and English as a child in Texas and then learned more languages in college."

"Are those your children?" I pointed to two pictures, a young woman in a graduation gown and a young man in military uniform.

"Yes, *mis hijos*," she said. "Rita graduated from law school five years ago. She's an attorney with the DA's office. Michael died in Iraq serving our country."

"I'm sorry about your son. He's handsome. You must be proud, and your daughter is so pretty."

"Thank you," she said. "I am so proud of both my children. You are proud of your son, too. I know that. Tell me why he's missing."

I told her about Kris's car crash in the desert and what the Phoenix police found—no sign of foul play and no reason to suspect kidnapping.

"What do you think?"

"Driver side airbag deployed," I said, "so the car must have slammed against the cactus. Maybe he suffered a concussion. If he got out of the car and wandered, a motorist on the highway may have picked him up. A tipster said they saw him at a truck stop. If a trucker gave him a ride, he could be far from Phoenix."

"Did the police search for Kris?"

"The police searched the desert. The Boy Scouts and Kris's

friends helped. Kris's father, my ex-husband, came from Seattle and stayed two months to help search. After awhile, the police focused more on why he drove into the desert. They asked about mental health issues. I told them, maybe I shouldn't have, how Kris suffered clinical depression when we moved to Phoenix from Seattle after the divorce. It wasn't just the blues, but serious depression. Kris was fifteen. With meds and time, he overcame the illness. At eighteen, he got a job and moved into his own apartment."

"So the police told you there was no reason to file a missing person report because he's an adult and may have chosen to leave without telling anyone, right?"

"Yes, the police stopped looking. I continued with help from friends and the media."

"What made him go into the desert, any ideas?"

"Yes, Kris had been going with a girl named Kate, but she found someone else. She broke up with Kris two weeks before he disappeared. Perhaps he felt heartbroken and went to the desert to be alone and think, maybe grieve. Kate has been helping me look."

"Did you get a tip to look in Los Angeles?"

"Not exactly. The local news stations ran the story, and tips came in, but the leads went nowhere. Months passed, and friends fell away. Only Kate hung in. After six months I felt desperate." I hesitated to tell Soledad what I did next.

She smiled. "Go on, please."

I took a breath. "A co-worker told me about Vesna, a psychic reader. After several readings, Vesna told me to look in Los Angeles, near the blue Steve McQueen. I had nothing else to go on. I took time off from work and came here to look for Kris. Do you think I made a mistake by listening to a psychic?"

"No, Gail, there are no mistakes. You are in the right place. We just need to figure it out. Gabby can give you fliers for places where homeless people get services. Good Samaritan Hospital is nearby. Check if they've seen a concussion patient resembling Kris. Where are you staying?"

"Mr. Damaso's apartment house on Eleventh Place, do you know him?" Soledad knew Mr. Damaso and lived near the apartments. She gave me her address and invited me to dinner on Sunday.

From the Sunrise Café and on to the hospital on Wilshire

Boulevard, I had found hope to inflate sagging resolve. Soledad had given me places to go, like spokes emanating from the blue Steve McQueen. Was he just breaths away, a disoriented Kris in a hospital room or a needy Kris in line at a help center? I imagined bringing Kris with me to Soledad's dinner party and regaling her family and friends how I found him. Hope is happy and intoxicating.

But no one had seen Kris at the hospital or at any of the homeless help centers. I revisited the centers each day, scanning the faces of others' sons. On Sunday I stopped before Steve McQueen as I walked to Soledad's house. The actor's blue eyes looked angry. Late afternoon sunlight played across the building and highlighted the grooves between the wood slats crossing his image. Did I dare ask him to speak, this Hollywood son with pursed, blue lips? He wasn't about to tell me where to find my son.

A small courtyard led to a yellow, stucco house with a red tile roof. The open double doors of the entryway revealed guests standing in groups in the living room. The sounds of conversations, laughter, and ice clinking in glasses competed with food aromas to welcome those just arriving.

Soledad took me by the hand and introduced me to others, among them her daughter, Rita, and Rita's fiancé, Mark Owens, a deputy sheriff. After selecting from the buffet table, I took my plate to a corner folding table where Rita invited me to eat with her and Mark. Rita, as poised and pretty as her mother, had told Mark my story.

"So, Gail, you're looking in LA because of a psychic, with no clues placing Kris here. Does the psychic have credentials?" he said.

"Yes, she's found quite a few people and has even helped the Chicago police on their cases."

"How do you know that?"

"Well, she told me." Hearing my own answer, it sounded foolish.

"Psychics claim to have extra sensory capabilities," he said, "but they don't. I used to work in a fraud unit. I hate to dishearten you, but I believe you could have thrown a dart on a map and just as well have chosen a place to look."

"Mark, you have a professional's view on how these things work," Rita said, "but we can't rule out possibilities."

"You mean what Soledad does," he said. "We've agreed to disagree on whether your mother is psychic."

"She doesn't claim to be psychic," Rita said.

"But her TV promotions billed her as a psychic."

"She's gifted at solving people's problems. My mother has helped many people, on and off her TV show."

Mark looked ready to say more but instead looked at his plate and pushed an olive around with his fork.

Rita reached over and squeezed my hand. "My mother will help you find Kris."

I went into the kitchen to help Soledad's nieces with the dishes. Soledad brought in another stack. She put her arm around me and apologized for Mark's skepticism.

"Please, you don't need to wash dishes," she said. "Mr. Damaso is leaving with his grandchildren. Walk back with them. I want you to come again tomorrow for dinner. We'll talk about finding Kris."

I walked hand-in-hand with Andrea while Mario and Mr. Damaso walked behind. Sirens wailed about somebody's trouble, and music blared about somebody's love as I bid goodnight and closed my door. After my shower, I checked my phone and returned a missed call from Kate.

"Kate, I haven't found any leads here. I'm glad you're still helping."

"I won't stop, Gail. By the way, I broke up with my boyfriend. He's not the one for me. Kris and I were better together."

"We'll find Kris," I said, "and he'll be happy to see you again."

The next evening, as I walked to Soledad's house, both Steve McQueen and Kris stared, Steve watching me from his mural and Kris looking out from posters on poles on both sides of the avenue. Soledad opened the door when I knocked.

"I worried about you last night," Soledad said as she hugged me. "Mark upset you."

"Mark's probably right about psychics."

"He doesn't know everything." She showed me to the dining nook in the kitchen. "We'll talk after dinner. I hope you like Mexican lasagna." After dinner we moved to the living room.

"Last night I thought about you and Kris and how much you are like me and Michael."

"How so?" I said.

"You and Kris have a strong bond, as did Michael and I. The moment *mi hijo* died a world away in Iraq, I knew. I sat in that green chair, waiting for the CNO team to knock on my door. It took them nearly six hours to come and tell me what I already knew."

"Soledad, such a loss. I wish I could have met your son."

"You've not given up on Kris. I will meet your son and we will celebrate."

"How can that happen?" I said.

"The police aren't going to help, and you don't have an army of friends to look everywhere. You have only one way to find your son. You must use your love."

"I don't understand."

"Gail, I speak many languages, but in all of them there is no more beautiful phrase than the Spanish words *mi hijo* or *mi hija*, meaning, *my son* or *my daughter*. It's a phrase of endearment connoting pride and love. *My son*, even spoken by a loving parent, doesn't convey such depth of meaning as *mi hijo*. If you hear *mi hijo* said by a Spanish-speaking parent, you hear love."

I remembered Soledad using those words when speaking of Rita and Michael.

"Your love connects you to Kris," she said. "This is August. You will have Kris back for the holidays. Just keep saying *mi hijo* over and over. Think it and say it aloud, at every opportunity, at all times."

I started crying thinking of Kris home for the holidays.

The morning I drove back to Phoenix, three weeks after arriving in Los Angeles, I whispered *mi hijo* to every saguaro I saw near the highway and every tumble weed that crossed the road in front of me. That helped me concentrate on the words. In the next weeks, as I drove to and from work and on errands, I said *mi hijo* deliberately, thoughtfully. In nighttime solitude before sleep and on waking each morning, I spoke *mi hijo* many times and wept, not because I feared Soledad was wrong, but because I pictured Kris sitting at the kitchen table, sneaking food scraps to Sparky, my dog who had been his dog until he moved to a no-pets apartment.

Kate and I continued our efforts posting on social media and contacting help services. I spent Thanksgiving Day with Kate at her parents' house. *Mi hijo, mi hijo*—I thought between exchanging pleasantries with Kate's relatives and passing the potatoes and cranberry sauce. *Mi hijo, mi hijo*—I hummed over Christmas music at the mall as November ended with a Phoenix dust storm.

Kate and her parents left for a family reunion in Pennsylvania, planning to return two days after Christmas. On December 23, Sparky and I watched a Steve McQueen movie marathon on TV in Kris's old room. I stared at the phones, Kris's and mine, on the stand next to the TV. The police had found Kris's phone in his car. I kept it activated in case he remembered his number and called. But when would he remember his number?

I thought back to Samuel Madrid. Soledad had sent me to Good Samaritan Hospital—Good Sam. At Good Sam I had bought a cup of coffee in the crowded cafeteria, where Samuel Madrid waved me to his table.

"There's no place else to sit, Ma'am," he said. "Please join me."

Samuel introduced himself as a medical student who planned to specialize in sports medicine. I introduced myself and told him about Kris. Samuel stared at me for a minute and then explained he had just completed a research assignment about post-traumatic amnesia in athletes after concussion caused by sports injury. What a coincidence! For thirty minutes Samuel answered my questions about amnesia and told me things I hadn't even known to ask about.

I stared at Kris's phone on the TV stand. *The athlete recovers in time, but how long depends on the severity of the concussion and the location of brain injury.* After eleven months, what might Kris remember? *The athlete may connect with early memories, but maybe not with anything that happened in the months or even years before the injury incident.* What would Kris remember first?

What about his older phone, the flip phone Kris had in high school? Would he remember that number? Out of service ten or more years, his old number, with Seattle prefix, was probably assigned to someone else's phone by now. What if it wasn't? What if Kris remembered and got a new phone with the old number? I had long ago updated my contacts file. Kate wouldn't have the old number either. Kris had his new phone before he met her, before he met anyone in Phoenix. I could think of only one person who might still have the flip phone number, Kris's father. I called my ex and, yes, he had Kris's phone number from ten years earlier.

My heart pounded when I dialed the number. Each ring seemed prolonged, but the ringing stopped. "No one is available to take your call. At the tone, you may record your message." I quickly pressed the red icon on my phone screen to end the call. I had reached somebody's voicemail, somebody using the generic announcement that comes with the phone. But I should have left a message, even to let a stranger know the call was in error.

I dialed again. My heart thumped. Sparky whined. The room swirled. I stood and started to sway. Ring-ring-ring-ring, then the same announcement and the short tone following. Silence, I couldn't think what I wanted to say. Time passed. I had to say something. More time passed. I blurted, "*Te amo, mi hijo.*"

"Blaaah," the dial tone replied. The swirling room slowed. Sparky settled down. My thumping heart quieted. The credits rolled for *Nevada Smith*. I turned the TV off. I sat for over an hour, whispering *mi hijo* again and again. The room darkened. I turned on lights and let Sparky out to the backyard. I took a hot shower and uttered *mi hijo* in a singsong as the water splashed against the shower wall. Then back in Kris's room, I squinted at my phone screen—missed call from Seattle. Not Kris's father, somebody else had called and left a voicemail.

My fingers fumbled to retrieve the message. I stopped breathing to listen to background noise, then, oh my God—Kris's voice! "I love you, too, Mom. Hey, why are you speaking Spanish?" I gasped. I cried. I fell to my knees and hugged myself. *Oh, mi hijo, mi hijo, mi hijo!* The phone jumped in my hand as I pushed each number.

Kris answered. We laughed and cried and asked and answered millions of questions. He was in San Diego, California. Father Perry had found him dazed on the lawn at his church and had taken him to a doctor. Yes, he had suffered a concussion. Kris was staying at the rectory and working at a car wash. I mentioned his car crash in the Phoenix desert. He knew nothing of it. *The athlete may never recover memory of the injury incident.*

I gave Kris phone numbers for him to call his father and Kate while I arranged for my neighbor to take care of Sparky.

Just past three in the morning, after my three-hundred-and-fifty-mile drive, Kris stood before my headlights, slimmer than before and wearing his hair shorter than I remembered. I parked and jumped from the car. I crushed him into my arms and wept. "Okay, Mom," he whispered over and over. I held him at arm's length to study his face, the face I had seen only in pictures in the last eleven months.

Kris handed me a mug of coffee as we sat in the rectory kitchen. I told him about Vesna and Soledad, about Samuel Madrid and Rita and Mark. He was surprised when I told him he disappeared in January. Father Perry found him on June fifteenth.

"Where were you between January and the middle of June?"

"I don't know. I don't even know how I got to San Diego." *The athlete may not remember events occurring in the months following the injury incident.*

"When will we get back to Phoenix?"

"Sometime Christmas Day," I said. I wanted to take Kris to Soledad's door and surprise her on Christmas Eve. "We'll see my friend in Los Angeles first and then drive home. Sparky's going to jump for joy when he sees you." Kris grinned when I mentioned Sparky.

More talk, tears, laughter—the hands on the kitchen clock spun. "You can lie down in my room, Mom. You must be tired from the drive. I'm going to make breakfast for the other men coming in to help hang decorations in the church and put out extra chairs for the Christmas Eve crowd."

In the afternoon, Father Perry brought us into his office. He asked about Kris's past and the car accident in Phoenix and invited us to return for a visit in the New Year. We hugged him and thanked him. Kris turned back and watched the church disappear as we drove away.

Rolling north along the freeway, we sang pop tunes and Christmas carols and watched the first stars sneak into the twilight sky. By the time we reached the Pico-Union district, the streets seemed unusually hushed. Christmas Eve celebrants must have secreted themselves into all the houses and apartments, where strings of colored lights trimmed eaves, windows, and stairway banisters, and nativity scenes shared porches with inflated snowmen.

We parked by the street light beneath the blue Steve McQueen. The actor's face looked softer than when I last gazed up at him.

"Wow, Mom, that's some mural! I couldn't picture it when you told me. What a great artist!"

I took Kris's hand and walked him along Union Avenue toward Soledad's house. In the dimness between street lights, I spied a remaining "have you seen" poster still affixed to a pole. I squeezed Kris's hand but said nothing. On this magical Christmas Eve, why draw my son's attention to a symbol of my earlier grief?

One of Soledad's nieces answered the door. "Come in, *Señora* and *Señor* Kramer," she said. "*Feliz Navidad.* We've been waiting for you. We are about to say grace." She must have been mistaken. How could they have been waiting for Kris and me? I didn't tell Soledad we were coming or even that I had found Kris.

Soledad waved us into the dining room. Many people sat at the dining room table, where folding tables at each end extended the capacity. I noticed two chairs, conspicuously empty, near the middle of the table. A small, white box, like a ring box, sat upon a napkin at the place setting in front of one of the empty chairs.

"Gail, Kris, Merry Christmas," Soledad said and stood up. She hugged us both. "Please join us. The box is for you, Gail. Open it and then we'll say grace." Inside the box, atop a little cotton pillow, my topaz earrings sparkled. Kris had given them to me the previous Christmas. I thought I had lost them. I looked to Soledad.

"After you left, Mr. Damaso found them in your apartment, on the bathroom window sill," Soledad said. "He wanted to mail them to you, but I suggested he wait and give them to you in person." Mr. Damaso and his grandchildren sat across from Kris and me. Andrea stared wide-eyed at Kris.

"*Gracias, Señor* Damaso," I said.

He smiled. "*De nada, Señora* Kramer."

Kris and I enjoyed *Nochebuena,* eating a traditional tamale dinner with our new friends. Mario and Kris bantered about football teams and the NFL. Mark asked about our plans after returning to Phoenix and if we might come back for a visit. Rita winked and whispered we should save the date, April fifteenth, for her and Mark's wedding. I felt so excited I kissed them both.

After dinner, dessert, and coffee, I stacked dishes and joined others helping in the kitchen. Andrea, who had been looking out to the dining room, turned to me and whispered, "*Señor* Kramer looks just like *Señor* Steve McQueen." Kris, wearing a blue shirt, sporting his shorter haircut and standing with hands at his waist, could have stepped out of the landmark mural. Past midnight Kris and I thanked Soledad and wished everyone *Feliz Navidad* as we left.

Christmas morning, Kris and I ate sausage and eggs at my kitchen table. Sparky, back from the neighbor, eyed Kris and pawed the floor in a doggy play invitation.

"Did you know Soledad was a psychic when you met her?" Kris said.

"Soledad is not a psychic. She's just really good at helping people."

"Mom, you didn't tell her we were coming, but she had your earrings on the table!"

I got up to get a coffee refill. Turning back I saw Kris sneaking half a sausage to Sparky.

Te amo, mi hijo.

Hippies in a Jar

MADELYN SOTO WITHDREW A letter from her briefcase and reread the stinging words as the light rail train pulled away from the airport station. Dr. Jason Sobey had signed the rejection letter with a flourish, the D and the J and the S huge beside the flat trailing lines of his signature. One smug bugger, she thought. She never did like him. She had presented her senior thesis in June, her last requirement for earning a BA in Integrated Studies at Utah Valley University. She had one last chance to overhaul her paper, *History of the Chumash Indians*, and present it to the committee again in September.

In the four years since leaving for college at age twenty-two, Madelyn had returned to Portland only once before, on the day of Grandpa's funeral. Her mother, Flo Bice, kept snail mailing newspaper articles about the gentrification of the old neighborhood. She's so low tech, thought Madelyn. Why doesn't she just text links to the articles?

North Mississippi Avenue, an historic Portland neighborhood, had continued repurposing itself, mixing new architecture with 1920s buildings to accommodate flourishing businesses, such as, Mellow Cakes Mabel, the bakery; Cheese Louise, the cheese and wine bar; and Wheel Sparrows, the bicycle repair and gear shop. Food carts, with lines of eager eaters, sprang up like mushrooms.

A year after Grandpa died, Flo grabbed up a vacant, vintage storefront and opened her shop, Hippies in a Jar.

"Sweetie, take the bus going north on Williams," Flo said when Madelyn phoned from the Rose City Transit Center, "fifteen-minute ride. Gosh, I can't wait for you to walk in. You'll just love my shop."

Other riders lined up for the same northbound bus. Madelyn boarded and stood, holding the overhead strap. She bent to look out the windows. The neighborhood of her last year in high school looked familiar but different, like an old friend wearing a new dress. She disembarked in front of her mother's shop and looked up at the pattern of windows on the second floor. Flo had told her about the two studio apartments above the shop. At street level, two display windows flanked the front door: on one side, a mannequin wearing a tie-dye t-shirt and cotton pants with embroidered flowers on the pockets, on the other, a mannequin wearing a floral print peasant blouse, denim bell-bottom jeans, and a wide headband crocheted in sparkling silver yarn.

Inside the shop Madelyn surveyed aisles of candles, sandals, headbands, hats, t-shirts, tea pots, posters, bumper stickers, belts, buckles, bells, dried flowers, vinyl records, sheet music, and other trinkets and memorabilia. The rubber runner on the wooden floor led to a glass display counter with jewelry inside and a cash register on top.

"Where's Flo?" Madelyn asked the girl with green hair, seated on a stool behind the counter.

The girl didn't look up as she texted on her phone and said, "She's not here."

"I spoke with her twenty minutes ago. She was here waiting for me."

"You know more than I do," the girl said, without looking up from her phone.

"I'm Madelyn, Flo's daughter. You must be Hannah. She told me she hired someone to help in the shop."

Hannah didn't reply or look up. Madelyn gave up waiting for Hannah's acknowledgment. She spotted an alcove, posted, "EMPLOYEES ONLY," and found space for her luggage in the small room, with its microwave oven, coffee pot, utility sink, three chairs, and a table. She dialed her mother, who should have been waiting for her.

"I'm at the shop. I thought you'd be here."

"Oh, so sorry, sweetie, a friend called and wanted to meet for lunch. I'm not far, back in ten minutes. Better make that fifteen."

Fifteen meant fifty. Madelyn hadn't forgotten Flo's penchant for making her wait. She dreaded the next ten weeks, anticipating frustration with her mother and boredom with the Chumash Indians. Rewriting sucked, especially rehashing her thesis to satisfy Sobey.

Madelyn read her research notes while several gaudy wall clocks just outside the alcove ticked on. Then she heard Flo's voice.

"Where's Madelyn?"

"I think she's in the alcove."

Flo swept into the alcove. "Sweetie, you look wonderful. I'm so thrilled to see you."

She wore a red peasant blouse, bell-bottom jeans, and a wide headband with gold sequins. Her long, blond hair hung straight, not in the soft curls of two years earlier. She looked thinner than Madelyn remembered. At fifty-two, she's reinvented herself again, Madelyn thought. Who's she trying to be now? Madelyn caught a glimpse of a wall poster she hadn't noticed before.

"Everybody says I look just like her. I had the poster made from an album cover. You probably don't even know who Jackie DeShannon is."

"Probably a hippie singer," Madelyn said, knowing her mother wished her to say she looked like the pretty young woman in the poster.

Flo seemed about to say more when the back door, marked, "NOT AN EXIT," opened, admitting a tall man carrying a cardboard box. He set the box down and shut the door to the alley behind him. A leather string secured his long, sandy-gray hair in a ponytail. His blue-gray eyes and gray moustache and goatee accented his rugged face. He hugged Flo and kissed her cheek.

Flo introduced him as Feathers, one of her suppliers. Which products might be his, thought Madelyn, the tie-dye t-shirts or the tea pots with painted pops of flowers?

Flo asked Feathers to carry Madelyn's luggage upstairs. "What do you think of him?" Flo asked after Feathers headed up the staircase behind the alcove.

"What kind of name is 'Feathers'?"

"His real name is Henry Perkins. In the sixties he wore hawk feathers in his hair. That's how he got his nickname. All hippies have nicknames."

"Are there still hippies? They'd have to be real old."

"They're all over the country, all over the world, in fact. Feathers can tell you."

Feathers returned, and Flo poured coffee for him and Madelyn before joining Hannah in the shop to wait on customers.

"So, what do you sell?" Madelyn said.

"The pendants in the jewelry case, Flo's number one seller, a walnut wood peace symbol with a crushed turquoise inlay." He took one out of his shirt pocket and set it on the table. "Pricey, but folks know quality, and it's the only handmade item in the shop. Native Americans in New Mexico make them and use the money for scholarships."

Madelyn picked up the pendant and ran her finger along the blue symbol on the dark wood.

"That one is for you," he said.

"Oh, no, thanks." She returned it to the table and pushed it toward Feathers.

"I insist." He pushed it back.

"Thank you. I really like it." She picked it up again, the only thing she had seen in the shop she didn't consider kitschy.

"You do anything else in Utah besides school?"

"Two part-time jobs, tutoring freshman and selling research papers to students who don't want to write their own."

"Flo told me you're intellectually curious."

"Too curious I guess. I've changed majors three times."

"That's okay, Madelyn. Early on, I changed majors more often than I changed my shirt. What brings you back to Portland for the summer?"

"Two things: finish my senior thesis and decide what I want to do next."

"Why are you finishing your thesis over the summer?"

"Yeah, I should have been done by now. I finished Capstone I and II classes in the fall and spring, but my thesis got rejected. I have another chance to present it when the committee members return to campus after summer break."

"You'll finish the thesis, but, goodness, as for deciding what to do next, I wouldn't want to be in your moccasins. I always advised my students to make decisions with their heart, not their head. It's not easy, but it's always right."

"You were a teacher?"

"Still am, and many other things."

After Feathers finished his coffee and left, Madelyn headed upstairs to unpack and repurpose an old silver chain to hold her new pendant. The couple who rented the apartment had gone to Costa Rica for the summer. They pushed their personal items into one of the dressers and into boxes under the bed to make room for Madelyn, a small inconvenience for them because Flo let them keep the apartment without paying rent while away on their trip. Flo occupied the other upstairs apartment.

Flo had put fresh linen on the bed and new towels in the bathroom. The bright and roomy studio apartment, with two windows overlooking North Mississippi Avenue, impressed Madelyn, who had imagined a dark hole with a tiny window above a back alley. The desk next to one of the windows would provide a good study space. The thoughtful tenants had left a post-it note on the wall with their password so Madelyn could access the internet. The room had a nice vibe, a good place for thinking and writing.

After closing the shop, Flo checked on Madelyn's unpacking. "Sweetie, I thought we might both wear one of my t-shirts at dinner tonight." She handed Madelyn a Hippies in a Jar t-shirt with psychedelic lettering and a cartoon picture of a hippie bus. Madelyn held the shirt out. Not her style, but she'd go along. They agreed on seven o'clock to walk to the food carts and then take their dinner picks to the nearby pub where a beverage purchase would entitle them to sit and eat inside.

After showering, Madelyn put on jeans and her new t-shirt and pendant. She looked down on the street below. The mellow, summer evening must have given all nearby residents the same idea, stroll-eat-drink. Lines formed in front of popular hangouts. Having not eaten lunch, Madelyn looked forward to picking out something large and tasty and then washing it down with a beer. She glanced at the time—fifteen minutes past seven—not a sound from Flo's apartment. She phoned Flo.

"Sweetie, I'm in the shop. I put the pendants in the display case and then decided to hang up a box of t-shirts. I'm almost done. After my shower I'll come get you."

Back in Portland only a few hours and trapped again in one of Flo's wait scenarios, Madelyn opened her notepad and sketched an old, familiar picture—a tree with empty branches except for a lone leaf on the top branch. She wrote beneath the drawing, "Here I go again, twisting in the wind."

An hour later and the avenue shops dark, a lesser crowd than before buzzed around the well-lit restaurants. Madelyn envied the restaurant goers in the outside eating areas she and Flo passed on their four-block walk to the food carts marketplace. Those people had seafood or pasta or steak or ethnic fare on their plates or remnants of such as they raised a beer or glass of wine or a cocktail and spoke and laughed with friends the way satiated people do. Hunger amplified Madelyn's anger at Flo, the self-absorbed mother who disappeared at lunch time, returned late, and then, probably not hungry herself, dawdled the time away while Madelyn waited for dinner.

"Sweetie, you have so many choices, and the lines are short because we waited. What do you feel like having?" Madelyn skirted around the other people, who stood in the lot and looked from one cart to another, pondering the menu signs. A mix of food aromas heightened her need. She stepped behind a man and woman ordering Mexican food. Flo fell in behind her and babbled something Madelyn ignored. She ordered a grande steak burrito and a chicken taco, and Flo ordered a taco salad.

They perched on stools at a table for two in the pub and ordered beers. "Don't you just love the apartment, dear? You didn't see mine yet, but it's the same, only a mirror image, so I guess you wouldn't call it the same." She chuckled. Madelyn ignored her and ate her taco before her beer arrived. Flo continued talking, and Madelyn continued eating and ignoring.

"Did you buy the whole building?" Madelyn asked after finishing her food.

"Yes, isn't that wonderful? I have a shop, lots of floor space, an apartment for me, and one to rent out. Rents keep going up. I have a gold mine."

"But you could have lived in Grandpa's house. It was paid for. You didn't have to sell it. You had a job at the bookstore. How do you know you can keep the shop going?"

"Grandpa's house sold for a fortune, so I was able to buy the building."

"But why take on a business? You don't have any business experience."

"I got the DNA from your Grandpa. His electronics business was like a money magnet. I'll do the same with my business, sweetie. Operating a shop is my life-long dream."

"It must have been a secret dream, one you never told me. Are you coming out ahead?"

"Madelyn, I'll turn it around soon."

"You don't even have a website."

"Hannah offered to help me with one, but I told her I didn't think I needed one."

Madelyn's weary brain tried to remember the saying about arguing with a fool.

In the next days, Madelyn worked on her senior thesis rewrite and helped Flo and Hannah in the shop. Feathers stopped in on Thursday.

"Sweetie, tell Feathers about what you're studying. He lived in California. He probably knows all about those Indians."

"You didn't come today to see my thesis," Madelyn said to Feathers.

He winked. "I'm curious about education in Utah. I'll take a look."

Madelyn retrieved her paper and Sobey's letter and laid them on the alcove table. "You two go ahead," Flo said. "Hannah's off today, and I'm busy in the shop."

Madelyn poured them coffee and watched as Feathers read.

"Well?" she said.

"Great thesis, I like your topic. Did you know the name Malibu has a Chumash origin?"

Madelyn nodded. Feathers knew about the Chumash.

"Well researched, well written, but Dr. Sobey's right. An Integrated Studies senior thesis must demonstrate analysis and connect disciplines, like History and Sociology, not History alone."

"I know. I could present more about Chumash influences in coastal California, but I'm just burned out. I wish I could start over, write something more interesting."

"Do it," he said.

"I can't. I'm supposed to fix my thesis and present it again."

"Write a new thesis and do it with passion."

Madelyn sighed. "I can't. I'd need approval to start a new topic, and what would that be?"

Feathers stood up and walked into the shop. Madelyn followed. He spread his arms and made a full turn.

"You mean Hippies in a Jar?"

"No, not this phony stuff," he said. "Tell the authentic story of hippies—hippies as a global, counterculture movement which influenced today's social structures."

Madelyn thought of the freedom offered by a fresh, blank page. "Wow, I love it! It would take lots of research and all the time I have left. Oh, I know I can do it, but should I? Should I even ask the committee? They might say no."

Feathers placed his hands over his ears, feigned a pained

expression, and shook his head. "The sky is falling, Madelyn. They might say, 'no'!" He brought his hands down and winked. "Look, every decision you make changes the course of your life, but you can't predict how. Use your heart, Madelyn, not your head."

Madelyn spent two weeks studying her proposed new topic before she crafted an email seeking Sobey's approval for the change. She labored over every word until satisfied her argument provided sufficient justification to change her topic. She reread her talking points before she hit "SEND":

> *The Chumash Indians had a limited, regional impact. My new thesis, "How Hippies Changed the World," will show how the hippie counterculture movement, started largely on the West Coast in the mid 1960s, spread throughout the nation and the world; influenced popular music, literature, art, and entertainment; promoted peace and love; exposed a wider audience to Eastern philosophy; and developed connections with the Peace Corps and civil rights movement. The hippie movement continues to influence environmental and energy policies, academia, politics, and other social structures.*

Sobey did not reply, posing a dilemma for Madelyn—continue work on the Chumash thesis or switch to the hippies thesis? Madelyn sought Feathers' advice. He emailed back, "Go ahead with hippies, my dear. You can wait until almost the last minute to shore up the Chumash, if you have to."

Two weeks later, Feathers suggested they meet at Mellow Cakes Mabel the next morning. Madelyn purchased coffee and a slice of pineapple cake and joined Feathers, with his coffee and raspberry scone, at a table in the bakery. The line of customers grew, and some with beverage and baked goods in hand waited for a place to sit.

"I wanted to meet here because Flo might distract us," he said.

"You're right. I love working upstairs, but she barges in and interrupts. I hide at the public library for peace and quiet."

"Peace and quiet?" he said. "What about peace and love?"

"What do you mean?"

"You've done a lot of research so far. Can you define hippie values?" He lifted his coffee cup to sip as if expecting a detailed answer.

"They were anti-war and anti-establishment."

"Whoa, my dear, don't use past tense," he said and put the cup down. "We promote peace in all of its forms, and we're still here, on the land and off the grid in modern-day communes and throughout academia, perennial students of the sixties who became life-long learners and teachers."

"What about love?" she said, thinking about San Francisco's 1967 Summer of Love.

"If everything you say and do is intended to promote peace, love follows naturally. How about you? Why don't you give peace a chance?"

Did he change the subject? She set down a forkful of pineapple cake. "Do you mean with my mother?"

"Yes, she told me she loves you, but she feels you push her away because she's not as intelligent as you."

"She's the one who says I got my brains from my father. I just want a normal mother-daughter relationship, but I can't change her. She just needs to accept that I don't want to be like her."

"We can't change people, but we can change our understanding of them by looking at what we share in common."

"My mother and I are not alike."

"I can prove you wrong," he said and held up his phone screen. "This album cover has a better picture than the one Flo chose for the poster. This angle shows Jackie DeShannon has a slight dimple in her chin, just like Flo and just like you."

Feathers surprised her because nobody ever noticed her dimple. "So we both have a dimple?" she said.

"There's more you two have in common."

"Okay, what?"

"You both love each other," he said and winked.

She had taken that for granted and compartmentalized it long ago. Did he expect her to take it out and analyze it? She didn't want to. She needed to change the subject.

"So what hippie song is Jackie DeShannon known for?"

Feathers leaned toward Madelyn and sang, just above a whisper, "What the world needs now is love, sweet love/No, not just for some, but for everyone."

She looked around the busy bakery to see if anyone had turned to see the singing hippie.

Four weeks after Madelyn emailed Dr. Sobey, she received an

email from Dr. Ortiz, one of the committee members working with Sobey. She read:

Dear Ms. Soto, Dr. Sobey is away in Europe on family business. He asked Dr. Vogel and me to decide on your request for approval to change your senior thesis topic and respond back to you. Dr. Sobey is not in favor of the change, but Dr. Vogel and I approve of your new topic. We must express Dr. Sobey's warning. As you have only one more chance to present your senior thesis, if it falls short of acceptance standards, even slightly, you will fail your senior year at UVU. He encourages you to submit your earlier thesis with the needed revisions. Sincerely, Dr. Ortiz.

Play it safe or reach higher? *Use your heart, Madelyn, not your head. It's not easy, but it's always right.* She completed her senior thesis on hippies.

Madelyn and Flo popped into The Raven's Tooth for dinner two nights before Madelyn would fly back to Utah. She had emailed her new senior thesis to Dr. Sobey and checked off one goal of her Portland visit, but not the other. How could she decide what to do next without knowing whether she would graduate? Sobey could torpedo her thesis no matter how solid her topic and research. He had that power.

"Did you send Feathers your finished work?" Flo said.

"Yes, but I haven't heard back. I've texted and phoned him. His voicemail box is full. Last I heard from him, he planned to go with a rescue team to help the earthquake victims near New Delhi."

After dinner, as they walked back, a chill breeze swept against them, and Flo reached out to pull Madelyn closer. Détente—they had managed a peaceful co-existence.

"I forgot to tell you about my renters," Flo said. "They've decided to stay in Costa Rica. They said to keep the furniture but asked me to send their personal items. Would you help me get the boxes ready? There's not that much to do since most of it is already in boxes."

Later, as they taped boxes, Flo urged Madelyn to come back from Utah after the presentation and stay in Portland. Madelyn ignored the suggestion. Flo pressed harder.

"I don't know. I need to see what happens in Utah." Madelyn's ploy to table the topic backfired and dashed détente.

"Utah, for goodness' sake, you could have gone to college right here."

Déjà vu, a Flo flare up—Madelyn knew the meltdown to come.

"You bolted to UVU to thumb your little nose at me. I've done nothing but love you, and you treat me so coldly. How could you, Madelyn? Tell me."

Tell her? Madelyn had already told her, years ago as a teenager in fights with her mother, how three marriages and three divorces equaled five moves in eleven disrupted school years and how Flo's rages had bruised Madelyn's childhood.

"Please stop," Madelyn said. "You're so high strung and dramatic."

"Calling me names, really?" Tears rolled down Flo's reddened face. "I've got two for you, sweetie—judgmental and self-righteous."

They had used all the tape, and one box remained open. Flo hurried downstairs and returned with two bumper stickers to secure the final box. She pressed them along the box flaps and left without another word.

Madelyn turned off the light and raised the window shade to look down on the street. Tree shadows played on the empty sidewalks below the streetlights. She really did love Portland.

After a shower and cup of tea, Madelyn pulled back the bedcovers. She and Hannah could take the boxes downstairs in the morning. She looked at the box on top of the stack, the one with the bumper stickers, "GIVE PEACE A CHANCE" and "ALL YOU NEED IS LOVE." She dialed Feathers and heard the mailbox-full announcement again.

She turned off the light and got in bed. Rain pelted against the windows. During dinner Flo had hinted at closing the shop in January if she couldn't turn it around. *We can't change people, but we can change our understanding of them.* Madelyn and her mother both faced the specter of failure, and Madelyn could understand her mother's anxiety. *Judgmental and self-righteous.* She turned over her damp pillow. *You both love each other.* She really did love her mother.

By the end of the next day, Madelyn and Flo regained civility. They bought their last dinner together at the food carts marketplace and enjoyed glasses of wine at the pub.

"Sweetie, you know business, those years you worked at the bank before you decided to go to college. You probably have ideas how I could save the shop."

"Yes, you could make a few changes," Madelyn said. "Sell quality pieces, not tourist trinkets. Folks who patronize trendy places to dine and drink have good jobs and good taste and money to spend."

"Who would be my suppliers, besides Feathers?"

"Have vendors who sell handmade jewelry and textiles send you inventory on consignment. Rent out space to artists and booksellers, and maybe host poetry readings to bring people in. And get a website, for goodness sakes."

"How would I find the vendors, and what would I call the new place?"

"Don't change the name. Just have a policy that all wares reflect hippie values. Find the vendors online. Google, 'handmade hippie,' and be selective with what you find."

"Google?" Flo grinned. "Maybe Hannah can help me with that."

The next afternoon, Madelyn's confidence flagged during her two-hour flight from Portland, two hours to think and regret changing her topic. Even her roommates, who picked her up at the airport in Salt Lake City and jollied her throughout dinner, couldn't dispel her anxiety as she stared at her food.

In the morning, alone in the same conference room where her prior presentation had failed, she wanted to talk to Feathers, but he remained unavailable. She heard the click of the handle on the conference room door behind her. Deep breath, game face—she turned. Sobey entered.

"Ms. Soto, I'm glad you're early. I want to tell you my disappointment on receiving your senior thesis. You switched topics despite my warning. You've exposed yourself to substantial risk. How did you even contemplate writing something so distant from your original topic?"

"I have a mentor knowledgeable in the new topic."

"On staff here?"

"No, it's a family friend." That sounded so dumb, she thought.

The other two committee members entered, shook hands with Madelyn, and took seats on one side of the table. Madelyn sat down on the other side. She liked Dr. Kenneth Ortiz, a tall, young man with an engaging smile, and Dr. Odelette Vogel, a short, old woman, with gray hair in a generous bun and rimless eyeglasses.

"We've all read your thesis," Sobey said. "We'll pose questions and give you the opportunity to defend each challenge." He looked down at a page of notes. "You already defended my first challenge via your email: how does one abandon a study of Chumash Indians in favor of an examination of hippies? Your defense satisfied my colleagues, but the committee must still deliberate on that point. I will yield the next challenge to Dr. Ortiz."

"Ms. Soto," Dr. Ortiz said, "How can you identify hippies in a scientific way to delineate who's in and who's out of your subject population?"

Madelyn hesitated. "Dr. Ortiz, I, uh, included references to methods used by doctoral candidates in their dissertations on hippies." She glanced at Sobey, who stared at her. "You are correct, Dr. Ortiz. I used a subjective model."

Dr. Vogel, who had been writing notes, looked up and said, "Dr. Ortiz, I believe Ms. Soto's approach is appropriate for a senior-level thesis. It offers an avenue for more quantitative research in a graduate program."

Sobey smirked and pounced. "Ms. Soto, have you applied for any graduate program?"

"No, I haven't decided yet." She couldn't think what else to say.

Madelyn heard someone enter the conference room. Addled enough facing Sobey, she feared an interruption might tip her over. With her back to the door, she hesitated to turn, but saw the man as he rounded the table. He wore a gray suit, white shirt, tie and— oh no—moccasins! Feathers had crashed her presentation. Worse yet, he grabbed both of Dr. Vogel's hands and leaned down to kiss her cheek. He didn't introduce himself or explain why he was there. What should she do? Feathers turned and winked. She noticed his tie, vintage Mickey Mouse paisley. She refocused on the committee members. What could they be thinking?

Dr. Vogel stood up and turned toward her colleagues, who had also risen. "Dr. Sobey and Dr. Ortiz, as I informed you yesterday, a colleague is joining us to witness this presentation. Meet Dr. Henry Perkins, an innovator in Education, an early advocate of Integrated Studies programs, a lecturer on many subjects, and director of several charitable foundations."

"I apologize for my late arrival. I just came from the airport," Feathers said. After handshakes, he sat in a chair behind Madelyn. His presence calmed her as she thought of all the coffee and wisdom he had shared with her. Her confidence returned. She felt ready for

Sobey, or so she thought before the ambush.

"Ms. Soto, I must inform you," Sobey said, "another student exposed you, told me you sell research papers to students who turn them in for their class assignments."

Sobey's torpedo rattled her. She hesitated and then squared her shoulders. "Yes, I sell papers, but I make buyers sign a disclaimer they'll use the paper as a starting point for research, not as a paper to turn in for credit."

"You know they're going to turn it in."

"Yes." She had to admit it.

"Crafty one, aren't you?" Dr. Vogel said. "When I wrote pirate papers as an undergraduate at San Francisco State College, I didn't think to ask buyers to sign something. However, Dr. Sobey, pirated papers is not an issue for a senior thesis defense."

Sobey aimed again. "With all due respect Dr. Vogel, that was not my point. I question whether Ms. Soto researched and wrote that hippie paper in just ten weeks. Perhaps Ms. Soto bought it from someone, or someone helped her."

Dr. Vogel gasped, and Dr. Ortiz looked stunned.

Madelyn placed her hands down on the table and leaned forward. "Dr. Sobey, I did all the research and writing. It took great effort, and I am proud of the result." She straightened in her chair, interlaced her fingers, and stared at Sobey.

"I believe you, Ms. Soto," Dr. Ortiz said.

"So do I," Dr. Vogel said and nodded.

The questions continued, and Madelyn responded confidently. When the committee members stopped questioning, Sobey announced the committee would meet in ten days and decide whether Madelyn's senior thesis passed. All shook hands, and the meeting Madelyn had dreaded for ten weeks ended.

Feathers and Madelyn regrouped over coffee and doughnuts at the student union.

"My dear, yours is the best senior thesis I've read in all my years of reading senior theses. Your defense, spot on." He wagged a finger at Madelyn. "I told you so."

"What do you mean?"

"I told you to use your heart, not your head, my dear. When you do something with passion, you do your best work. There's no way your thesis will fail. Your other dilemma, what to do next—are you close to a decision yet?"

Madelyn nodded. "Changing my topic showed me my direction. I wrote with passion, in Portland and with my mother. I truly love both. I'll stay in Portland and help my mother repurpose her shop. The upstairs apartment is a wonderful place to think and write." She offered up her coffee cup as if making a toast. "My first book will be, *On the Land and Off the Grid, Hippies in America Today.*"

Flo boxed t-shirts, Hannah dismantled racks, and Madelyn swept growing expanses of empty floor, readying Hippies in a Jar for new products and displays. The mailman came in and left several pieces on the counter. Flo sifted through them.

"Hey, sweetie, a large, brown envelope from the university—this must be it." Madelyn reached for the envelope, but Flo stepped back, opened it, and withdrew the diploma. She turned away from Madelyn to read the words before relinquishing the document to its rightful recipient.

"THE DEGREE OF BACHELOR OF ARTS/WITH A MAJOR IN INTEGRATED STUDIES"—Madelyn stared at the certificate: the university logo, the date spelled out, all the requisite signatures, the gold seal—much ado about four years of her life. For her, the diploma changed nothing because she already decided what to do with her life.

Flo snatched the certificate back and pecked Madelyn on the cheek. "I'm so proud. I'll get a frame for it. We must show it off! Oh, I forgot to show you what Feathers sent. It came yesterday." Flo withdrew something from an envelope on the counter. "It's one of those old photos of a hippie couple posed at the corner of Haight and Ashbury in San Francisco. You recognize the guy, don't you, sweetie?"

Feathers, young and skinny, with full beard and wearing feathers in his long, sandy hair, held hands with a short girl, barefoot and wearing shorts, a sleeveless top, and beads. Madelyn read the caption on the back, "1967, Henry and Odelette." She looked again at the girl with Feathers. A young Odelette wore rimless eyeglasses similar to those she wore at Madelyn's presentation of *How Hippies Changed the World.*

Yosemite Punch Video Goes Viral

"Believe only half of what you see and nothing that you hear."
—Edgar Allan Poe

Sunday

I RAN MY TONGUE around the left side of my mouth as I had done a few dozen times that afternoon while speaking with law enforcement. "You should get checked out at the hospital. We'll call an ambulance. You may not feel like driving." I declined again and again until they stopped urging me. I just wanted to get back to Keith.

If Keith hadn't suffered diarrhea that morning and opted to remain in the hotel room while I ventured out for a few more pictures, he would have witnessed the punch. Thank goodness he didn't. A mouthful of Keith's rage might have provoked a serious beat down.

Squad cars had arrived in minutes. The first deputies handcuffed both men and escorted them to separate cars without trouble. Other deputies pushed back the tourists who pressed in to snap cell phone shots of the suspects. An officer drove me to the substation while another followed in my car.

A female deputy glanced at my cheek and groaned. She came back with a hand mirror. I expected a red splotch of a bruise. The tiny welt, puffy and blue, surprised me. Makeup would cover it. She snapped photos of my cheek and the tear in my jeans where I had scraped against a rock when I fell to the ground. She offered coffee and a doughnut. Yes to coffee and no thanks to a doughnut. I hoped to be on my way soon, with a story for Keith over a late lunch at the diner near our Oakhurst hotel, just outside Yosemite National Park.

Another deputy chatted with a man holding a camcorder, a man

I recognized from the scene. As other tourists with cell phones had clicked away at the strange coyote by the side of the road, this man panned the entire scene, turning his humming video recorder from coyote to crowd and back again.

"Lauren Wade?"

"Yes," I said to yet another interrogator. He introduced himself as Detective Ross Hamlin and ushered me into a side room. I sat across a desk from him as he confirmed facts in the sheriff's report.

"You must be careful, Mrs. Wade," he said. "You have a Portland address. Coincidentally, the boys are also from Portland."

"What boys?" I hadn't seen any boys with the men. The mustachioed man in the red shirt who punched me stood at least six feet, two inches, two hundred pounds. The other man, clean shaven, stood a bit shorter and slimmer. I guessed them to be in their early to mid twenties.

"Derek Hibler, the one who punched you, is seventeen," Hamlin said. "He goes to Jesuit High School and plays on the football team. His brother, Jordan, is nineteen and attends the University of Portland. If charges are filed by the DA, you might end up on the same airplane when you return to testify. The DA won't want you speaking with them or their attorney."

I didn't want to speak with them either. "Should I get an attorney?"

"Well, not for the criminal proceedings," Hamlin said. "The prosecuting attorney will represent the State. Other than that, all I can say is sometimes these things can go sideways."

What did he mean? Before I could ask, he handed me his business card and said, "Do get a medical evaluation, if not today, as soon as you get back home. Fax the medical report to me."

He escorted me to my car and gave me directions to the hotel. I figured Keith might be mad at me. He couldn't call me because I forgot to take my phone when I left midmorning to photograph rock climbers on the face of El Capitan. I had thought of borrowing a phone to call Keith, but then thought better of it. I had the car. He'd be frustrated to learn what happened and then not be able to drive to where I was. I checked the car clock when I pulled in at the hotel, 3:10 p.m.

"What took so long? You left your phone here. I couldn't call you." Keith spat his words, then pursed his lips and shook his head.

Pouty husband had no idea what he was about to hear. I savored my words before answering.

"A punch to the cheek," I said, turning for him to see the welt, "a ride in a squad car, questions, reports, photographs, and warnings. That's what took so long."

He touched my cheek. I winced. "Babe, are you okay?"

I nodded.

"What the hell happened?" He sat down beside me on the bed.

"Just before I got to the park entrance, I saw cars lined up beside the road, both sides. I stopped to see. A dozen or more people watched a coyote, and he watched them, like he wasn't even afraid. You know me, Keith."

"Yeah, I can guess. You had to help the coyote."

"Sure, I figured the coyote must have come out looking for water, you know, with the ongoing drought and the scorching temperatures these last few days. I took my plastic bowl from the trunk and put it about ten yards from the coyote. I filled it with bottled water and moved back so he could get to it. A few people nodded and gave me thumbs up."

"Then what, did the coyote attack?" Keith looked pale. I hadn't even asked him if he felt better, but I'd finish my story first.

"No, he stood still. Somebody said to move the water closer so the coyote could smell it. A man in a red shirt stepped in front of me, like some macho guy. I didn't want him to scare the coyote. I told him animals are usually less afraid of women than men, and that I would move the water. When I stepped beside him, I must've touched his arm. He punched me and I went down." I showed Keith the tear in my jeans.

"Did he hit you again?" Keith said, red faced, fists clenched.

"No, another man, his brother, asked if he could help me up. Then things got nasty. A guy in a dew-rag and tank top, lots of tattoos, cursed and called the brothers names. A gal with him helped me up. They almost started a fight, but the cops showed up by then."

"You didn't go to the hospital, did you?"

Keith knew my aversion to hospital waiting rooms, tests, and needles. "No, but I'll see Dr. Singh when we get back. I'm okay, really. I felt more embarrassed than hurt when I slipped."

"Did you slip, or did the punch knock you out?"

"I wasn't knocked out. I lost my balance. That's all."

"You're too easygoing about this," Keith said. "Under no circumstances should a man ever hit a woman. Don't you agree?"

Keith continued his questions over early dinner at the diner and ordered us glasses of wine to cap off the strange circumstance of our last day at Yosemite. We'd get home late Monday and go back to work Tuesday. I heard Keith on the phone while I showered before bed.

"Who called?" I asked when I emerged from the bathroom.

"The news guy," he said.

"Local news? Should I call him back?"

"You can't. He didn't leave a number, and the call log shows, 'RESTRICTED.' He said to tell you you're in for a bumpy ride."

"What does that mean?"

"The hell if I know, Lauren. He just said what I told you and hung up."

Monday

We didn't wait for the free continental breakfast. We left before six, with Keith driving the first leg of our twelve-hour drive. We listened to music on subscription satellite radio, no commercials or static from local stations. I thought of nothing in particular as the music played and the farmland rolled by.

"Mom and Dad, where are you?" Briana's phone call silenced the radio. I heard uneasiness in her voice over the car speaker.

"Dad and I are on Highway 99, past Merced already. Anything wrong?"

"Mom, you're on YouTube. Greg called me at work. I pulled up the video and saw the black guy punch you. Are you okay?"

Keith turned to me. "Lauren, you didn't say the guy who hit you was black."

"I didn't think about it. The deputies arrested him. I didn't need to describe him, just confirm he was the guy who hit me."

I assured Briana I felt fine and promised to see my doctor, and she explained to us how to view the video on our phones. She said she and Greg would stop by Tuesday evening.

At the next roadside rest area, Keith turned his phone sideways for a larger view of the video. We watched me step beside the guy in the red shirt and say something, no audio. I moved and brushed his arm. He looked at me, a double take. His arm shot out, his fist strik-ing my cheek. Next, the video showed the guy's brother bending to-ward me, saying something, and me, on the ground, making a face.

"Looks like I'm scowling," I said, "but I was checking my mouth by wiggling my jaw."

Keith put a finger to his lips to silence me. The audio had be-gun. The man with the camcorder must have remembered to press a button. The dew-rag guy with the tattoos stepped forward and screamed, "Get back, asshole, or I'll knock your teeth out, both you thugs." I heard voices in the background but couldn't make out words. The video panned back to me standing with my mouth open. That was all. The video ended.

"Gosh." Keith slapped the steering wheel. "What a bad situation! I wish I'd been there." He reached over to hold my hand. "You didn't tell me everything, Lauren."

"You're right. I missed some of what happened. I was focused on getting up quickly and still thinking about the coyote. No wonder Briana sounded worried."

Tuesday

With our morning coffee in front of the TV, we always watched the first twenty minutes of *Your World Now* before heading out for work.

> *Female YWN host, Siobhan Wrigley*: "We'll join Katie for the national weather, but first this viral video from Yosemite Nation-al Park. Mitch, what do you make of this one?"

> *Male YWN host, Mitch Sheldon*: "Siobhan, I had to watch twice. We'll let the viewers tweet in on this one. Warning, it's graphic. We've blurred the face of the underage subject and bleeped the expletives. Take a look."

Keith and I looked at one another. We both recognized the video on the TV screen, but it wasn't the same as on YouTube. In the video on TV, when I stepped over to the red shirt guy and moved my lips, a bleep sounded, as if I had said something offensive. The blur over red shirt guy's face and right arm obscured the punch he landed on my cheek. The video skipped to me standing, mouth open. Next the video displayed the tattooed guy's menacing actions, his words bleeped. Editors had also bleeped some, but not all, of the indiscernible voices at the end of the video, as if they had been able to pick out specific words.

"That's been doctored!" Keith said. "That's not what we saw and heard yesterday on YouTube. It didn't even show the punch."

"Yeah, and the misleading bleeps . . ." I stopped speaking to listen to the TV commentators.

> _Siobhan_: "Mitch, you can see why so many views on social media. Who would expect a near riot in the woods of Yosemite? Sources tell us Madera County deputies arrested the young boy and his brother, but not the tattooed man or the woman with him. Go figure, huh?"

> _Mitch_: "Yes, Siobhan, we'll be watching this one. Please tweet us at #yosemitepunchvideo. Next up, Randall Richie, our consumer reporter, will turn your stomach with undercover video at popular fast food restaurants. You need to see this, but first these messages."

Phone calls, emails, Facebook messages, text messages—friends and relatives deluged us all day. Are you okay? Why did they say you were with the tattooed guy? Where was Keith? Did Keith shoot the video?

Later emails and messages reflected growing internet buzz: How'd you meet the tattooed dude? Are the cops blaming you or your friend for punching the boy? Do you have a good lawyer?

That evening, Briana and her fiancé, Greg, brought hot pizza and cold beer. Greg also brought his knowledge of viral video licensing. A communications wonk closing in on an MS degree in Communication Studies, he proposed a toast with a bottle of beer. "To Lauren, may the news cycle spit you out soon." We tapped our bottles together.

"What about the video?" Keith asked Greg.

"Yeah," I said, "how did the guy with the camcorder get his video on the internet and on TV so fast?"

"The guy posts the video on YouTube, and it goes viral. Okay. Then he signs a contract with a licensing company. TV stations pay to use the clip, and the licensing company gives the guy part of the proceeds."

"So," Keith said, "any guy with a camcorder can get paid, even if he's not trying?"

"Keith, people also make video clips with their cell phones. They look for scenes they can record and post, hoping to make money. Natural disasters and civil unrest get them rushing out their doors."

"Okay," Keith said, "but people seem to think the tattooed dude is Lauren's friend and either Lauren or the dude punched red shirt guy. Isn't that fake news? I think *Your World Now* doctored the video to confuse people, but I don't understand why."

"Blurring the boy's face because of his age, that's okay" Greg said. "But obscuring the punch opened the clip to interpretation, and Siobhan's comments misled viewers."

"She lied," Keith said.

"No, Keith, editors control content. They need a villain and a victim. But the villain can't be the young African-American. That might offend viewers' sensibilities. So editors crafted Siobhan's remark to place villainy on Lauren and the tattooed dude."

"That's unfair," Keith said.

"Sure, but it worked—lots of buzz. More buzz, more viewers, more advertising dollars. Watch for more from Siobhan and Mitch tomorrow."

Wednesday

We drank our morning coffee in front of the TV and watched *Your World Now* with the sound muted as Katie pointed out the jet stream on a giant map and clicked buttons to initiate video clips of baseball-sized hail in Texas, flooded city streets in Virginia, and overnight lightning displays in New Mexico. A dozen commercials followed, and then we listened to the program hosts.

Mitch: "We showed you the Yosemite punch video yesterday. Quite a reaction and we have a startling update. But first, let's see it again."

(The video played.)

Siobhan: "Mitch, our producers followed up with the Madera County DA and learned the young boy seen in the video is in a Portland, Oregon hospital, said to be undergoing brain surgery. We don't have any word yet on his condition.

Mitch: "Yes, Siobhan, startling news. We reached out to his family. Their attorney will join us tomorrow in our studio. I'm sure many viewers will tune in."

Siobhan: "Right, Mitch. And sources tell us Lauren Wade, the woman seen in the video with the tattooed man, also lives in Portland, Oregon. We'll ask the attorney about that connection. Don't miss it. Now, our food editor, Jenny Stevens, will show you how to save money on your next backyard barbecue party."

"Call the DA," Keith said. "Find out if Derek Hibler really is undergoing brain surgery."

That afternoon I left work early to see Dr. Singh. She examined me and found no problems. I phoned the DA while waiting for the doctor's assistant to print the visit summary. The DA confirmed Derek's brain surgery but had no other information.

Thursday

I brought a pitcher of ice tea and glasses from the kitchen as Keith, Briana, and Greg settled in front of the TV. "I should have popped some popcorn," Keith quipped. He had recorded the *Your World Now* morning broadcast so we could watch it together after work.

Siobhan, away from the anchor desk, sat face-to-face with a man she introduced as Anthony Robinson, the attorney representing Derek Hibler.

Robinson: "Thank you, Siobhan, for inviting me. The Hiblers would have come, too. But as you know, Derek is recovering from brain surgery."

Siobhan: "Yes, we'll ask you about the surgery and his condition. But first, please update us on the charges in Madera County. And why was Jordan, Derek's older brother, also arrested? Has he been charged with anything?"

Robinson: "Deputies didn't arrest Jordan, Siobhan, but handcuffed him at the scene. That was appropriate because they had no way of knowing his role, if any, and they needed to provide safety while interviewing witnesses. He was released at the sub-station, and no charges were filed. A misdemeanor battery charge is still pending against Derek."

Siobhan: "Mr. Robinson, isn't the jury still out, as they say, whether Derek should even have been arrested and charged? I mean, we've all seen the video."

Robinson: "Siobhan, the DA showed me the complete video from the scene, no editing. We can stipulate Derek struck Lauren Wade. We've never claimed otherwise."

Siobhan: "Forgive me, but you sound more like the prosecutor and not the defense attorney."

Robinson: "Let me say this, we're asking the DA to withdraw the charge against Derek because of the underlying circumstance on the day of the incident."

Siobhan: "Which was?"

Robinson: "Derek is an honor roll student and an Eagle Scout and volunteers at the Rescue Mission. He's never been in any trouble. But in late spring he began failing in his classes. He suffered agonizing headaches. Doctors discovered a brain tumor, benign but still responsible for cognitive and behavioral symptoms. I'm told his brain misfired when Mrs. Wade brushed his arm. His action was reflexive, not intentional."

Siobhan: "Why was Derek at Yosemite, considering his condition?"

Robinson: "Jordan took Derek to Yosemite to help take his mind off the impending surgery."

Siobhan: "Okay, thank you, Mr. Robinson. We're almost out of time. Please, quickly, tell us how Derek's doing."

Keith hit pause. "See? The attorney didn't say what Siobhan wanted to hear so she cut him short."

"I love it," Greg said. "Live broadcast and she didn't see that coming." Keith hit play.

Robinson: "Yesterday Derek underwent stereotactic radiosurgery. It's *a one-treatment hospital procedure with no incision. He's recovering well. His family thanks everyone for their prayers and well wishes."*

<u>Siobhan</u>: "I'm so sorry we're out of time. Viewers should know we reached out to Lauren Wade, the woman seen in the video, and her attorney. They declined our request for comment. Now a few messages and a love story you shouldn't miss, when we return."

"Mom, did anyone from the show contact you?" Briana said. "Do you even have an attorney?"

"Siobhan's lying," Keith said. "We've caught her in a lie. Lauren, doesn't that infuriate you?"

"Mom, why are you smiling?"

"I'm just happy to know Derek Hibler didn't mean to hit me. Now I understand what happened. I feel so much better."

"Congratulations, Lauren," Greg said. "The video has no more shock value. You're out of the news cycle now."

Five Weeks Later

Briana suggested we meet for lunch at Deux La Rue, our favorite weekday lunch spot and a short ride from my office using the MAX, Portland's light rail train. Briana's soon-to-be wedding dominated all of our conversations, and I looked forward to hearing more about her honeymoon plans.

On the MAX, I sat in the section where seats line the windows on each side, leaving room in the center for folks standing with bicycles. Everyone seated stared at phone screens, except the young man who sat across from me, Derek Hibler.

He looked at me. As far as I knew, the DA still didn't want me to speak with him. I hesitated and then smiled. He smiled and mouthed the words, "I'm sorry, Mrs. Wade."

If his lawyer had been there, he might have objected, but then Derek hadn't actually spoken with me. I blew him a kiss. Great mimes think alike—the fast-reacting athlete plucked my kiss from the air and tucked it into his shirt pocket. He formed a heart shape with his hands in front of him. I returned the gesture. The MAX stopped, doors opened, and Derek left.

The Bird on Silver Strand

Hollywood-by-the-Sea, California – July 4, 1929

SADIE PULLS UP HER coat collar against the brisk ocean wind this sunny Thursday morning. A lady, scarf wrapped around her head, tendrils of light brown hair whipping her face, crosses Ocean Drive to meet Sadie on the sea side. "Little girl," she says, "you can't recognize me bundled up as I am against this cruel blast. Behold Gloria Swanson, famous on the silver screen."

"Glad to meet you, Miss Swanson." Sadie says. "I've seen your wonderful movies."

"What's your name, young lady?"

"Sadie."

The lady pulls paper and a pencil from the depths of her coat pocket, scribbles, and hands the autograph to Sadie. Sadie curtsies, thanks Miss Swanson, places the autograph in her pocket, and continues her stroll south toward Silver Strand. Gloria Swanson treks north.

Sadie's friend Milton is on the beach as usual, head down, walking lines two feet apart, parallel to the shore, eyes scanning the sand for copper or silver coins.

"Milton, I just met the Gloria Swanson imposter." Sadie pulls the autograph from her pocket.

"Look, Sadie," Milton says, "I found a silver dollar, first one ever. It was right there." He points down the beach where screaming seagulls fight over their own found treasure.

Sadie ruffles his hair and obligingly observes his find. At age ten, Milton is one year Sadie's junior and, with his boundless energy and curiosity, serves as the little brother she wishes she had. Milton's a year-round resident. His father works at the sugar beet factory in

Oxnard. Sadie is summers only. Her family stays at the forty-room, beachfront hotel. They'll remain through the Independence Day celebrations and return home Saturday to the upscale Holmby Hills neighborhood of Los Angeles.

Sadie shows Milton the autograph. The paper Miss Swanson wrote on is an envelope, Oxnard address on one side. Gloria Swanson is not the addressee. On the flap side it reads, "Dear Sadie, enjoy me in the movies. Love, Gloria Swanson."

"She tries to disguise herself with the scarf and coat. You know what gives her away?"

Milton shrugs.

"My father says the real Gloria Swanson is only five feet tall. The imposter is taller than my mother, and she's five-six." Milton appreciates his friend's insider information. Sadie's father works for the Max Factor Company. He meets with movie studio executives to sell flexible greasepaint and other makeup products specially developed for the new movie industry.

Automobiles crawl up Ocean Drive as Angelenos arrive after the sixty mile coast drive, the rich in Chryslers, Duesenbergs, and Packards—the envious in Fords, Studebakers, and DeSotos. Parking spaces fill, hotel guests withdraw leather travel bags, picnickers unload baskets and blankets, campers pull out canvas bags with essentials for a Thursday to Sunday beach stay. A dog runs on the sand nearby.

"Hey, this is worth a penny," Milton says. "My neighbor pays me each time Buster gets out and I bring him back." A quick good-bye to Sadie and the Buster chase begins. Sadie quits Silver Strand to rejoin her parents at the hotel.

The Independence Day events will take place later at Hollywood-by-the-Sea. Prime viewing spots already claimed, later arriving beachgoers settle for Hollywood Beach to the north or Silver Strand to the south. Picnickers Ted Smith and fiancée Opal Calvert are among the first eyeing Silver Strand. They traipse closer to the water. The chill wind of earlier is replaced by the calm of warm noontime air.

A young man, hair wet from ocean swimming, stands in his striped, full-body swimsuit, a straw hat on the sand at his feet. He waves to Ted and Opal. "Please, can you help me?" he says. They approach.

"A dog mauled this poor bird I've captured, here, under the hat. I must go get my sister. She takes care of injured birds. Looks like you're staying for a picnic. Would you please spread your blanket here by the bird and make sure no one disturbs it? My sister has a bird cage. I'll be back shortly."

"Let's have a look," Ted says. He bends with outstretched hand to lift the hat.

"No, no, please! The bird can fly, but his leg is broken. If you let him get away he'll certainly run into more trouble down the beach." He points toward several dogs playing with children in the surf.

"Ted, this is a good place for our picnic." Ted nods, and Opal spreads their blanket next to the hat.

Ted sets the picnic basket on the blanket and extends his hand. "I'm Trevor Daring and this is my fiancée, Opal."

Opal shakes her head. "That's his screen name. His real name is Ted Smith."

"Glad to meet you both. I'm Chase Chandler," the young man says. "Screen name, huh? Are you in movies, Mr. Daring?"

"Not yet. I'll be discovered, and moviegoers will know me as Trevor Daring. You can call me Ted for now. Your name, is that real? It sounds like a movie screen name, a really good one."

Chase hesitates. "My father is part-owner of Paramount Pictures. I changed my name when I appeared in one of his movies. He's always looking for talent." Chase watches Ted's reaction, which is an ear-to-ear grin. "When I come back for the bird, we can discuss the movies."

Chase turns and runs across the Strand toward Ocean Drive. "Don't let the bird get away," he shouts.

"I sure won't," Ted shouts back.

"What'd I tell you, Opal? I knew if we came here often enough I'd meet a Hollywood kingpin. I'll be rich soon. I'll be able to buy you that engagement ring you want."

Early that morning Opal had made sandwiches for the picnic in the small kitchen of the North Hollywood bungalow where she lives with her parents. Opal's engaged-to-be-engaged status worries them their twenty-year-old spinster daughter may never marry, especially if she continues seeing Ted Smith.

Ted leans back on the blanket and stares at the hat to watch for any movement. Available picnic sites are disappearing fast when Sadie's family spreads a blanket nearby. Her father sets down a basket containing food prepared by the hotel chef: fried chicken, bread rolls, salads, and slices of apple pie.

Milton runs up to them. "Do you remember me from last summer, Mr. Landrum?"

"Yes, of course I do, Milton," Sam Landrum says.

His wife Beatrice says hello to Milton. "Sadie thought you might join us today so we brought extra food."

"Gosh, Mrs. Landrum, thank you." Then he notices the straw hat next to Ted and Opal's blanket. "Does that hat belong to anyone?" He recognizes it as a cheap hat like ones local boys steal from the Chinese hat vendor on Ocean Drive.

"It's mine," Ted says. "Don't touch it."

"There's an injured bird underneath the hat," Opal says.

"There you go, Opal, spilling the beans. Now you've drawn attention. Why can't you just keep it quiet?"

"I'm sorry," she whispers.

"Look, son," Ted says, "Chase Chandler, whose father is a Hollywood kingpin, is coming back for the bird. He entrusted me to keep it safe. Now just mind your own business."

"Okay," Milton says. "I know his brother. Jack Chandler goes to my school."

"His brother's name is Chandler, too?"

"Yep."

"I don't think you know what you're talking about," Ted says. He turns toward Sam Landrum. Milton flashes a half-smile at Sadie.

The Landrums exchange pleasantries with Ted and Opal and learn of Ted Smith's screen name. "So Ted," Sam says, "have you acted in stage plays or taken acting lessons?"

"No, but I'm a natural. A lot of people say I look like Gary Cooper. What do you think?"

"I'm not that familiar with Gary Cooper."

Seagulls hover, eyeing the lunch fare Beatrice and Opal distribute from their picnic baskets.

"What do you do?" Ted says.

Sam hesitates. "I'm a schoolteacher." Beatrice and Sadie exchange a glance.

"You probably don't see many movies."

"We go often to the Egyptian Theatre and to the Broadway movie palaces," Beatrice says. "We attended the premiere of *Noah's Ark*."

"Sam, how'd you get into a premiere?" Ted says.

"Oh, just lucky I guess. Ted and Opal, do you know the story of these beaches?"

Opal smiles. "I know they've made movies here."

"That's right. When filmmakers wanted Arabian-looking scenes, the sand dunes here worked perfectly. Hollywood filming made the Oxnard area so popular, real estate developers built up Hollywood Beach and Silver Strand. Later, the developers flattened the dunes and stripped away the fake palm trees to transform Oxnard Beach into Hollywood-by-the-Sea. The hotel and the lots offered for sale drove the filmmakers away."

"I'm sure they're still here," Ted says. "They still come from Hollywood to relax. They probably stay at the hotel."

"We're staying at the hotel, Ted. We haven't seen any Hollywood big shots," Sam says.

"Well, you'd have to know what you're looking for."

"Well, Ted, if you sat as close to someone with Hollywood connections as you are sitting to me right now, how would you know?"

"The smell," Ted says.

"What?"

"Hollywood people reek of money."

Milton jumps up. "Mr. Smith, I think that's Chase over there, sitting on that beach log with two boys." Milton points to a threesome wearing knickers and cotton shirts.

"No, son," Ted says. "Chase had on a swimsuit, and he's older than those boys."

"He must've changed clothes. That's Jack's brother all right."

"Shouldn't Chase have come back for the bird by now?" Sam says.

"He'll be here. He wants to talk to me about movies."

An afternoon breeze picks up. The hat wobbles. Ted jumps to pin the brim of the hat with his fingers and realizes the capricious breeze will require his holding down the hat until Chase's return.

Independence Day events start with the arrival of a marching band and a cadre of clowns wearing red, white, and blue costumes. Two stilt walkers and a man and wife with a dog circus of five performing Chihuahuas and a Great Dane fall in behind the clowns. The mayor of Oxnard, with his megaphone-broadcasted greetings, cannot be heard over the band's "I'm a Yankee Doodle Dandy" as celebrants fill in beside the parade route along Ocean Drive from Silver Strand to Hollywood-by-the-Sea.

"Beatrice, should we head back to the hotel?" Sam says.

"Aren't you gonna watch the fireworks?" Ted asks.

"Yes, we'll watch from the balcony of our room. Best place for viewing. All of you are welcome to join us. We'll have hotel staff bring up plates for dinner."

"We should go there, Ted," Opal says.

"I can't go until I talk to Chase. Go on ahead, Opal."

"I'll stay here with Mr. Smith," Milton says.

Milton observes Chase and his buddies. They watch young women in swimsuits strolling to the surf. The boys turn their eyes toward Ted during lulls in the parade of beauties. Ted awkwardly lies across his blanket and holds down the hat brim. Milton hears early fireworks explosions and expects the big displays will start soon. He fears Ted Smith will not give up his wait for Chase, not even when the sun dips into the Pacific.

"Mr. Smith," Milton says, "as far as I know, Chase's father is a milkman, and I see Chase watching you right now."

Ted looks as Milton points to the threesome of laughing boys. "Why didn't you tell me this before?" he roars.

"Because you told me to mind my own business."

Ted, red-faced, snatches up the straw hat and flings it. Milton watches the aerial fluttering, the dip to the sand, and then the hat floating away in a foamy, receding wave. Ted squints at the dark, inert form on the sand at his feet. It could be a dead blackbird, but it isn't. The boys hold their sides, jumping up and down. One yells out, "Trevor Daring, starring in *Adventures of the Dog Poop Bird*."

The chase is on. The fleet-footed boys weave between picnic blankets and hurdle shell-seeking children. Milton runs behind Ted, who catches up to the boys near the crowded Hollywood-by-the-Sea concession area. Ted throws a fist upward toward the taller Chase and lands a blow to Chase's throat. Chase chokes and steps back. Ted steps forward. Chase's thrown fist meets his chin. Ted buckles and cusses. Chase and the other boys disappear into the crowd as a policeman emerges from among the onlookers. He yanks Ted up and scolds him for causing a fracas.

Starlight clusters in the sky punctuate each booming explosion as Ted trudges to Silver Strand to retrieve basket and blanket. He arrives back at Hollywood-by-the-Sea after the official fireworks display has been spent. Beachgoers' dwindling caches of sparklers and small Roman candles are playing out. The Landrums and Opal greet him in the hotel lobby.

"Did Chase ever return?" Sam asks.

"Yeah, and that stupid skunk got his ass whipped for lying to me about the bird and his father's connections."

"Hey, watch your language in front of the ladies."

"Oh, sorry. Opal, are you ready to go?"

Opal thanks the Landrums for their hospitality. "You did tell your father I'd be bringing you home late, didn't you?" Ted says as he opens the passenger door of the Studebaker he always borrows from his brother when he takes Opal beyond streetcar range. It will be after midnight when Ted escorts Opal to her front door. Her father will be waiting up.

At dawn Sadie slips from the hotel lobby and embraces the early morning quiet. She muses on stories of a time not long ago when sand dunes and papier-mâché palm trees dressed the beach. Today Hollywood-by-the-Sea is dressed in colorful mounds, sleeping celebrants left over from the Fourth, covered head to toe in blankets. Milton won't look for coins on this beach.

Sadie heads toward Silver Strand. Yesterday's plethora of picnickers promises a bonanza for her friend. Milton sees Sadie and abandons his coin labor. As he runs toward her, Sadie feels his excitement.

"Something, isn't it?" Milton says. His grin hurts, but he can't straighten his face even to lessen the pain from his deliciously round, swollen shiner. "It's darker now than last night. My father says it will turn all shades of purple and green before it fades, and that might take two weeks."

"What happened?" Sadie says.

"Mr. Smith got mad at Chase, and Chase knocked him on his keister. After a policeman broke up the fight, some other fellows started to brawl. I just wanted to watch, but Chase's brother Jack started waving his fists in front of my face like a prizefighter. I waved my fists in front of him." Milton throws up his arms to demonstrate. "It seemed like we were dancing until he threw a haymaker."

"What about him?"

"I tripped him when I fell. Didn't mean to, but he broke his nose. Best of all, we're buddies now. Chase is going to teach me and Jack how to swim in the ocean."

"Why didn't you come to the hotel for the fireworks? Was your eye too sore?"

"No, I went to show my father my eye. Then I went over to the neighbors' yard because they still had a lot of flash-light crackers."

"What did your mother say about the black eye?"

"She's mad at me, won't look at me. That's OK. My father's proud of me, says I'm like Jack Dempsey." More grin, more pain as Milton touches sandy fingers to the sore spot.

"I'll miss seeing it heal," Sadie says.

"Oh, you're leaving tomorrow. Are you coming back later this summer?"

"No, I won't see you again until next summer. Your eye will be healed by then."

Milton's shoulders drop, and he turns to face the ocean. "Let's go sit down," Sadie says. They walk to a bench near the concession area. Vendors will soon cart out their wares, but for now Sadie and Milton are alone. Sadie is the smartest girl Milton knows, maybe even the smartest person. He feels like a grownup when he and Sadie sit and talk.

"Why did your father lie to Mr. Smith about his job?" Milton says.

"He does that when he thinks someone will hound him about knowing movie actors. Mr. Smith seems fanatic about make believe. He doesn't even like his real name."

"Do you like make believe?"

"We all pretend," Sadie says. "Sometimes it's wishful thinking. Sometimes it's lying. Sometimes it's just a way of being nice."

"Like pretending to believe the Gloria Swanson imposter?"

"Yes, we were both being nice. She thought she was making me happy by giving me the autograph. I wanted her to be happy believing I believed her."

"What about make believe movies?"

Sadie smiles, pleased Milton seeks her opinions. "When Gloria Swanson plays a strong woman on screen in her fine clothes, girls believe they can grow up to be somebody, not just a typist or a wife."

"So what do you want to be when you grow up?" Milton says.

"I'm going to be a reporter."

"Do they let girls be reporters?"

"They'll let me. What about you? What are you going to be?"

"I'm going to be a pilot, a barnstormer. At first I wanted to be a wingwalker. I saw them in newsreels. It's dangerous and daring. But my father says I'll get more jobs and make more money if I fly a plane, not just walk on its wings. I can get a job carrying mail or taking rich people wherever they want to go."

Mr. Wang, the hat vendor, wheels his hat trees outside. Food vendors prop up awnings, and a policeman begins his foot patrol. A few of the beach sleepers stir.

"I can't come to the Strand tomorrow morning. We'll be getting ready to go home."

"That makes me really sad, Sadie."

Sadie pulls a wrapped taffy sucker from her pocket and hands it to Milton. "I'm going to miss you. Next time I see you, you'll be taller, and your hair will have sun streaks from swimming in the ocean."

"I might be taller than you by next summer."

"I think you will be. You know, Milton, there's something I really love about you."

"What?" Milton is stunned she said, "love."

"You are yourself. You don't pretend. I can always count on you being you." Sadie stands up and kisses Milton's forehead before turning to leave. A few steps away, she turns and waves. Milton waves back and watches her walk to the hotel and disappear through the lobby doors.

The salty breeze picks up, ruffling Milton's hair and buffeting seagulls in flight. What a wonderful day to be ten and in love! Milton wishes he had summoned the courage to kiss Sadie and ask her to be his first girlfriend. He missed his chance, but next year he'll be taller and bolder. Today he has a black eye and a taffy sucker his girlfriend-to-be gave him.

Milton stretches out his arms and crosses Ocean Drive to run home for breakfast. He dips his arms, banking to the left, straightening, and then banking to the right. He can visualize his Jenny biplane in the newsreel, theater audiences applauding his airborne feats. Today he can make believe he's a pilot married to a girl reporter. It's the best day of Milton's life, even better than yesterday when he found a silver dollar on Silver Strand.

AMBER Alert

Peter, Friday morning

THE SCHOOL BUS STOPPED, red lights flashing, in a San Diego, California suburb and belched children, with their books and backpacks, from both front and rear exits. Some children sauntered toward the school building, and others dashed toward the playground. Parked across the street, Peter watched, eyes darting back and forth. The bigger kids hopped out the back. He looked for someone petite, a girl with long blonde hair he would cut with scissors he brought in a bag containing a dark wig and girls' size twelve clothing. Sweat beaded on his forehead, worrying him his penciled eyebrows might wash away. His heart pounded as burly boys and chubby girls disembarked. He hoped she would exit out the rear of the bus so the driver might not see him approach her.

He glanced at his watch—7:38 a.m. Per his instructions, the courier would deliver his letters between half past one and two o'clock to the sheriff's office and to the attorney's office, the attorney who had spewed lies in court five years earlier. With a six-hour head start, Peter could drive far enough to remain unhindered through the weekend.

Ten-year-old Addison, the last child out, hugged her books against her red parka.

Cathy, Friday afternoon and evening

Cathy waited in the driveway while Rachel made several trips to an upstairs apartment to get her belongings. On each trip up and down stairs, she glared at a bony woman, with carrot-orange hair and leathery skin, leaning against the landing railing. The woman glared back. When Rachel finally settled into the car, Cathy asked about the woman.

"That's Powder Mom, my cocaine-addicted mother," Rachel said.

Cathy waited for more explanation, but Rachel stared at her phone and texted with her thumbs.

Cathy had left work at half past four, ready for a solo road trip from Reno, Nevada to Humboldt State University in Arcata, California to pick up nineteen-year-old daughter Carrie, but Carrie phoned in a favor—would Cathy give friend Rachel a ride? Twenty-one-year-old Rachel, visiting her mom who, coincidentally, also lived in Reno, needed to get back to school for summer classes.

As they merged onto Highway 395, Cathy said, "We'll get past Susanville by nine thirty."

"What about stopping at the shoe tree?"

"It's gone, Rachel. They cut it down recently."

"You're wrong. I'll show you."

"No, I'll show you, Rachel. I read in the newspaper the road department cut it down because most of it was dead."

"I never read that. The state clears up the shoes now and then. That's probably what you read."

What an attitude, thought Cathy, telling me what I must have read! She dreaded six hours in the car with Rachel.

Traffic dwindled past the Reno outskirts. The June sun hovered in the West, smothering the highway and sandy desert with a heat blanket. Cathy looked forward to forest scenery west of Susanville.

She turned into the wide turnout on Highway 395, just outside of Nevada and inside California, where the Hallelujah Junction Shoe Tree, a lone juniper, had stretched limbs to the sky, laden with hundreds of shoes. "See, Rachel? It's gone."

"Are you sure this is the right spot?" Rachel got out of the car and walked a few yards, as if to pay respects to a departed friend. Cathy walked beside her, glad to stretch her legs.

An old, beat up sedan stopped, and two men got out. Rachel whispered, "Here's trouble."

Cathy had no chance to question Rachel. The two men bounded toward them and stopped uncomfortably close.

"You ladies from Reno?" the older man said.

"Yes, Reno is home," Cathy said, trying to sound casual to mask her uneasiness.

"We're gonna switch cars," he hissed.

Switch cars, switch cars—her brain stuttered until she willed her mouth to form, "Oh, no!"

"Shut up, bitch," he shouted.

The younger man watched Rachel the way a cat watches a spider on the floor. Rachel stood as if frozen, only her eyes darting to the highway and back. Cathy's chest squeezed her heart. Sweat came from nowhere and dripped on her shoe. She couldn't move or speak. The older man stepped even closer. "Lady, I'll knock your teeth out if you don't give me your keys right now."

She handed him the keys.

He told the younger man to take the keys from the old sedan but leave it unlocked. The younger man followed orders, and then they drove away, toward Reno, with phones and purses in Cathy's Subaru.

The two women stood, stranded along a two-lane desert highway with the last glimmer of sunlight painted on the western horizon in bands of pink, purple, and indigo and a blanket of black velvet unfurling from the East.

Cathy panted until she caught her breath. "Rachel, what if they come back? What can we do?"

Rachel seemed unfazed. "They're not coming back. We're lucky. They're in a hurry to get far away."

"How'd you know they'd be trouble?"

"Dressed alike, even down to their cheap shoes, and the way they walked—I figured them for escapees. There's a prison in Susanville."

The cloudless sky turned black, and a million twinkling stars popped out. The temperature had dropped quickly. Cathy suggested they get in the old sedan to stay warmer. "We'll also stay safer from other hoodlums seeing us alone." A fan of true crime TV shows, Cathy knew better than to flag down a motorist or trucker or be seen in the sedan. Best to hunker down and hide until patrolling CHP officers stopped to check the abandoned sedan.

Marijuana odor assaulted them when they opened the car doors. They pushed aside trash and empty beer cans. Cathy settled in front. Rachel took the backseat. Now and then headlights punctuated the dark highway.

Late Friday night or early Saturday morning

Metallic scraping sounds awakened Cathy. She hoped Rachel's snoring wouldn't alert the person or animal scratching or clawing at the front bumper, but Rachel stirred, dislodging a pile of beer cans which cascaded in a rumble. Somebody popped up before the windshield, a big silhouette head backlit by starlight and cast on the breath-fogged glass.

"Sorry, I didn't know you were in there." Male voice, a liar because anyone knows fogged windows mean people breathing inside. "I'll put the license plate back on. No need to get out."

Cathy gasped when Rachel opened the back door and shouted, "Dude, what are you doing?" Out of the sedan, she yelled again to the guy with the big silhouette head. She inched around to the front, where her silhouette joined his. Cathy got out, too.

The man held a dim penlight up to his face. His facial stubble, perhaps a start at a beard and mustache, contrasted with thin eyebrows drawn on his middle-aged face. He held a screwdriver in his other hand.

"Don't you have a better flashlight on your phone?" Rachel said.

"I left my phone at home."

"Well, we need to contact CHP," she said. "Two dudes carjacked her car and left us this one, with no key. They probably stole it. Not wise for you to take those plates. Anyway, we need a phone."

"I'll drive you to Susanville."

Cathy looked at his silver Honda Civic. "No," she said, "we'll wait for CHP."

"Ma'am, it's cold out and maybe dangerous for you and your daughter to wait here. Come, meet my daughter. She'll charm you into accepting a ride to Susanville. She's ten, going on forty. You can report your stolen car to CHP in person there."

Cathy looked again at his car. A small face looked back through the passenger window. A child out in the middle of the night—the mother in Cathy ached at the sight. The child should be at home, tucked into a warm bed.

"We'll say hello to your daughter and then discuss what's next," Rachel said through chattering teeth. "What time is it?"

He shined the penlight on his wristwatch. "Three forty. C'mon, ladies, I'll light the way."

The girl stepped out of the car, and the man reached in to turn on the headlights. He, maybe five feet, seven inches, wore navy blue slacks and a light blue shirt, topped by a cream-colored hoodie. The four-foot tall girl wore a red and blue plaid dress, black leggings, and a red parka. She also wore a long, curly, black wig.

"I'm Harvey and this is my daughter, Dory."

Cathy introduced herself and Rachel.

"Mother and daughter?"

"No," Cathy said, "Rachel and my daughter both go to Humboldt State."

"Great school, is that where you were headed?"

"Yes," Cathy said. "And where are you two headed?" Would he tell the truth?

"Dory and I are on vacation. I wrote a list to make this road trip an adventure. I didn't know the shoe tree had disappeared. Next up is the Sundial Bridge in Redding. Now, can we give you a lift to Susanville?"

"Rachel and I should discuss it," Cathy said.

"Sure, ladies." He took Dory's hand, and they walked in the headlight beam a short distance along the highway shoulder.

"He's not dangerous. Let's get out of the cold and on to Susanville."

"You don't know he's not dangerous," Cathy said. "Why does he want a different license plate? What's up with the girl's wig and his drawn-on eyebrows?"

"We'll ask him. If he's shady, even more reason to go with him. Perhaps Dory needs our protection." When the man and girl walked back, Rachel asked Cathy's questions.

"No worries, ladies, Dory likes to play dress up with the wig. My eyebrows? Look, I inherited my father's bushy, Mediterranean eyebrows. They look like chinchillas perched on my forehead if I don't trim them every other day. For vacation, I just wax them and draw new ones with an eyebrow pencil. Is it okay for women to do that but not men?"

"What about the license plate?" Cathy said.

"Actually, you know, that's none of your business." He still smiled, but his sharp tone startled her. "Without asking your permission, Cathy, I'll just go ahead and purloin those plates."

Rachel slid into the front passenger seat and waved for Cathy to get in the backseat.

"Wait a minute, Rachel. He didn't answer everything."

"He doesn't have to answer our questions. Get in. It's cold."

Cathy stood by the open car door while Rachel settled in the seat. "We'll wait for Harvey to get the plates, then on to Susanville," she said and closed the door. Dory jumped in the backseat and waved for Cathy to join her.

Not one vehicle had swept past since Harvey stopped his car. No more stars. A soft, pink light washed the eastern horizon. Cathy eased into the backseat so she could reason with Rachel, but Rachel and Dory chatted about a talking fish with short-term memory loss.

"Let me guess," Rachel said, leaning between the front seats to look at Dory. "Harvey is a rabbit."

Dory giggled. "Wow, Rachel, I didn't think you'd know that. It's such an old movie."

Rachel looked over the seat at Cathy. "I know more than some people think I know."

Harvey returned from the sedan and tinkered at the Honda bumpers.

Cathy considered options: Get out, go back to the sedan, and watch Rachel leave with him? Try to talk Rachel into staying? Or go along and hope for safe arrival in Susanville soon? Alone by the roadside, she'd still face danger and didn't want Rachel to drive off by herself with a stranger. Talking with know-it-all Rachel probably wouldn't help. She decided to go along. Best case, they'd be in Susanville soon—coffee, doughnuts, and a phone to borrow to let Carrie know why she was late. Worst case, things might go sideways, and she and Rachel would protect Dory. She sighed and glanced at Dory, who took her hand, raised it to her lips, and kissed it.

Twilight ushered in the dawn. Wispy, white clouds patterned a changing hue sky. Dory, tucked in a ball on the seat, dozed while scenery not worth watching whizzed by. Rachel and Harvey chatted up the mundane: movies, muscle cars, music, and California politics.

Dory stirred, stretched, and unfolded her legs. Her wig had fallen beside her. Her short, straight, strawberry blonde hair needed combing.

Harvey checked the rearview mirror. "Dory, dear," he said and tapped his head.

She pulled the wig on. Cathy helped her push blonde strands under the wig. Dory reached down to straighten things on the floor to clear space for her feet. She piled up schoolbooks, a notepad, and a clear plastic pouch containing pink ballet shoes. Cathy read a name printed in marker on the plastic, *Addie Bakas*. Dory caught her looking at the plastic pouch.

"Ballet class is on Fridays. I brought my school things because Daddy surprised me with our vacation. We left yesterday when I got off the bus at school."

Abduction, or is it considered kidnapping or child endangerment?

The car slowed. Harvey glanced at Cathy in the rearview mirror. She didn't want him to know Dory's words sparked her suspicion. "Thank goodness, Dory," she said, "I thought maybe you study all the time instead of having fun."

Harvey's eyes returned to the road.

After passing trucks and slower vehicles, Harvey slowed the car, exited the highway, and drove onto a back road. The scenery reminded Cathy of a true crime TV episode. She looked at the back door locks, both in the down position. Safety locks controlled by Harvey?

"Harvey, where are we going?" she said.

Rachel turned around. "You missed the sign, Cathy—Honey Lake Rest Area."

"I'm sure we can all use a pit stop," Harvey said. "I'll park by the restrooms. I see benches on the grass over there. Nice place to relax a bit."

Dory pulled off her wig. Harvey handed a comb over the seat. She made a part, combed her hair down on each side and in back, and then spread bangs evenly across her forehead.

"Good job, young lady," Harvey said. She handed back the comb and got out of the car. Harvey handed Dory clothing from the car trunk.

"Daddy bought me new play clothes for our vacation," Dory said as she walked with Rachel and Cathy. When they left the women's restroom, Dory, in striped cotton capris and a cat-themed jersey, joined Harvey on a bench overlooking a play area.

Cathy pointed to a sign for a pay phone around the corner of the building. "I'll phone Carrie. She must be wondering where I am." She worried Carrie may have called her number and gotten either no answer or, worse, heard one of the carjackers answer.

"Do you have money?" Rachel said.

"Yeah, those jerks didn't get my wallet. I put it in my pocket after gassing up in Reno."

They walked around the corner and found the pay phone had been vandalized—cord dangling, receiver missing. "I should ask someone to phone CHP for us," Cathy said, "How about that old woman? I bet she'd make a call for us."

"Let's just go with Harvey."

"Rachel, I'm not comfortable with him. Look, Dory's real name is, 'Addie.' I saw it on her school stuff."

"We don't know what's best for her. We need to find that out first."

How could Rachel not share her suspicions? She'd confront him and get the truth or refuse to get back in the car and not let Dory go with him. She'd get others at the rest stop to help her.

She and Rachel approached Harvey on his bench. "Cathy will blab unless you explain yourself," Rachel said. Harvey's jaw dropped and his eyes bore holes into Cathy's head. She wished Rachel had used more tact.

"I'm concerned because you didn't tell us your real names," she said, "and I still don't understand about the license plates."

"People can have vacation names, Cathy, so what?" He stared her down.

That tore it for her. She strode toward two young men, one holding a cell phone.

"Wait, Cathy. I'm sorry. Our real names are Peter and Addison." Cathy turned and stepped back, curious what more he'd admit.

"Ladies, I picked up Addie without my ex-wife's permission because we have an ongoing battle. Sheila and her sister perjured themselves in family court to limit my access to my daughter. I haven't gotten to spend Addie's birthday with her in five years."

Harvey paused and glanced to where Dory smiled and laughed with other children.

"Tomorrow is her eleventh birthday. That's an important one. Soon she'll become boy crazy, glued to social media, and too important for old dad. Right now she is sweet and happy to be daddy's girl. I just want to spend all of her eleventh birthday with her."

"You'll get arrested if a cop runs the license plate," Rachel said.

"Sure, I know." His face seemed to have softened. Perhaps he felt more comfortable with truth than with lies. "The plates are just for sightings by John Q. Public. If there's an AMBER Alert and motorists see it, they can't match the car or the occupants. The wig, well it only works from a distance, too conspicuous up close. Having you two ladies along helps."

"Where are you running from?" Rachel said.

"San Diego. I sent letters to Sheila's attorney and the sheriff saying I would surrender on Monday morning to police in a coastal city."

"Good strategy," Rachel said, "mitigation against felony charges, but now what?"

Cathy felt her jaw tighten and her face flush when Rachel said, "felony charges." Yes indeed, now what?

"I want Addie to have a real vacation, so Sundial Bridge in Redding next and then on to Bigfoot country. I brought a small tent and sleeping bags. Addie loves camping. I'll rent a tent site near Big Flat, and we'll go hiking and rafting all day tomorrow. Monday morning, we'll show up at the Eureka Police Department." He raised two fingers. "I have two objectives—spend Addie's entire birthday with her and turn myself in without being arrested first. Now that I've told you, please just keep using our vacation names."

Rachel nodded. "Shall we beat feet to Susanville now?" she said to Cathy.

Cathy answered as if in a daze, her mind still processing all he had said. She believed him and didn't want Dory to see her father arrested. "Yes, let's go now." She sighed. "I need to phone Carrie and also report my stolen car."

In Susanville, a young CHP officer wrote up the crime report. "Yep, you're lucky," he said. "Escapees are unpredictable. Nice of the Good Samaritan to drive you here, but you must always be careful when accepting a ride."

When Cathy got off the phone with Carrie, an officer drove Cathy and Rachel to Jake's Diner. They had agreed to meet Harvey and Dory for breakfast and go on with them to Redding. Dory wanted them all to see the Sundial Bridge together. Cathy knew Redding well, having lived there before her divorce, and looked forward to spending a few more hours with Dory. She would rent a car in Redding and purchase a new phone at the mall there.

Throughout breakfast Rachel kept up a patter with Dory and

Harvey. When Dory and Rachel left for the restroom, Cathy turned to Harvey. "You're taking chances being seen."

"The police aren't expecting someone from San Diego to show up here. I'm hiding in plain sight if I don't draw any attention." He held up his car keys. "But it might help if you drive us to Redding while I nap in the backseat."

At the mall in Redding, the sunny Saturday morning drew a stream of shoppers. "You girls do your shopping," Harvey said. "Meet me back at the car at eleven thirty, and we can decide on lunch."

Rachel and Dory window-shopped near the electronics store. When Cathy came out with her new phone, Rachel waved her over to a glass-enclosed message board. Dory and Harvey smiled out from an AMBER Alert poster. Dory, identified as Addison Bakas, age ten, four feet, three inches and sixty-five pounds, wore her hair long in the photo. Harvey, identified as Peter Bakas, age forty-six, five feet, eight inches and one hundred fifty pounds, appeared clean shaven, with glasses and bushy eyebrows. The poster included a description of Harvey's Honda.

Dory, mouth open, looked from Cathy to Rachel and back. "Cathy, please don't turn us in. Please wait an hour or just half an hour before you call the police. Give us a chance, please."

"We won't let you down," Cathy said. "C'mon, it's almost eleven thirty. Let's meet your dad at the car and leave here." Dory hurried as Rachel and Cathy followed through the parking lot.

Dory saw them first and stepped behind Rachel. "Don't let them see me." Three policemen, two mall security guards, and a tow truck driver hovered over Harvey's car.

"Harvey's not there," Rachel said. "Maybe he saw them first. I'll schmooze one of the security guards and find out. You and Dory meet me at the food court."

Cathy and Dory walked through the mall, watching for Harvey. "Dory, we need something here," Cathy said as they came upon a "lid" store. She found green bill caps with Seattle Seahawks emblems—perfect disguise—matching caps for a mother and daughter from the state of Washington.

Cathy and Dory, bill caps pulled low on their foreheads, sat at a food court table with sodas. A security guard swept along the food concessions, looking back and forth between people waiting in line for food and people eating at the tables. He positioned himself near the food court entrance and smiled at Rachel as she sauntered by.

"Love the caps, girls," she said. "Fill you in later, but first let's get a rental car over here so we can leave."

———————

Once in the rental car, Cathy asked Rachel what she had learned

"Would you believe the coincidence?" Rachel said. "An off-duty Susanville cop shopping in Redding recognized the license plate number because he wrote the report Friday when the escapees carjacked the sedan. Redding cops connected the Honda VIN to the AMBER Alert. They're searching the mall for Harvey and Dory."

"We'll have to take Dory back to the mall security office."

"No, Cathy, please just find Daddy," Dory said. "He'll go to the Sundial Bridge. Please go there."

"Dory's right," Rachel said. "He may try to meet us there. How far is it?"

"Wait, Rachel, we need to notify someone she's with us."

"No," Rachel said, "we need to reunite Dory and Harvey. Let him decide what to do next."

Cathy liked Rachel's idea of passing the baton to Harvey, if they could find him. A four-mile walk, he could get there. They drove to the Sundial Bridge without seeing Harvey on the way and parked in the visitor lot. The cloudless sky and quick afternoon warm up reminded her of the summer days when she and Carrie tracked the giant sundial shadow.

Rachel got out and searched the far side of the bridge and along the trails. No Harvey. Then she stayed in the car with Dory while Cathy looked. Cathy phoned Carrie as she walked and told her they were waiting to give somebody a ride. Carrie complained, as Cathy expected she would. The sundial shadow fell across the three marker. No Harvey yet.

Several police cars entered the parking lot. Officers fanned out on foot, eyeing visitors.

"Harvey's still free," Rachel said. "Otherwise, the cops would look for us, not him. They're eyeballing men only."

"Wait longer?"

Rachel shook her head.

Cathy hadn't expected Rachel to give up right then, but she agreed—no Harvey, no hope for their ill-fated mission. The sun promised more hours of daylight, but the tree blossoms and flowers took on faded hues. Dory sat up and pushed her cap back. Her sapphire blue eyes had turned pale as sea foam.

"Dory, I'm sorry," Rachel said, "your dad's not meeting us here, too many cops. This is the end of the line for us."

Dory remained still, eyes forward, focused on a point far away.

"Dory, sweetheart," Cathy said, "please understand. We have no way to find your dad."

Dory smiled, as if to herself. Cathy remembered Harvey describing her as ten-going-on-forty. To Cathy in that moment she looked forty-going-on-old-soul.

Minutes passed, and then she spoke, her voice brimming with resolve. "He will meet us at the campground, Cathy. He won't let me down on my eleventh birthday. He'll keep his word."

"He has no way to get to Big Flat, and the police are after him."

"I know he will take me camping tomorrow."

"Dory, how can you know that?" Rachel said.

Dory waited while people returning to the SUV beside them loaded up their kids and dogs and left, and then she scooted to the middle of the backseat and leaned forward. She held up her hand. "When a baby is born," she said, "God carves the baby's name on the palm of the parent's hand. You can't see it, but there's a way for the parent to feel it. It keeps him thinking about his child every minute of every day. Did you know that?"

She paused and caught a tear on her cheek with the ribbed cuff of her cat jersey sleeve. "The parent will keep every promise no matter what it takes because the child is precious to him."

"How do you know all of this?" Cathy said.

"God told me." Dory caught another tear with her cuff.

"When did He tell you?" Rachel said.

"He told me just before I was born." She punctuated her revelation with a nod.

Rachel's face turned ashen, and tears rolled down her cheeks. Cathy reached over and took her hand. She could not envision

RACHEL carved on Powder Mom's palm.

———————

Cathy phoned Carrie to tell her about her plans to go camping with Rachel.

"Rachel always pulls this kind of crap," Carrie said.

"Carrie, we want to help the little girl celebrate her birthday. Her dad's having car trouble. You can understand." She decided to wait to explain in person about the AMBER Alert and police.

"I'm stuck in the dorm by myself, except for Anne. Her brother is picking her up Monday."

"Good, I'll get there about ten Monday morning. You and Anne can keep each other company."

Dory told them the name of the campground, and Rachel looked it up on Cathy's phone. "One hour and seventeen minutes on Highway 299," she said. "Jerry's Camping and RV offers tent sites, RV hook-ups, and cabins. Rafting, hiking, and fishing nearby."

"How is it okay for us to take Dory to Big Flat?"

"Cathy, we're in no more trouble at Big Flat than at the Sundial Bridge as long as Harvey doesn't get arrested and shows up at a police station on Monday."

Rachel seemed so matter-of-fact. Is that why Cathy kept going along with the young woman she hardly knew?

"Rachel, how do you know so much about legal stuff?"

"My major is CJS."

Cathy shrugged.

"Criminology and Justice Studies," she said. "Did you think I was Theater Arts like Carrie?"

"Okay, so what happens to us on Monday?"

"Maybe nothing, but we'll be contacted later. The DA will decide whether to charge Harvey with a felony or a misdemeanor."

"So, maybe more trouble for us if Harvey gets arrested before he turns himself in?"

"Right, so pray he shows up for Dory's birthday and turns himself in on Monday."

"I prayed already," Dory said. "I prayed for Angel Gabriel to help Daddy."

Cathy prayed too. They needed more help than just one angel.

A bearded man in the campground office offered a cabin with two sets of bunk beds. "Just you three gals staying with us?"

"No," Cathy said, "we expect my brother to get in late tonight."

"Cabin 3, down the driveway, toilets and showers here in the main building, towels available. No heat in the cabins, lots of blankets but you'll still need to bundle up tonight."

The gift shop yielded matching sweatshirts—cranberry colored with a white outline of a mean looking Sasquatch and white lettering, "Bigfoot Country/Big Flat, CA." Cathy also bought gray sweatpants, toiletries, packaged sandwiches, chips, sodas, and Bigfoot slippers for Dory. They ate in the cabin and then headed to the women's showers. The last sunlight shafts filtered through giant pine trees, as they, dressed alike, strolled back and greeted others they passed.

"How will Harvey find us here?" Rachel said.

Dory stopped beside the rental car, in front of Cabin 3, pulled her cat jersey from the clothing in her arms, and spread it across the hood. "Daddy will recognize this."

By nine o'clock Cathy convinced Dory to go to sleep and promised to wake her when Harvey arrived. But she doubted he could get there. Rachel climbed into the bunk above Cathy's. They spoke softly, with the light out, so Dory could sleep.

"Rachel, why did you visit Powder Mom?"

"She phoned a week ago and told me how much she loved me, how she really wanted to see me, how she's getting sober. I knew she was lying. She just wanted me to bring her money."

"If you knew that, why did you even bother coming to Reno?"

"Cathy, when it comes to your mom you always hope."

Cathy heard the choke in Rachel's voice. A distant coyote howled, and the chatter of campers walking to and from the toilets and showers carried over the night stillness.

"What will you do with CJS?" Cathy said.

"Get a job in law enforcement. I want to take children away from bad parents."

More coyotes joined the pine forest chorus. Rachel and Cathy fell silent. Rachel started snoring. Cathy's thoughts meandered through Carrie's childhood until she slept, too.

Cathy woke to a figure by her bed, tugging at the blankets. "I looked at your phone," Dory said. "It's eleven forty-six. I wanna wait outside for Daddy."

"It's too cold outside. He'll knock on the door when he sees your cat jersey, but he may not come until later."

"He said he'd spend my whole birthday with me. My birthday is about to start."

Rachel stirred. "Let's listen for him, Dory. I'll turn on the light." She eased down the wooden bunk ladder, and they waited. Dory held the phone and announced the time every five minutes. Near one in the morning she ceased her announcements and merely stared at the phone.

Rachel, sitting yoga-style next to Dory on the other lower bunk, sprang up when a car rumbled past their cabin. It stopped. A door banged, and a woman's voice shouted something indiscernible. The car passed their cabin again, leaving the campground. Rachel, like a deflated balloon, shriveled back into the bunk, but Dory smiled. She heard the footsteps approaching the cabin before Rachel or Cathy did.

A tap on the door and then dad and daughter hugged at the threshold. Harvey picked Dory up and twirled into the cabin while Cathy pushed the door shut against a chill blast.

"Daddy, I'm so happy you're here."

"Me too, honey, but I'm so sorry I'm late." He put Dory down to hug Rachel and Cathy. "Thank you for taking care of her."

"How in the world, Harvey?" Rachel said. She and Cathy took positions on one lower bunk, ready for a story, while Harvey sat with Dory on his lap on the other lower bunk.

"I asked a kid on a bike for directions to the Sundial Bridge, but then I saw police cars going that way. I ducked into a hole-in-the-wall bar with Harleys lined up in front. Perfect, I thought. I used to ride motorcycles and figured I could blend in with the bikers."

Dory slid off Harvey's lap to come and sit between Rachel and Cathy. "But how did you get here, Daddy?"

"Hold on, grasshopper, I'm getting to that. The bikers chugged beers while I sipped sodas and played darts with them. One guy, a real talker, told me he lives in Junction City, just down the road from here. He was too drunk to drive his bike home, so I offered to help. He pulled his girlfriend's pink helmet and denim jacket from the saddlebag on his bike, and off we went along Highway 299, me wearing girl's gear and driving his Harley with him on the back."

"Wow, what a hoot!" Rachel said.

"Yeah, quite a picture. When we got to his house, we waited for his girlfriend, Nevaeh, to get home from work. Then she drove me here in her Camaro."

"Daddy, what was the guy's name?"

"I don't know his real name, but the bikers called him, 'Gabby.'"

Dory held her palms together in front of her, fingers upward, and whispered, "Thank you, Gabriel."

Sunday

"Row, row, row your boat gently down the stream." They all sang, and the birthday girl, in the backseat with her dad, moved her arms like a music conductor. The Trinity River kept companion with the highway as they rolled along and stopped at trailheads for short hikes along pine needle-covered paths in the brisk morning air.

By noon they reached the rafting center, where they ate lunch, toured Bigfoot exhibits, and waited for a turn with guide Michael on an inflatable raft. Michael helped them don life jackets and demonstrated proper paddle use. The birthday party of four, plus Michael, maneuvered along the river shoreline.

"I saw a fish jump," Dory said and pointed to the river's center. An osprey glided above the raft, and crows cawed from trees as they floated by. Michael entertained with regional history and folklore.

When the sun began its bid for repose in the West, Harvey raised his paddle skyward, invited Cathy and Rachel to do the same, and offered a salute to the "smartest, prettiest, and sweetest lady in the world."

Rachel led the birthday song, and Dory blew kisses to everyone.

"Eleven years ago I experienced the best day of my life," Harvey said, "and I feel as blessed today as then."

Monday morning

They drove past Humboldt State on the way to Eureka. Cathy looked in the rearview mirror. Harvey, wearing Dory's Seattle

Seahawks cap, kept his eyes on his daughter, perhaps to capture a mental video, a vivid memory of chatter and laughter, sweet-little-girl smiles and poses, sapphire blue eyes contrasting the big green eyes on her whimsical cat jersey.

The birthday vacation ended. They parked across the street from the police station and got out of the car for hugs and good-byes. Addie and Peter Bakas walked to the police station front door, Addie clutching her Bigfoot slippers and Sasquatch sweatshirt. A policeman leaving the building held the door for them as they entered. Addie looked back through the glass on the door, reminding Cathy of when she first saw her, early Saturday morning, looking out the window of her father's car.

After stopping for gas, bottled water, and granola bars, Cathy and Carrie sped onto the highway. Landmarks from the day before rolled by: the turnoff to the rafting center, trailheads, Jerry's Camping and RV. Cathy told Carrie more about the weekend, filling in details about Harvey and Dory, the AMBER Alert poster at the mall, the Sundial Bridge, the campground, and the river rafting birthday party.

"Mom, you left me stuck in the dorm to go camping and partying with Rachel and even hiding fugitives. She's a bad influence."

Cathy had not yet processed all the influences from the weekend.

The highway unfolded before them, leading them home, with alternating stretches of old asphalt and new blacktop. Carrie and Cathy alternated between stretches of easy conversation and comfortable silence. A green signboard loomed with mileage posted for Redding and Reno.

"I like road tripping with you, Carrie." Cathy lifted her hand from the steering wheel and checked her palm. There indelibly—*CARRIE*.

Year of the Pig

"When I think of talking, it is of course with a woman. For talking at its best being an inspiration, it wants a corresponding divine quality of receptiveness, and where will you find this but in a woman?" –Oliver Wendell Holmes, Sr.

Los Angeles, 1971

NEAR TWO IN THE morning on Sunday, January 24, Lori Kaplan drove Wendell Mah home along Wilshire Blvd. to the Brookbend Apartments in Mar Vista. Her husband, George, one or two *sakes* away from passing out when the trio had emerged from the China Palace restaurant, piped up from the backseat. "Explain exactly, Wendell Old Boy, why you're hiding from your neighbors tonight."

Wendell thought he had already explained the reason. "This weekend's theme is Chinese New Year, and I'm the only Chinaman in the complex," Wendell said. "Need I say more?"

"Yeah, buddy, what a bitch," George slurred, "all the bikini babes would have singled you out and chased you around the pool in celebration. I understand the problem." He rolled his eyes and winked at Lori.

"I get it, Wendell," Lori said. "You're not cut out for this hedonistic hyperactivity."

George, a sociology professor who hoped his friend would find a wife, had coaxed Wendell, a China History professor, into moving into the Brookbend Apartments, a "swinging singles" complex, where a social director filled the weekly calendar with mixers, climaxing in a themed dance party on Saturday night, hangover brunch late Sunday morning, and poolside barbecue with sing-along or "risqué charades" on Sunday night.

"You'll have to sneak by the pool," George said. "Shall we walk you to your door in case somebody tries to drag you into an orgy?"

"No, by now the pool rats are blind drunk. They won't even see me," Wendell said. "Thank you both for saving my Saturday."

Wendell kept to the dark side of the meandering path around the pool enclosure, away from the spotlights cast below the lampposts, and hurried past Buildings H and I to ascend to the third floor of Building J. Green door, with gold numbers, 328, above the peephole. When he had moved in, he considered it a good omen, his birth month and year, March 1928. But the good omen disappointed. Brookbend hadn't offered up an antidote to loneliness.

Before going to bed, he pulled exam blue books from his briefcase and placed them on his dining table. Reading and grading essay answers about the Boxer Rebellion would consume most of Sunday afternoon and evening.

Monday afternoon along Bruin Walk, students held up anti-war posters and offered political pamphlets to passers-by. Wendell walked across campus toward his office in Haines Hall. Tall eucalyptus trees cast long shadows in the bright winter sunlight. UCLA seemed a world away from UC Berkeley, his alma mater, birthplace of the Free Speech Movement and where he taught until moving to Los Angeles.

He found a package on his desk with return address in San Francisco and withdrew from it a bound journal with wooden covers. Though he couldn't read the raised, red, Cantonese characters adorning the front cover, he knew he had run his fingers across that cover long ago and felt the textures of the leather cords holding together the covers and the pages between them. He opened the journal and leafed through pages which had delighted him in childhood. His father, holding Wendell on his lap, had translated the freshly inked, intricate strokes of each day into English, his voice filling Wendell's ears with magical words. He recalled on one of those pages Mah Jing had explained why he named his son after the poet, Oliver Wendell Holmes.

A manila envelope and a separate note had fallen out of the same package. Wendell read the note:

Dearest Wendell,

A few weeks after Sylvia's funeral, I found Mah Jing's journal and letters in the basement, on the top shelf of Sylvia's old secretary. Jing wrote in his journal from before you were born until the time of your mother's deportation. The letters are ones Jing sent to Sylvia, telling her of conditions in China. I apologize for the delay in sending them to you. The loss of my sister has been so devastating for me and for you, too, I know. She and Jackson loved you, couldn't have loved you any more if you had been their natural born son. Lai-Guk and Mah Jing, Jackson and Sylvia, may they all rest in peace. God bless you. Call on me any time, dear friend. Love, Gloria.

Wendell poured the letters from the envelope. Sylvia had told him his father wrote to her about the Japanese invasion of China in the months before his death. Wendell had his own letters from Mah Jing.

Wendell realized the power of this unexpected treasure. Who better than his own father to teach the teacher about China History? That night as his Brookbend neighbors enjoyed happy hour at the pool, Wendell spent an evening with his father, or at least the next best thing, an evening with his father's letters to Sylvia, written in English.

The next day Wendell popped into George's office, placing the journal on George's desk and telling George about the package from San Francisco. "I read and reread the letters all night, but the journal is written in Cantonese. Do you think your friend in the Linguistics Department can find someone to translate my father's journal for me?"

"I think so. After my lecture today, I'll make an inquiry."

"Terrific! Thank you." Wendell looked down at the red characters on the journal cover. Decades had passed since his father's voice had given color, substance and meaning to life in a new land for Jing and an only land for Wendell. He thought of his mother, Lai-Guk, who lived in those journal pages. She had loved him, cared for him, and spoken to him in Cantonese. He had long ago forgotten Cantonese but never forgot the last time his mother hugged him and kissed him good-bye.

"Wendell, are you okay?" George said.

Wendell straightened in his chair, cleared his throat, and pulled his mind back into the conversation. "Sorry, George, I got lost in thought. Oh, did you tell me what you're lecturing on today?"

"*Societal Impacts of the Women's Liberation Movement.* I hope the students pay attention. The stuff going on now with women will have far-reaching consequences, some unintended."

"More job opportunities, equal pay for equal work—sounds good to me."

"Volunteerism down, some labor markets flooded, soaring child care costs, more single-parent families, women having no choice but to work—that's the other side of the coin." George let out the sociologist sigh Wendell always heard when George got started on unintended consequences.

"Oh, one more thing," George said, "Lori said to give you this." He pushed a slip of paper toward Wendell. "You didn't take your fortune from the fortune cookie. Lori put it in her purse."

Wendell squinted at the tiny letters, "Your forever will arrive tomorrow." Wendell shrugged. "What does it mean?"

"Lori says it means something wonderful will happen tomorrow and change your life forever," George said and grinned, throwing out his hands. Wendell tucked the slip of paper into his shirt pocket. Women sometimes came up with the strangest ideas.

Students filing into the lecture hall on Wednesday greeted Wendell with, "*Gung hay fat choy*," and he returned the well wishes, happy they knew the correct date of the Chinese New Year, the start of the Year of the Pig. Someone left a stuffed toy, a red pig with yellow polka dots, on the lectern. Students applauded when he grinned and held up the pig for all to see.

After class, he sauntered back to his office, enjoying the sunshine and sounds of robins along the way. *Gung hay fat choy*, "Good luck, may fortune come your way." Fortune had come Wendell's way in education, career, finances, and friendships, but not in love. In his last letter to Wendell, his father had written, "Son, live with honor and perseverance and you will find love. Love is the master key that opens the gates of happiness."

Where had he gone wrong?

With fifteen minutes before the weekly faculty meeting, Wendell decided to simply sit and think. He pulled and released a metal sphere in the Newton's cradle toy on his desk. *Plink*—the sphere struck the row of other suspended spheres. *Plink* again and again as the end spheres took turns transferring energy. Sylvia, a gadget enthusiast, had sent him the desk toy. Sylvia, also a problem solver, had taught Wendell her favorite problem solving technique. "Wend, my dear," she would say, "write your problem in question form, jot down answers, and question each answer. Write it, don't just think it. Writing revs up the power of your subconscious. You'll discover what to do."

Plink-plink-plink—he picked up pen and pad and wrote:

> *Why am I still unmarried? Jenny broke our engagement. Why? Parents didn't want her to marry Chinese. Why? Nebraska's ant-miscegenation laws.*
>
> *Jenny broke our engagement. Why? Didn't want to disobey her parents. Why? They convinced her society would make life hard for mixed-race children.*
>
> *Why am I still unmarried? Can't find another woman to love. Why? Still broken-hearted.*

He looked at the clock and sprang from his chair, with just enough time to dash to the faculty meeting. Down the stairs, out the door, and crossing to the Humanities Building, Wendell caught a glimpse of helmeted police aligned in front of the Administrative Building and remembered seeing posters announcing a sit-in protest in the chancellor's office. He hop scotched around protesters carrying signs on their way to the police line.

Back from the meeting, Wendell cleared his desk and slid his problem solving notes into his briefcase. He would pore over them at home. The telephone rang.

"Not going home, Wendell," George said.

"Yes, just about to leave. You're lucky to catch me."

"No, Wendell, I mean you're not going home. The police staged their vehicles across the roadway by the faculty parking lot. We can't get out."

"You're kidding."

"Not kidding, but I have to stay anyway. A former student wants to talk with me about a project. I can see the parking lot from my window. I'll phone you when the cops leave."

"Thank you, George."

"One more thing, I found a translator and sent your journal over to him. In a few days, maybe a week, he'll have it done for you."

Confined to campus until the police withdrew, Wendell pulled his problem solving notes from his briefcase and stared at them. They stared back and whispered old, cold facts. Sylvia told him, if you've written stale answers, look for fresh perspectives. He stared harder and jotted more notes:

AM laws repealed too late. Jenny married someone else. Fresh look— reassess prospects of falling in love with another woman.

The telephone rang.

"You're free to leave," George said. "The cops scampered away."

Wendell stayed and turned back to his notes.

Qualities I desire in a wife may exist in women but are hard to discern. Why? Women changed in the last ten years. Why? Women's lib.

He would think about that on his drive home.

He turned off the office light, locked the door, and left. At the stairs, he heard the telephone in his office ringing. He hesitated. How could a ringing telephone sound so insistent? But it did. He unlocked the door, assuming he'd miss the call, but somehow he lifted the receiver in time.

"Good, you're still there," George said. "I have a grad student I want to send over."

"Right now?"

"Yeah, if that's okay. She has a project she needs to start on. She'll explain it to you. You can spare an hour, or do you have wild plans for tonight?"

Wendell opened his office door all the way. Prudence dictated leaving the door wide open when meeting with students, especially females. His office looked presentable, better than George's, with his hodgepodge piles of newspapers and magazines everywhere. Wendell spied a tiny slip of paper on the floor, near the wastebasket. He wanted to pick it up, but footsteps in the hall announced the student's arrival.

"Dr. Mah, I'm LeAnn Moore." She seemed to know him already. "Dr. Kaplan said you might be able to help me."

Wendell offered her a seat across the desk from him. "You were in one of my classes, weren't you?"

"Yes, I majored in sociology, but I took many electives. Your lecture, 'Why So Many Chinese Restaurants in the United States,' fascinated me."

"That one seems to resonate with students."

"Clever! Most Americans love Chinese food, but few know they're abundant because of the Chinese Exclusion Act of 1882. I hardly breathed when you explained the hardships Chinese immigrants endured at Angel Island and in Chinatowns across the country."

Good, at least one student had understood his most passionate speech at the lectern, passionate because his own Chinese immigrant parents came through Angel Island.

"I'm humbled by your recall of my lecture, Miss Moore. How can I help you today?"

"I'm on a graduate committee, Student Filmmakers for Social Change. We're writing a grant proposal to produce an historical drama film. Dr. Kaplan said you have an interesting story about your parents coming to America. Do you mind telling me about them?"

LeAnn's impromptu request stunned Wendell. He had spoken the events of Mah Jing's and Lai-Guk's lives only to people with whom he felt close. He felt uncomfortable speaking to a stranger about them. Maybe a short summary would suffice.

"Well, Miss Moore, my father emigrated from South China to San Francisco and worked in his *paper uncle's* restaurant. He and my mother married, and I was their only child."

LeAnn jotted notes as he spoke, but then looked up. "What are the dates of those events?"

"Oh, yes, the dates," he said. "My father was born in 1901 and emigrated in 1918. My parents married in 1927. I was born in 1928." He had given away his age, but that shouldn't matter.

"When was your mother born?"

"I don't know." Nobody knew, but that would be a long story.

"Please, go on."

"My mother was deported in 1935." Perhaps she wouldn't ask the circumstances. "My father asked his best friends, an American couple, to be my guardians. He went to China to find my mother. They both passed away in China."

He stopped. She looked up and waited, pen poised above her notepad. His mind spun like a Rolodex as he sought any more facts he could concisely provide. He found none. During the long pause, his wall clock ticked louder than usual.

She closed her notebook and dropped her pen into her handbag. "Thank you, Dr. Mah. Your parents' story is interesting. I will confer with the committee. Thank you for your time."

That was it? She seemed to have dismissed him. Had he acted too buttoned-up? She was ready to leave. He didn't want her to. She had been so receptive about his lecture.

"Miss Moore, did Dr. Kaplan tell you I have a journal, written by my father and documenting his life from the nineteen twenties through nineteen thirty-five?" Talking with her had been enjoyable. He didn't want the conversation to end. "I also have his letters from China up through nineteen forty-three."

She looked down and shook her head. He waited for her words.

She took a deep breath and sighed. "I can hardly believe what you just said."

"But it's true, Miss Moore."

"Well, of course it is. I mean I can't believe I found someone with a documented, first-hand, contemporaneous account of the early Chinese experience in America. May I show the journal and letters to the committee?"

"Yes," he said. Her request kept the conversation going, perhaps leading to another meeting. "The journal is being translated into English. I have the letters at home. I can get copies made. Perhaps I can phone you when I have everything ready." He handed her a pen and paper from his desk caddy and watched as she pushed strands of her light-brown hair away from her glasses and wrote her name and number.

"One more question, Dr. Mah, what is a 'paper uncle'?"

"Oh, it's very complicated. *Paper families* were a way to circumvent immigration restrictions by claiming relationships with unrelated Chinese already in America. For example, my father called a man, 'Uncle,' who wasn't really his uncle."

"It must hurt to the core to lose one's true identity and family structure," she said, surprising Wendell with her perception and empathy.

After she left, Wendell bent to pick up the slip of paper he saw on the floor earlier. "Your forever will arrive tomorrow." He flicked it into the wastebasket, turned, turned back, and retrieved the little omen—nothing wrong with keeping it in his desk.

On his drive home, Wendell didn't think about how women's lib had changed women, as he had planned to do. Instead, he thought of how LeAnn Moore had climbed into his head and poked around as a museum visitor might take in exhibits, stopping to read and digest the little cards in display cases. She had been inquisitive and receptive, or had he imagined her level of interest? He wondered how old she was.

A week later, George phoned Wendell at his office. "Good news, I have your translated journal on my desk. Do you want me to drop it by?"

"Thanks, George. Yes, I need a copy for the student you sent over last week. I also need copies of my father's letters."

"You're helping LeAnn. Good for you. I'm going to send an order to the print shop. Bring your letters and I'll send everything over together. Kenny at the print shop always gives me fast turnaround."

Nothing seemed fast in the next few days. Clock hands moved as if being held back by little, unseen dragons. What if LeAnn gave up on the copies and chose another story for the committee? A sunny afternoon made a good excuse to stroll through Westwood Village. Wendell had patronized the print shop a few times in the past.

"Dr. Mah, what can I do for you?" Kenny said.

"Dr. Kaplan sent you a print order. If it's ready, I'll take it to him. Some of my materials are in the same order."

"Dr. Kaplan picked up his items. You just missed him. But LeAnn picked up your copies earlier. She said she needed to start on a film project. She left the originals here for you. She's your girlfriend, right?"

"No, she's not my girlfriend." Wendell considered himself too old for anyone to think LeAnn would be his girlfriend.

"Oh, that's too bad," Kenny said. "If she's not your girlfriend, then she's somebody else's. Such a hottie is not alone."

Wendell gathered up his originals, mumbled a thank you, and stepped outside. Hottie, not alone—LeAnn, five feet, six inches and lithe, with long, light-brown hair and a poised and intellectual bearing—she probably had a boyfriend. Whether she did or not was none of his business.

He waited a week to phone her. "Have you talked to your committee about my family's story?"

"Yes, Dr. Mah," she said. "The committee wants to move forward with it."

"That's wonderful. So what's next? Should we meet and discuss the film?"

"Not yet. First I'll write the drama in story format to submit with our proposal."

"That sounds like a lot of work. Do you want me to help you?"

"That would be wonderful. Perhaps you could give me feedback on the draft."

"Of course I will."

"I'll mail you my pages."

"Wouldn't it be better to discuss it in person, Miss Moore?"

LeAnn agreed to contact him in a few weeks. After three weeks, he stared at the phone. He paced. Maybe she was busy with a boyfriend. In the meantime, George invited him to dinner.

Mexican food suited Wendell, George, and Lori. George tipped the restaurant's mariachi musicians to play a couple of songs for Wendell and wish him *feliz cumpleaños* on his forty-third birthday.

"Wendell Old Boy, how's it going with LeAnn?" George said.

"What do you mean?"

"Is her committee going to make the film?"

"Oh, the film project, I don't know. She's working on the grant proposal. I'm supposed to help."

"Have you asked her out?" Lori said.

"Of course not, Lori, LeAnn is too young for me."

"Wendell, you want to get married, right?"

"Yes, but I think I should find a lady closer to my age."

"Wrong," Lori said. "You're too old to date someone closer to your age. Think about it. If you want to have kids, you need to find a wife younger than you, someone still in her twenties. Women can't wait until their thirties to have babies. It's too risky."

"You watch," George said, "childbearing years will be extended through medical advances, maybe even into the late thirties."

"Maybe someday, but not yet," Lori said. She fidgeted, seeming to dance in her seat.

"Tell him our news, Lori." George looked like a Cheshire cat.

"We're expecting a baby!"

No more talk of LeAnn or the film, Lori and George gushed

about baby names and plans to transform a den at home into a nursery. They asked if Wendell would consider being the godfather.

That night in his apartment, Wendell listened to the clock on his dresser, tick-tick-tick. He wanted to be a father, a good father, like Mah Jing, but he had clutched his broken engagement so long he had become too old to marry someone his age. Tick-tick-tick.

He phoned LeAnn the next day. She had completed a draft of the first few pages, and they agreed to meet Sunday afternoon in Lafayette Park, near her apartment in the Westlake district of Los Angeles.

"Dr. Mah, I'm sorry to have you drive over here," she said, "but I work part time. The office is two blocks from here. On Sunday, Tuesday, and Thursday I go in and update client ledgers from five until nine."

They found a park bench away from family gatherings and children at play. The early afternoon sunshine played with the wind in the trees to dress the ground in a moving filigree of intertwined shadows. LeAnn withdrew a binder from her tote bag and handed it to Wendell. "Please read it and tell me what you think," she said.

"Oh, no, Miss Moore, I hoped you would read it to me. I'd like to hear the words in your voice." Maybe that came across a little pushy.

"Well, okay," she said. "The working title is, *China Sons*." She read:

> *By the dim candlelight, Jing discerned dark cloth behind the drums and a child hiding, face pressed against the cabinet back. He dropped his stick, pushed oil drums out of the way, and pulled the child out. The child, with hair chopped short and uneven, wore boy's clothing, all black and too large, and stood rigid and silent, eyes cast down.*

LeAnn looked up. Perhaps she sensed Wendell's puzzlement. "Is there something wrong?"

"No, of course not, but I'm surprised you start with my father finding my mother as a child. That was 1923, in San Francisco. His story started in South China in 1901."

"Dr. Mah, it's an historical drama, not a documentary. Hans encouraged us to create the dramatic scenes needed to expose the social issues of the time period."

Strands of her hair had fallen forward, and he wanted to reach out and brush them back into her silky tresses. He watched her push them back.

"Is Hans someone on your committee?"

"No, he's not a student," she said. "He's our faculty sponsor. You may have heard of Dr. Hans Dahlgren. Not only is he a professor in the Fine Arts Department, he's a director and has made several major films. He was nominated for an Oscar."

"You call him by his first name?" Wendell leaned forward.

"Sure. Hans asked us to because we're all working together."

"Then perhaps you should call me Wendell."

"Okay. Then please call me LeAnn." She smiled. He imagined he could swim in her green eyes.

She read more. He listened and closed his eyes. Her steady voice transported him to early childhood, a time of joy and dreams. The afternoon breeze softened. Traffic noise lessened. Fewer voices shouted or laughed.

She stopped reading. He opened his eyes and watched her put her pages back in her tote bag.

"Is that all you have now, LeAnn?"

"I have more pages, but I have to get to my job."

"Do you have time for a sandwich or a soft drink, maybe?"

"I don't really, Wendell. Let's meet later in the week. I'll keep writing."

At home, Wendell thought of Sylvia and took pen and paper to the dining table and wrote:

*Why am I not LeAnn's boyfriend? I haven't told her my inter-
est. Why? Afraid of rejection. Why? Don't know what she thinks
of me. Why? She's not said. Why? Maybe she needs time to feel
comfortable.*

They met at the same place on Wednesday afternoon. LeAnn dug into her tote bag and presented Wendell with a book, *The Professor at the Breakfast Table.*

"Wow, Oliver Wendell Holmes!" Wendell flipped the cover and perused the front matter.

"A belated birthday present, Wendell."

"Oh, no, I couldn't accept such a gift, LeAnn. That's so sweet, but I can't."

"You must. I'm grateful for this project and your help. Not just that, but your family story has become dear to me. Such an honor-able man was your father, and he never gave up."

Wendell remembered the birthday letter from Mah Jing—*Son, live with honor and perseverance and you will find love.*

"You know my father well."

"I know you well, too, Wendell."

"What do you know?"

"You're an honorable man because your father taught you his ways. I know this from his journal."

If Wendell were to swim in her green eyes, he'd have to take a plunge. "I like you, LeAnn."

"I like you, Wendell." She blushed.

The book, the blush, her words—he would hardly remember how the rest of the afternoon and evening unfolded, his mind skip-ping back and back, like a stylus caught in a groove on vinyl, think-ing of what just happened. She read more. Dusk fell. They ate at Langers Deli. He walked her to the door of her second story studio apartment on Sixth Street.

They met five more times to review the story. They sat at her dining table, nibbled crackers, drank hot tea, and refined details re-quiring his childhood recollections. He admired the artwork on her walls and the books in her bookcase.

Then the times together ended. The committee submitted the grant proposal and waited. Wendell phoned LeAnn. She had loaded on more hours at work and had to prepare for final exams.

In the middle of June, Wendell surveyed the mountain of final exam blue books on his desk. The telephone rang.

"Wendell, it's LeAnn, we got the grant!"

"That's wonderful, LeAnn. Let's celebrate."

"That's why I phoned. There's a party Friday night. It's at the home of Hans's friend in Malibu, a movie producer. You're invited, too."

The committee had titled the project *China Sons*, and as one of the China sons, Wendell felt obliged to attend, but going to a busy party to celebrate with LeAnn fell short of his hopes.

"We should go together," he said. "I'll pick you up." She agreed, thank goodness. He would have been disappointed if she had al-ready made another arrangement.

Friday night, Wendell squinted at the Thomas Guide map and

located the Malibu address. He handed LeAnn the guide to place back in the glove box. Her hair gleamed golden below the car dome light as she bent forward. He didn't want to go to the party, but he could think of no excuse to change plans.

Wendell punched in the gate code and followed the driveway to a paved parking pad beside a two-story Tudor home. Hans came to the door. LeAnn hugged Hans and introduced Wendell all around.

Wendell watched LeAnn move among the partygoers, talking and nodding, laughing and embracing. Hans struck a fork against a glass until conversations quieted and the partygoers circled him. "When LeAnn pitched *China Sons* to the committee, we almost celebrated right then. What a powerful story! LeAnn brought us historical social issues with current relevance: discrimination, immigration, deportation, restrictive housing, extortion and human trafficking. Here's to LeAnn, Dr. Mah, committee members, and all who helped us get this far. Let's make the best historical drama film imaginable."

The party kept going—eleven o'clock, midnight, one in the morning. Wendell didn't want to pull LeAnn away from colleagues and friends wishing her well-deserved congratulations. Near one-thirty, as he talked Bruin basketball with a movie cameraman, LeAnn came over and tapped his arm. "Shall we leave before bar drunks get on the freeway?"

On the way, she gushed about the party and everyone's excitement about making the film. "This will be an important film, Wendell. I appreciate your involvement."

They arrived on Sixth Street, and Wendell parked to walk LeAnn to her door.

"Please come in for a few minutes. I've been thinking about something, and I want to ask you."

They entered the apartment. She switched on the light.

"What do you want to ask me?"

"I haven't spoken to Hans or the committee. I'll ask you first. I'd like to re-title the film."

What better title than *China Sons*, a film about his father and him, how his father had rescued and loved his mother, how he had chosen between his love for his wife and his love for his son, and how he sacrificed his heart so his son would grow up in America?

"What do you suggest?"

LeAnn drew up before him, close, closer than ever before, and put her hands on his shoulders. She leaned in, brushed his face with her cheek, brought her lips to his ear, and whispered, "*Pretty Chrysanthemum.*"

His mother, the child with no name found hiding from her abusers! Mah Jing named her Lai-Guk, Pretty Chrysanthemum, the flower one waits for. On the afternoon she disappeared, Pretty Chrysanthemum hugged Wendell and kissed him good-bye before he skipped beside his father on their way to the Fan-Tan parlor. LeAnn was right, the story was Lai-Guk's, not his father's and certainly not his. LeAnn, divinely receptive to his family story, proved divinely perceptive about the gaping hole in his heart, the void left when Pretty Chrysanthemum disappeared.

His throat knotted, and tears welled up. He couldn't let LeAnn see. He pulled her closer and concealed his tears in her tresses. She embraced him, as Pretty Chrysanthemum had. He sought her lips. At once, she was his mother and his lover.

"Can I stay with you?" he said. After kissing her, he couldn't imagine leaving her.

She turned off the light and moved to the window to open the blinds above her bed. The moon cast its light on them and reminded Wendell of the window in the storeroom he shared as a boy with his father and mother—the same moon, the same moonlight, the same feeling of being where he belonged.

On October 27, Wendell and LeAnn celebrated her twenty-seventh birthday. The valet parking attendant opened the car door for LeAnn. Wendell took her arm as they entered the Benson House restaurant on Santa Monica Blvd., with its mahogany appointments, crystal chandelier, and special area for romantic dining in secluded, curtained booths.

"You'll have to wait until dessert to open this." Wendell placed a wrapped box on the seat beside him. She would never guess a rung pig for a birthday present, a recycled present at that! Earlier that day, he had mused, as he threaded a needle, on how long before she would catch on.

He checked his watch. The waiter asked: which wine, half liter or by the glass, need more time with the menu, any appetizers, soup or salad, which salad dressing, mixed in or on the side, out first or with the entrée, bread while you wait, French or sour dough, any questions? Pink's Hot Dogs on La Brea would have been easier and faster.

"Wendell, have you asked the Kaplans if they can come to the film screening?"

"I forgot the date you said." He dropped his knife while trying to butter the bread.

"January twenty-eighth. Do you think Gloria will come from San Francisco?"

The salads came.

"I have no idea if she travels. She's older than Sylvia was." He spilled a drop of Roquefort dressing.

The waiter came back. "Your dinners will be out shortly." He turned and disappeared.

"LeAnn, I can't wait any longer."

"I'm sure he headed to the kitchen. He'll bring our dinners in a minute or two."

"No, I mean, please open your present." He almost knocked her water glass over when he passed the present to her.

She removed the paper, lifted the top of the box, and drew out the stuffed toy pig, red with yellow polka dots, diamond ring sewn to its snout.

"Oh, how wonderful, this is so unique! Thank you. My grandfather kept three rung pigs in his yard. Of course, he didn't want them rooting in his plantings, thus the rings."

The waiter brought their plates, and, to Wendell's horror, LeAnn placed the pig back in the box, set it by her wine glass, and surveyed the dinner. He stared at the box and then looked at her. While he waited for her to say something, his heart stopped.

She looked up. "Yes."

"Yes, the dinner looks good, or yes, you will marry me?"

"Both."

He sprang up, leaned across the table, and kissed her. "I'm so happy, LeAnn!"

He pulled the pig from the box, removed manicure scissors from his pocket, snipped the thread on the pig snout, and slid the ring on her finger. She moved her hand toward the candle on the table and showed him the diamond's sparkle.

"Please pick the date, LeAnn, but don't make me wait too long."

She took his hand in hers. "How about February fourteenth?"

"Perfect." He knew she thought of Valentine's Day, but the Year of the Pig would end on the same date. He had started the year meeting her and would end the year marrying her. He thought of the tiny slip of paper with the fortune he read the day before he met her: *Your forever will arrive tomorrow.*

Mr. Williams' School Bus

I WAS THE FIRST OF the teachers to take a seat in the front row of folding chairs below the stage. Mrs. Goode, the school district superintendent, sat onstage with Mr. Pittman, the school principal. Other teachers joined me as Mrs. Goode called the hearing to order.

"Mr. Pittman asked me to convene this hearing because he received a letter of complaint from the mother of one of our Deerwood Park Elementary students," Mrs. Goode began. "The letter indicates inappropriate behavior by our school bus driver, Walter Williams."

She seemed ready to say more, but Pittman stood up and interrupted her. "Mrs. Goode, I will be addressing problems with Mr. Williams' job performance in addition to the serious accusations in the letter."

"Yes, I know, Mr. Pittman. You may question Mr. Williams about all concerns."

Mrs. Goode turned to me. "Mrs. Rose, I see only teachers and one parent present. Are other parents coming?"

On Friday she had asked me to notify parents of the Tuesday night hearing in the school auditorium and told me inappropriate and potentially criminal activities involving Walter Williams had been reported.

Both Bruce Pittman and Walter Williams were new at the school this year. The teachers had all become fond of Walter, or "Wally," as we called him. Wally lived at the end of the bus route in Eagle Creek, so he hung out in the teachers' lounge each day, mostly reading while waiting to drive children back to their stops at the end of the day. The teachers, less fond of Pittman, considered the new principal more concerned with the politics of administration than with the concerns of teachers, parents, or students.

"Mrs. Goode, the parents work and most don't have cars. So they will ride together later on the school bus—the same route Mr. Williams drives, west along Old School Road from Eagle Creek to Deerwood Park, sixty-one miles."

"Our school bus?" Pittman said.

"Yes."

"Mr. Williams is here, so who's driving?" Mrs. Goode said, nodding toward Wally, also seated onstage.

"Darrell Henderson, owner of the A-1 Garage in Eagle Creek," I said. "Mr. Williams borrowed Darrell's tow truck after he finished taking the kids home so he could return on time for the hearing."

"Oh yes, Henderson. He bills the district for bus repairs," Pittman said. "I don't know that he is authorized to drive the school bus."

"Mr. Pittman," I said, irritated by his remark, "Darrell knows more about that bus than anyone. He's helped the district maintain it for many years."

"I'm getting text messages from Darrell at each stop," I told Mrs. Goode.

"We can't wait," she said and nodded to Pittman.

Bruce Pittman, bald headed and square jawed, glared down at Wally. Pittman's large frame and booming voice would intimidate anyone. Wally, short and slim, looked childlike in his chair as he sat woodenly, waiting for Pittman's words.

Pittman drew a page from a folder. "According to our bus log, except for the first two weeks of school last fall, the bus was late one hundred percent of the time, fifteen to twenty minutes most days and one to two hours late on several occasions. Last year, when Mrs. Randall drove, she maintained punctuality ninety-eight percent of the time. Why, Mr. Williams, is this year different?"

Wally looked at Mrs. Goode and then turned back to Pittman. "Well, it's different because I changed one of the stops," Wally said. "By the time we reach the reservation each morning, some kids have been on the bus a long time and need a restroom break. The tribal kids used to walk a mile down the hill from the tribal center to meet the bus, even in the cold or wet weather. I talked it over with Mr. Tall Bear." Wally glanced at Mrs. Goode. "We agreed I would drive up the dirt road to the tribal center, and he would let children use the restrooms there. That added maybe fifteen minutes."

"Why don't you start out earlier?" Pittman said.

Wally looked back and forth between Mrs. Goode and Pittman, as if surprised by the question. Mrs. Goode nodded. He turned to Pittman. "Well, the Eagle Creek parents can't walk their school age kids to the school bus stop any earlier. They meet me at five fifty-five as it is. Some of them also have toddlers to get ready before they board the town bus for a daycare stop near the factory where they work.'

"I guess we'll just have to change the school day, not just for the bus riders but also for all the other kids who live in Deerwood Park and arrive on time and ready to learn." Pittman turned toward Mrs. Goode, perhaps to emphasize his sarcasm.

He turned back to Wally. "Do you have any special needs children on your bus?"

"One autistic boy," Wally said.

"Yes, I'm glad you know about Tobias Ramirez, part of the district underserved population which also includes students who must learn English as a second language. We don't have funding for teacher aides to tutor those needing more help, and we certainly don't have funding for Special Education. Mr. Williams, you are responsible to get our bus-riding students to school on time so they have the same opportunities as our students who don't ride the bus. Every minute of education adds value to the school day."

Pittman lapsed into a speech many of us had heard before. "Funding and grants for targeted programs require us to strive harder for our underserved population. We also report to the Bureau of Indian Education, which is responsible for tribal schooling. Mr. Tall Bear and the bureau decided Deerwood Park Elementary would be the best place to teach our local tribal children. We can't let them down."

"I agree, Mr. Pittman," Wally said.

Mrs. Goode turned to me. I looked at the last text message from Darrell and announced twenty minutes as the parents' ETA.

"Let's move on," she said and nodded to Pittman. He pulled a letter from his folder.

"Mr. Williams, I will read this letter, leaving out the name of the mother and daughter. Mrs. Goode and I agree the names should remain confidential. After I read it, you may respond to the charges."

Pittman cleared his throat, stepped behind the lectern, and read:

Dear Mr. Pittman,

My daughter is a top student in the sixth grade at your school. She has told me disturbing information about the district bus driver. I have four concerns. First, the bus driver drove the children on an unauthorized, off-campus outing. Second, he has singled out three of the female students and given them the inappropriate nickname, Mermaids.

Wally sat expressionless. I hoped Wally was preparing his defense in his mind as Pittman continued:

Third, the bus driver provided spray paint and encouraged a boy to deface the school bus. Fourth, and most disturbing, he downloaded pictures of scantily clad, under aged children to his computer in the bedroom of his apartment while in the presence of a twelve year-old girl, a girl who rides on his bus.

For the safety of our children, please check into the bus driver's behavior.

Sincerely,

Pittman stopped and looked at Wally.

I heard someone seated behind me sniffling. A teacher sitting next to me took a tissue from her purse and passed it back. I wanted to turn around but didn't want to appear rude.

"Can you explain?" Pittman's voice boomed.

Wally surprised me by answering in a booming voice unfamiliar to me.

"Of course I can. But first I want you to know that letter contains so much that is true it had to be from someone who knows all about my bus and what we do on the bus. But it's all so wrong the way it's worded. It's as if somebody wants me to lose my job. You won't tell me who wrote that letter. But the only student on my bus who fits that description, top student in the sixth grade, is Althea Johnson. And I know Mrs. Johnson didn't write it."

Normally mild-mannered Wally seethed anger. I felt anger too, but also relief. I knew the truth.

The sniffling behind me sounded more like stifled sobbing.

Wally continued, "I didn't name the girls, 'Mermaids.' Naomi, Mr.

Tall Bear's granddaughter, came up with the name for herself, Erika Diaz, and Althea. I think the name came from a movie the kids like. It became a convenient way to refer to the three girls."

I turned slightly. I could see a woman behind me, head bent down, weeping.

"I took the kids swimming at the pond we pass on Old School Road. The kids were getting out early on a Friday because of teacher training. Some on my bus are latch-key kids. I worried it wouldn't be safe for them to arrive home so early. The Mermaids had confirmed everyone had swimsuits to bring. The boys stood outside the bus with me while the girls stayed on the bus to change into swimsuits. Then the girls stayed outside with me while the boys changed on the bus."

Wally stopped and looked at Mrs. Goode before continuing. "Althea wants to be a photojournalist. She took pictures at the pond with the new camera her mother gave her for her birthday. Her mother's computer is old, and her printer doesn't have the slot needed to download the camera's memory card. Mrs. Johnson phoned me and asked if she and Althea could come over to my apartment to download the swim outing pictures. I printed the pictures for Althea."

Mrs. Goode interrupted, "Mrs. Johnson is not here yet. Can we somehow verify your account?"

I raised my hand and stood. "Althea is in my class. She told me about going to Mr. Williams' apartment with her mother to download pictures. She showed me the pictures."

"Thank you, Mrs. Rose. Mr. Williams, what would you like to tell us about how the bus was defaced?"

"Oh, Mrs. Goode," Wally said, "I want to tell you all about that. Every morning we see one deer by the pond. The kids love that deer. It stood back in the tree line when the kids were swimming. Althea zoomed in and got a great picture, antlers and all. She gave a copy of the picture to Toby. Toby sketched it, just beautiful, so life-like. So I bought three cans of spray paint—black, brown, and white—and asked Toby to paint the deer on the hood of the school bus. If you haven't seen it yet, Mrs. Goode, you should take a look. The kids love it. It's like a logo for the school, you know, Deerwood Park Elementary—a deer on the bus."

Mrs. Goode looked stunned. "Do you mean Toby Ramirez?"

"Yes, Mrs. Goode. I don't understand how he does it, but I think maybe he's an autistic savant. I'm sure you know more about that than I do."

Mrs. Goode had been a teacher at the school before becoming district superintendent. Toby had been in her second grade class three years earlier. In each grade, Toby's teachers tried to get him to engage. No one had succeeded.

The parents arrived and quietly filed into the rows of chairs behind the teachers. Mrs. Goode seemed not to notice. "Mr. Williams, please tell me about Toby."

"My first week at school," Wally began, "Toby sat at the back of the bus with his head down. He didn't speak to anyone, and no one spoke to him. My nephew is also autistic. My sister and her husband ease his anxiety by telling him in advance about upcoming things, like a dental appointment or a relative coming to visit. I took Toby's arm and guided him to a front seat. It took several times before he started sitting up front on his own. As I drove I told him about the day ahead, like an assembly in the auditorium or what would be served in the cafeteria."

"Did he start talking to you then?" Mrs. Goode said.

"No, but one day Gilbert told me Toby is artistic. I said I already know he's autistic. He said, 'No, Mr. Williams, Toby can draw pictures. He has a pencil but no paper.' Sure enough, Toby had a pencil behind his ear. I found a sketchbook in the supply cabinet in the teachers' lounge. I put it on Toby's seat. He just held it on his lap, but after a few days he started drawing. He wouldn't let anyone look at what he was drawing.

"One day Gilbert told me Toby needed a pencil sharpener. I got one, and when I handed it to Toby, he said, 'Thanks,' and sat down. The other kids started talking to him after that."

"Is he talking to them?" Mrs. Goode said.

"Not consistently. He responds to situations, but he doesn't talk much."

"I'm amazed, Mr. Williams. It seems like a miracle." Mrs. Goode smiled. "Now, would you please tell me about the Mermaids?"

The nature of the hearing had changed. Without more accusations, Pittman sat down. Mrs. Goode's questioning of Wally seemed a friendly conversation between colleagues.

"Mrs. Goode," Wally continued, "I felt discouraged the first week of school. Don't get me wrong. All my kids were well behaved, but they weren't motivated. They didn't do anything on the bus. Some talked with others, but most looked out the window or sat with their heads against the back of the seat in front of them.

"Three kids were different. Sixth-grader Althea, fifth-grader Erika, and fourth-grader Naomi were always reading, not just for school assignments, but fun subjects like photography, stamp collecting, and origami. They were diving into the world through books instead of wasting our bus time. I thought about them as I stared at my bus through the window in the teachers' lounge. I read the lettering, 'School Bus.' Aha! I thought. 'School' comes before 'Bus.' I realized I was driving a learning environment on wheels.

"I asked the three girls why the other kids weren't reading. Althea told me some of the first and second graders hadn't learned to read yet, and some of the older kids had trouble with some words. I asked the girls if they could help the other kids with reading. That's how it started.

"I asked the school librarian for multiple copies of classic children's books for each grade. The three girls started reading with groups of kids."

"Why are you so passionate about reading?" Mrs. Goode said.

"Well, Mrs. Goode, I loved school when I was little. But by about the third grade, I started falling behind the other kids. Fact was, they could read and I couldn't. I tried hard to learn. I struggled. I did poorly in other subjects because I couldn't read my assignments. When I got to high school, I feared I would never be able to graduate.

"Mrs. Emmons, my eleventh grade English teacher, recognized my problem. 'Walter,' she said, 'you are the smartest boy in my class, but you are dyslexic.' She stayed each day after class teaching me to read. Thanks to Mrs. Emmons, I'm a lifelong learner. I love reading about astronomy and the Old West, but I read other subjects as well.'

"Mr. Williams, any other thoughts?" Mrs. Goode said.

Wally looked down while biting his lip. "I'd like to go back to something Mr. Pittman said."

Mr. Pittman stood up. "Yes?"

"Mr. Pittman, you lectured me tonight on the value of the school day. You implied I shorted the underserved population by arriving late to school. You know, or should know, that's not true. The teachers told me that on the most recent state reading tests, all Deerwood Park kids scored well, but my kids improved the most. I don't take credit for their scores. The teachers do a remarkable job with all of the kids, and the Mermaids have helped so much."

Wally hesitated before continuing. "You also know, or should know, my kids' attendance is higher than last year. Many of my kids did not miss one day of school. Being at school adds value to the school day, too.

"Mr. Pittman, my kids have more school time than the in-town kids, a few having almost four hours a day more. My kids stay on the bus and read or study even when the bus breaks down and we have to wait for Mr. Henderson to get us started. My kids use their time well. That's what I wanted to tell you, Mr. Pittman."

The other teachers and I exchanged concerned looks up and down our row of chairs. I worried, and guessed the others did as well, how Pittman might react to this push back from Wally.

Pittman looked downward for a long time before speaking. "Mr. Williams, the purpose of a hearing is to find the truth. You have provided much more truth than I think any of us expected. As for me, I learned a great deal from you tonight. I learned I misjudged you and underestimated your value to the district. I spoke to you in a tone that was condescending and accusatory. I was wrong. I apologize."

Mrs. Goode turned toward the rows of parents. "I'm impressed to see so many parents. If you would like to say something, please stand. I'm interested to hear your inputs."

Mr. Tall Bear, seated at the end of a row of folding chairs, had placed a large, round basket on the floor beside him. I wondered what it was for. The elder tribesman stood. "Mrs. Goode, the school bus holds forty passengers, not room enough for all who wanted to come tonight. The tribal parents asked me to speak for them. This school year our children are alert and excited about school, more energetic than ever. They help their parents more and listen better to the stories of our traditions. We appreciate Mr. Williams."

When Mr. Tall Bear sat down, Mrs. Diaz stood up. "Mrs. Goode, those who came with me tonight are not so confident in English. So I speak for all. We are families of farm workers. The work is hard.

Education is most important for better lives for our children. Mr. Williams helped them learn much. My daughter, Erika, is proud to be a Mermaid. Thank you."

Mrs. Johnson rose. "Mrs. Goode, the other parents in Eagle Creek have small children, so they could not come tonight. They asked me to tell you how grateful they are to Mr. Williams. I would like to address Mr. Williams directly."

"Yes, go ahead, Mrs. Johnson."

Mrs. Johnson turned to Wally. "My father once told me that praise embarrasses humble men. Walter, I respect your humility, but you must suffer my praise. I credit you alone for the amazing change in my daughter. Althea has gone from a girl to a young woman this year. Of course she's been on a great trajectory as top student every year. This year that trajectory skyrocketed."

Wally smiled as Mrs. Johnson made a sweeping upward gesture.

"Althea used to tell me she wants to be a photojournalist so she can travel and meet important people. Now she tells me she wants to be a photojournalist so she can help people see beautiful places through her lens and learn about important events throughout the world. Althea sees herself as a world citizen now. You gave her the opportunity and inspiration to help others with her talents. Inspiring others is your special talent, Walter. I thank you from the bottom of my heart."

Mrs. Johnson put her hands together and bowed toward Wally. Wally stood and bowed back.

Mr. Tall Bear stood up again, this time drawing up the basket. "Mrs. Goode, all of the parents would like to shake Mr. Williams' hand if that's okay."

Mrs. Goode nodded.

The parents formed a line behind Mr. Tall Bear, who placed the basket next to Wally's chair, shook Wally's hand, and then presented him with an apple. Each parent climbed the few steps to the stage while pulling an apple from a coat pocket or purse. By the time Wally had three apples to hold, he realized the purpose of the basket beside him.

After about a dozen parents had shaken Wally's hand, the scbbing woman behind me left her seat and disappeared through the auditorium side door.

Juan Ramirez, Toby's grandfather, held apple thirty-nine out before him. Wally accepted it and reached out his hand. The tiny old man with bent shoulders thrust his arms around Wally, burying his head momentarily in Wally's chest. I knew Wally was a non-hugger, uncomfortable with the hugging response so natural to many of us. He stood motionless until Toby's grandfather released him. He looked relieved as Mrs. Johnson, at the end of the line, smiled and offered apple forty and a handshake.

It was past nine when Mrs. Goode closed the meeting. Mr. Tall Bear carried Wally's apple basket as the parents and Wally headed to the bus. I walked to my classroom to get my purse and keys. I switched on the classroom light and heard footsteps behind me.

"Mrs. Rose, may I talk with you, please?"

I turned to see the sobbing woman. I offered her a chair by my desk. "How can I help you?"

"I'm Glenda Reynolds, Lucinda's mother. I wrote the letter Mr. Pittman read tonight."

I knew Lucinda, a sixth-grader in Mr. Gray's class and Althea's best friend. "Why did you write that letter? It was misleading. It could have caused problems for Mr. Williams. You live in town. Your daughter doesn't even ride on his bus."

"I'm so sorry. Lucinda never lied to me before. She told me awful things, and I believed her. When I learned at the meeting what a fine man Mr. Williams is, I went out in the hall and phoned Lucinda. She admitted everything. I feel so guilty about the letter." Mrs. Reynolds dabbed her swollen, red eyes with a limp tissue.

"Why did Lucinda lie?"

Mrs. Reynolds shook her head and took a deep breath. "Althea is top student every year and Lucinda is always number two. The local Soroptimist Club honors the top two sixth grade girls each year. The last Monday of school, they will take two girls for a university tour and luncheon on campus. Lucinda really wants to go with Althea. She knows two other sixth grade girls on Mr. Williams' bus who have improved their grades so much one of them might beat her out for the number two spot. She thought if Mr. Williams got fired the other girls might fall back in their studies before the semester ends."

"So your daughter lied because she is jealous. I feel sad for her and for you, too. Is there anything I can do?"

"Mrs. Rose, my daughter and I are really close. I know she and I will work this out. But I've heard you are friends with Mr. Williams. Would you apologize to him for me?"

I thought maybe she wanted me to speak with Lucinda, but what she wanted was out of the question. "No, you must do that yourself," I said.

"But he will be so mad at me."

"He isn't like that. He'll accept your apology." I handed her a tissue from the box on my desk. "His bus will arrive tomorrow at eight fifteen or so. You should meet him then and apologize."

As Wally's kids filed into class the next morning, I glanced out the window to the parking lot. I saw Mrs. Reynolds standing before Wally. She pulled an apple from her coat pocket as they spoke. He took the apple and they shook hands.

Six weeks later, the entire student body sat in the auditorium, one giant fidget away from summer break. Pittman rapped on the lectern to get their attention for the last business item of the school year. Ten teachers and Mrs. Goode sat on stage with Pittman.

Pittman waved his hands up and down in front of him, signaling all to cease their conversations and horseplay. "Please everybody, come to order. You will be free as the wind momentarily. But now it's time to announce the Teacher of the Year Award. The teachers vote by secret ballot. This year we had a write-in candidate. You teachers," Pittman turned to us, "have chosen unanimously Mr. Walter Williams as Teacher of the Year. Please come up, Mr. Williams."

The audience exploded as Pittman's eyes scanned to find Wally. Reaction started with the bus riders and spread to the in-town kids. All jumped up and down, girls shrieking, boys whistling and shouting. I worried Wally would be outside on his bus, waiting for his kids to board for their last ride of the school year.

Gilbert popped up and scurried to the back of the auditorium. Wally emerged, and Gilbert coaxed him forward amid thunderous applause.

Pittman motioned Wally up to the stage, handed him a plaque, and held onto his hand after a firm handshake. "Wait a minute, Walter, before you leave. You have done a magnificent job this year. We hope you will choose to stay with us for many school years to come. However, I must ask you to change in one respect. I have it on good authority you do not like to hug or be hugged." Pittman looked past

Wally to wink at me. "But educators are huggers. It's in our DNA. This award confirms you are an educator. You will have to learn to give and receive hugs."

Pittman wrapped his arms around Wally, who held his award in one hand while he slapped three times on Pittman's back with his free hand, like a wrestler tapping out for release. Once freed, Wally looked ashen and deflated as if Pittman had actually squeezed the air from him. He gasped and regained his color and volume.

There was no holding back the children and no reason to. Chaos in the auditorium spilled outside as in-town kids ran to waiting parents in the parking lot and bus riders ran, skipped, and danced their way to the school bus. We teachers hugged Wally ever so gently as we said good-bye. I watched as the school bus exited the parking lot and turned east on Old School Road.

Riley, Redeployed

SOMETIMES DEPLOYMENT SEPARATES A soldier from his or her dog. It happened to Sergeant Martin Halloran and his dog, Riley. A desperate Martin turned to social media to find a safe place for Riley for six months, giving up on the agency that was supposed to help when the family the agency found to foster Riley reneged five days before the deployment date. Patti, an animal activist friend of mine, had shared the post.

"Dave, do you know what we need?" I said.

"No, Linda, but you're about to tell me."

"We need a temporary dog." I held out Martin's social media post on my phone for Dave to read.

Two years before, Dave buried our Jack Russell terrier, Petula, by the gardenia bush behind the house. Her little heart had weakened, and euthanasia was kindest. Grief poured like a mudslide through our lives, knocking us down as we tried to get up and get on. A pet bereavement group introduced us to "The Rainbow Bridge," a poem with a comforting description of a paradise where pets and their owners reconnect on their way to Heaven. With the group's help we recovered but agreed not to adopt another dog. Our hearts couldn't handle another loss.

"Fostering would be different," I said. "We would enjoy a dog for six months, and then, following a joyous reunion between dog and soldier, we would walk away happy."

"What if the soldier gets killed?"

"We'll have to ask that and other questions before deciding,' I said. "Quickly though, the guy is in a tight spot."

As Dave drove the sixty miles to the dog park Martin had designated for our meeting place, I looked up information about boxers—clean, short hair, faithful, energetic, playful, and good with children. Martin hopped out of his red pickup truck. Riley, medium sized, brindle with white chest, trotted beside him, tail wagging. When Martin introduced Riley to us, Riley broke out in a full body wiggle. We laughed because it seemed so over-the-top.

"He's just that way with everyone," Martin said. "He's a cuddly baby, totally non-aggressive."

Martin unhooked the leash and gave Riley the "run" command. Riley galloped away, looking back now and then, circling the bench where we chatted with Martin. Riley soon came and sat beside Martin, nudging his knee until Martin patted his head.

"I've no place to turn," Martin said. "My parents are on assignment in Paris for the State Department. My only other relative, my grandmother, can't keep him because of her health. My friends are on deployment themselves."

"What if we had Riley and something happened to you?" Dave said.

"My best friend, Bobby, will be returning to base four months from now," Martin said. "He's agreed to find Riley a new home if I get killed or gravely injured. But that's not going to happen."

Martin asked how we spent our time as a retired couple, why we wanted to foster a dog, and questions about our pet history, home, yard, and neighbors. He seemed accepting of us but wanting to delay. "I think I mentioned Riley is six now and I had him from a puppy," Martin said, looking intently at Riley, who sat at his feet. "My wife and I picked him out. Ex-wife, that is. When I got back from my first deployment, Kristen had my things packed and told me to take Riley with me. I bumped into her a year ago in a coffee shop. She's remarried and has a child. She didn't ask once about Riley."

Martin pulled a tennis ball from his coat pocket, threw it out for Riley, and walked away, giving Dave and me time to talk. It was time for him and Riley to talk as well. Martin sat on the grass, hugging Riley.

"They're gonna miss each other so much," I told Dave.

"Should we help?"

I nodded.

Martin brought Riley on the leash to us and handed him to Dave. "I want Riley to go with you, if you agree. I wish we had more time to decide, but we don't. I know you are good people, good dog people." Dave told Martin we'd feel honored to keep Riley safe while he was away keeping us safe.

Martin retrieved paperwork and Riley's bed, bowls, food, and box of toys. "Please wait with Riley until I've driven away," he said. Riley pulled on the leash as Martin walked away and pulled hard when Martin got in his truck. Riley looked from us to the truck as it turned from the parking lot. He whined and wagged his tail and then sat, watching the road.

As we walked him to our car, Riley kept staring in the direction where the truck had disappeared. He hesitated and then jumped in the back seat, perhaps expecting us to take him to Martin. We drove in the opposite direction.

Riley seemed still hopeful as we brought him in through our garage, taking his bed into our bedroom, bowls and bag of food into the kitchen, toys into the family room. Once Riley determined where the front door was, he stationed himself in front of it.

For the next few days Riley remained mostly at the front door, responding to commands—come, sit, stay—as trained, but not using his bed or eating. Finally, steak bones from the dinner Dave grilled outside tempted him. After that, Riley slept in his bed, ate his dog food, fetched balls in the backyard, and watched TV with us. When not otherwise engaged, he stayed by the front door.

In the weeks that followed, Riley adjusted to our routine, his favorite ritual being Friday night T-bones. He abandoned the front door station in favor of a corner in the kitchen. We exchanged email with Martin, usually on Sundays. Two months into fostering, emails from Martin ceased.

Three more weeks passed without hearing from Martin. Then Audrey Dash, Martin's grandmother, phoned. Martin had been injured in a bombing and transported to a hospital in Germany, where he died. Mrs. Dash asked Dave if we'd give her a few days and then bring Riley to her.

When we turned off the highway, Riley jumped to the window, tail whipping side-to-side. Maybe Riley thought Martin was nearby. Riley went crazy as we pulled up to Audrey's house. Riley ran up the walk, barking and jumping until Audrey opened the front door of the stately old home. Riley performed his full body wiggle and then ran inside.

"Mrs. Dash, I'm Dave. This is my wife, Linda."

"Call me Audrey," she said. "Please come in and sit down."

Throughout the living room and adjacent dining room, boxes were stacked and tags affixed to furniture. Riley had disappeared.

Audrey, connected via tube to an oxygen bottle, used a walker. "I'm moving to assisted living next week. My neighbors are helping me pack. I don't even go upstairs anymore. Martin couldn't get base housing with a dog, so Martin and Riley moved in here, just four miles from the base. After awhile I couldn't take care of Riley. Martin left him at doggy daycare and brought him home in the evenings." Audrey's eyes spilled tears.

"We're sorry for your loss, Audrey," Dave said.

"Thank you," Audrey said. "The funeral was Thursday. My daughter, Isabel, and son-in-law left for the airport this morning. Isabel picked out some of Martin's things she wants shipped to Paris."

"Riley must be upstairs," I said.

"I feel so sad for him. He's looking for Martin in their old room. Would you please get him? Go left at the top of the stairs."

I found Riley on the floor beside the bed, curled up atop a dog-wadded, camouflage Army uniform. I coaxed, but Riley wouldn't budge, so I went downstairs and asked Dave to get him.

"Riley must have pulled the uniform off the bed," Audrey said. "Isabel laid it out."

Dave carried Riley down. "Is he allowed on the sofa?" he asked Audrey.

"Yes, of course," she said.

Dave placed Riley across my lap. He remained motionless, even when I scratched his ears. As I realized the depth of his disappointment, my teardrops fell and rolled down his fur.

Audrey dabbed a tissue beneath her wet eyes before speaking. "You know, Riley is such a good dog because Martin poured him full of love. Will you continue to care for Riley until Martin's friend Bobby returns and finds him a permanent home? I can't keep Riley and don't know anyone who can."

Dave and I exchanged glances. I ached to think of Riley needing a new home. Foster, yes—adoption, no. We had thought to protect our hearts, but life works otherwise. Dave knew my thoughts and I his. I patted his knee.

"We'd like to adopt Riley," Dave told Audrey.

Audrey smiled, we smiled, and everyone fought back tears. I offered to bring Riley to the assisted living facility for visits. Audrey declined, saying that wouldn't be best for Riley. She gave me the facility phone number and asked me to call once in awhile. Audrey hugged Riley and said good-bye.

Suddenly we became the owners of Riley, the dog we had fallen in love with in the last three months, the brokenhearted dog separated from Martin and Audrey. We walked Riley to the car, his head and tail pointed downward, a much different dog than just an hour earlier. Our challenge became making Riley's life happy again.

Riley stayed by the front door, ate his dog food, went for walks, but seldom wagged his tail and never did the endearing full body wiggle. Andy, Dave's dog trainer friend, agreed when we said Audrey thought it best not to bring him for visits. He said it would be like breaking his heart over and over again. He told us to look for anything that perked him up and then do more of that. We clung to the tiny bit of animation Riley showed when riding in the car. Over the next few weeks we took him everywhere: car wash, post office, grocery store, dry cleaner. Every errand we ran, Riley rode.

The grocery store was busier than usual. I had to park several storefronts away. Coming back to the car with groceries, I saw a young man at the passenger side window. Riley stood on the seat, paws on the window, performing an outrageous full body wiggle.

"Oh, your dog is so friendly," the man said. "My dogs aren't that good with strangers."

"I'm glad to see him this happy," I said.

"Yeah, dogs are usually a bit more reserved around uniforms."

The young man wore a camouflage Army uniform. Riley continued acting crazy in the car. "Would you let me pet him?" the man said.

When Riley and I entered the house, Dave said, "What's up with Riley? He looks different."

I told Dave about the young man in uniform and how Riley had reacted. I told him about the Army recruit office tucked away in the corner of the storefront complex and the young man's suggestion I bring Riley for visits. Dave phoned Andy, unsure if the visits would be good for Riley.

"Sure," Andy said. "He's not going to think those men are Martin.

His nose will tell him the difference, but he'll react positively to their uniforms and their youth."

Once a week Riley visited Greg, the man we had met, and Erik, another young man in uniform. Riley regained the happy dog aura we had noticed the day we met him.

On one visit, Riley and I encountered Erik just inside the door. "Greg," he said, "I have to go to the hospital. Alex is in trouble again."

"Just go," Greg said. "I'll take care of things here."

Erik slipped out the door after saying hello to me and patting Riley's head.

"Erik's nephew is ill," Greg told me. "He's in Children's Hospital."

The next time I brought Riley, I asked Erik about his nephew. "Not good I'm afraid," he said. "The doctor said Alex may not live more than two months. My brother and his wife are devastated. Their only hope now is to make Alex as comfortable and happy as they can." Erik seemed distracted by Riley, who was wiggling and wagging. "Maybe, do you think I could borrow Riley? The hospital allows pets in to cheer up the kids. I could take him now and be back in two hours, maybe bring him to your house, if you want."

That's how it began. Erik took Riley to Children's Hospital once a week to cheer Alex. The third time he brought Riley home, Erik said, "My brother, Peter, and his wife, Marie, would like to meet you and introduce Alex. Would it be possible for you to take Riley to the hospital tomorrow morning?"

Everyone at Children's Hospital knew Riley by name. Riley stopped in at each patient room, where he traded wiggles for giggles. Parents squeezed our hands as if we were royalty. In Alex's room, Peter and Marie Spencer sat at either side of Alex's bed. They rose and hugged Dave and me and then gushed over Riley, who gushed back in his own way and then jumped on the bed. "Riley, get down," Dave said.

"It's okay," Peter said. "Alex can't hug Riley unless Riley is on the bed. The nurses understand."

Marie introduced Alex, age eight, and his brother, Connor, age six. Riley snuggled up to Alex, not disturbing any of the many tubes connected to the pale boy with dark circled eyes. Alex reached to scratch Riley's ears, and Connor reached across Alex and his tubes to scratch Riley's chest.

"Alex's test results have stabilized in the last two weeks," Marie said. "We're told there's no cure, but we're holding out for time and quality. Riley's been a godsend. You see Alex now, but two weeks ago he was worse. Linda, Alex needs Riley."

"I'm glad Riley is helping," I said. "We want Riley to continue visiting." Tears streamed down Marie's face as she looked to Peter. I felt something hanging in the air, a shared secret or undisclosed desire.

Peter turned to Dave. "Perhaps you and Linda would join me out in the hall and let Marie and the boys enjoy Riley a bit." We stepped out of Alex's room with Peter.

"If I may ask," I said, "what is Alex's illness?"

"DIPG," Peter said, "fast growing, inoperable tumors at the base of the brain. Chemo and radiation slow the tumors, but that's all we can do. Alex may be eligible for a clinical trial, but that's not much hope."

Peter sighed and bit his lip. "Would you let us keep Riley, just until Alex passes?" he said, with a choke in his voice. "If we could take Riley home and bring him to Alex every time one of us is here, which is almost always, Alex could be happier in the remaining weeks. We would take excellent care of Riley, and you could visit any time." Peter paused. "Please talk it over." He turned and reentered Alex' room.

"How can we say no?" Dave said.

"It would be really disruptive for Riley. He's just now getting use to us."

"Linda, we've seen that Riley is adaptable. We should help that poor boy. Those parents are having such a hard time. It's in our hearts, Riley's heart, too, to help."

That evening Dave took Riley and his bowls, bed, food, and toys to the Spencers. While Dave was out, I phoned Audrey. "That'll be good for Riley," she said. "He loves people. That's just who he is."

Marie phoned every other week, reporting good results about Alex. As two months passed I began to think Alex might get better. We would get our dog back, and Marie would get her son back, too. Marie repeated Peter's offer for us to visit Riley, but I declined as Audrey had. Not that I thought it would break Riley's heart to see and then not see us, but I worried it would break our hearts to see and then not see Riley. I held out for the day he would come home permanently.

I hadn't heard from Marie in over a month when Peter phoned Dave. "Is Alex okay?" Dave said. "We haven't heard from Marie lately."

After his conversation with Peter, Dave filled me in. Alex's condition had changed. His doctor was letting him come home two days a week. The Spencers were optimistic. They even took Alex and Riley for a visit at school.

"Did Peter say when they would give Riley back?"

"No, Peter just said he would keep us posted."

In time Peter announced Alex was being treated as an outpatient in the last phase of a clinical trial. Next he reported Alex was placed in the "no evidence of disease" category and said he and Marie were optimistic he might continue doing well.

That autumn, after keeping Riley for just over six months, Peter reported Alex would be attending school half-time and taking Riley to class with him.

"Peter asked if Alex could keep Riley forever," Dave said.

"No!" I said. "They agreed to give Riley back."

"Things changed, but Alex still needs Riley."

"They hijacked our dog," I said. "Now he's at their house. How can we get him back? They have all of his stuff, and they're not going to hand him over. What's our recourse?"

Dave knew my thoughts and I his. He wasn't my ally. He stared at me, wanting me to relent. I felt Riley slipping from me.

"Linda," Dave said, "it's not about us. It's not even about Alex. This is about Riley, what makes him happiest. He started out as a young man's dog. Martin got him as a puppy. It's in him to be with a young man. We're not the right ones for him. To separate Riley from Alex would be selfish."

"The Spencers are being selfish."

"Everyone is being selfish," Dave said, "except Riley."

Dave made coffee the next morning. "Peter asked me to phone tonight. They hope we'll say yes."

"You mean we could say no?"

Dave selected my favorite coffee mug from the cupboard and poured my coffee. "Peter again told me we can visit any time and mentioned if something changes, we might like to take Riley then."

"What's going to change?" I said. "They'll give Riley back when he's old, has cataracts, and can't control his bladder?"

"Linda, why don't you phone Audrey about this? After all, she had Riley at one time, too."

I hoped Audrey wouldn't mind me calling so early. The receptionist who answered hesitated when I asked to speak to Audrey Dash. "Are you a relative or close friend?" she said.

"I'm an acquaintance," I said.

The woman put me on hold. In a minute another female voice spoke. "I'm sorry. Mrs. Dash passed away the end of last month. The funeral was last week. Is there anything I can do for you?" After a few courtesies on the phone, I hung up and told Dave of Audrey's death. Riley's connection to his past was over. I then realized what Dave already knew. In Riley's life, Dave and I had served as a conduit. Riley was in his right place.

"Olivia didn't even get to meet him," I said. Our granddaughter had wanted to meet Riley at Christmas when she and our daughter and son-in-law would fly in from Denver. I had expected Riley back before Christmas.

"So what are you thinking?" Dave said.

"I'll have to send the Spencers a Christmas card every year."

"Why?"

"They need to have our address and keep thinking of us over the years."

Dave looked confused.

"Maybe in later years they'll decide to return Riley," I said.

"You'd take Riley back, blind and peeing himself?"

"In a heartbeat."

Marie and I exchanged notes in our Christmas cards over the years. Marie always enclosed a recent picture of the boys and Riley. In one note she announced she and Peter were expecting a baby girl. "That's great for Riley," Dave said. "You know how he loves children." Christmas pictures then included all three children with Riley.

One springtime brought an unexpected note from Marie. "Dear Linda and Dave, with much sorrow I inform you Riley died. The veterinarian said it was aortic stenosis, a heart condition. We are all deeply saddened. Our consolation is that he lived longer than average for boxers. We know you share in our loss because you loved Riley, too. We are so sorry. Love, Marie, Peter, and the children."

In the next days we grieved for Riley and sent a condolence card to the Spencers. "Dave," I said, "do you know where we should go tomorrow?"

"No, Linda, but you're about to tell me."

"I'll drive us and surprise you."

Sunshine, shadows, and showers graced our morning drive. Tucked away from thoroughfares, Oak Grove Memorial Park seemed the perfect place to repose for eternity. I parked in front of the cemetery office.

"Is the flower shop open?" I asked the lady at the counter.

"Yes, dear," she said. "I can help you pinpoint the plot you want, and then we can go into the flower shop. The flowers are all fresh this morning."

I joined Dave outside and handed him two bouquets, one tulip and iris and the other lily and daisy. I studied the map on which the lady had marked a circle. "Just on the other side of the duck pond," I told Dave.

Our path took us along a narrow wooden bridge over a water lily pond, where ducks quacked and flapped at our intrusion. On the other side, I found a headstone for Sergeant Martin Halloran and beside his, one for Audrey Dash. I arranged the flowers after getting water from a nearby spigot to fill the in-ground vases.

Dave said a prayer for Martin and Audrey. We sat on a bench beneath a giant oak and watched clouds, hurried by a steady breeze, skip over clearings in the gray-blue sky. As we walked back to the car, I shielded my eyes. The late morning sun held sway over the few remaining rain clouds.

"Linda, turn around," Dave said, as he ambled along behind me.

I turned and gasped at the beauty, the best rainbow I'd ever seen. The full arc spanned the cemetery plot beyond the duck pond, the colors vivid—red, yellow, green, violet. Dave waited in the car while I stood, rainbow-struck, gazing at the sky. I thought I heard a dog bark. Refocusing on the pond, I saw the ducks in disarray, beating their wings and quacking as they darted among the lily pads. I heard more barking, but I didn't see the dog.

The Accidental Life Coach

THE DUCK RINGTONE STARTLED Vincent, who had fallen asleep in his recliner.

"Hi ho."

"You sound groggy, Vinnie. Were you asleep?"

"No, I just dozed off in the chair. Thank goodness it's you, Angela," meaning thank goodness not Ma. Conversations with Ma always seemed endless and pointless and perhaps a little judgmental as she quizzed him about his dating frequency and whether he thought an Italian dating website might help him find a girlfriend.

"In your voicemail, Vinnie, you mentioned a class," Angela said.

"I've been thinking about changing careers."

Thirty-year-old Vincent Santorelli had worked nearly ten years at Domoto International Tracking Systems, known as DITS, as a customer support technician, fielding customer calls and writing problem reports.

"I'm all for that, Vinnie. You deserve more."

Vincent didn't own a car and walked to work. On weekends, he cleaned his apartment, washed clothes in the building laundry room, and watched TV or took the bus to Angela's house to have lunch with her and his brother-in-law, Lanz.

Vincent's mother, Gianara Santorelli, with many fifty-something best friends, regularly pressed Vincent to call so-and-so's daughter and take her out. He phoned the attractive ones for a second date, with no luck. He started asking the unattractive girls for a second date and was rebuffed with thin excuses as well. One girl seemed more genuine. She said, "Vincent, you're really nice and not bad looking, but I don't want to ride the bus on dates."

"It's a two-week community college course, *How to Become a Life*

Coach, Monday and Wednesday from seven to nine in the evening," Vincent told Angela. "It starts next week."

"How can somebody become a life coach with just four classes?"

"The college helps with job placement," he said. "I phoned the college counselor. She said some firms hire without requiring special accreditation."

On Monday night, Vincent slid into a student desk in the back row of the class and watched as others filled in all the seats.

"Popular class, it seems," he said to a young, red-headed woman sidestepping into the row in front of him.

"Easy 'A,'" she said.

He smiled, but she had turned.

The instructor, middle-aged Muriel Bennett, began her lecture before the sign-in roster and last copy of the syllabus reached Vincent.

"Let's be clear," Mrs. Bennett said, "life coaching is not therapy. You can achieve a satisfying career in life coaching without the educational requirements for becoming a therapist. Specific goals, that's what life coaching is about. You will learn how to help your coachees identify specific life improvement goals and reach those goals through actions. Simple, isn't it? Just one caution—don't try to solve their problems for them."

Vincent phoned Angela Monday after class and asked for her help with his first homework assignment, a list of improvement goals for his own life. On Wednesday evening, as students ambled into the classroom, he pulled a paper folded in quarters from his sweater pocket and smoothed the paper flat.

"Did you finish the homework?" he said, leaning forward to engage the redhead, who again sat in front of him.

"No," she said, "my friend who took the class last term told me Bennett doesn't collect the homework. We're only graded on the final test, multiple-choice."

He listened carefully to the lectures but didn't bother with the homework going forward. Three days after the test, his phone quacked. Mrs. Bennett congratulated him on earning an 'A' for the class and offered to forward his name and number to a friend in the life coaching industry who needed additional associates.

A week later, the bus lurched to a stop one block from the County Children's Learning Center, which had contracted with Linda Hyatt

& Associates to provide life coaching services to children in protective custody. Linda had given Vincent a briefcase with her company logo on the side and instructions for his first assignments, one at the county school and the other at Mystic Woods Community, an assisted living facility. Unready to commit to the career change, he had arranged a couple days off from his job at DITS to try the life coaching assignments.

"These children have endured family dysfunction," said Bonnie Wilson, the county school director, as she escorted Vincent around the facility, with its classrooms, living areas for the children and house mothers, and outside, a well-appointed playground surrounded by a chain link fence with a locked gate for security. "They have uncertain futures. I want them to feel they have a degree of control over their outcomes. I trust you can help them."

Mrs. Wilson showed Vincent into the library alcove where preteens, three girls and seven boys, fidgeted in their chairs at a conference table. "This is Mr. Santorelli," Mrs. Wilson told them. "He'll help you learn new things about yourselves and have fun, too." She made a slight bow and left the room.

Twenty eyes focused on Vincent, a sea of eyes ready to drown him, take him down by exposing how unsure he felt. His face and neck burned. These formidable children before him, outnumbering him ten to one, might refuse to cooperate. What could he do? A red neon sign flashed, "FAILURE," in his aching head.

"Mr. Santorelli," a small voice interrupted his plague of thoughts. "Mr. Santorelli, there's a spider on your briefcase." Eyes off Vincent, the children stared at the spider atop the ampersand in the "LH & A" logo on the briefcase he had laid on the table.

Vincent's first impulse, to take off his shoe and beat the spider, dissolved as he looked into the faces of the young wards of the county. The pulsing, red neon sign in his head turned green and flashed, "HERO." He pulled a pen from his shirt pocket and pushed it under the terrifying little monster. The spider clung to the pen. Vincent walked to the window, opened it with his other hand, and shook the spider outside. He shut the window and let out his breath. Applause and cheers rocked the alcove. The children gave him thumbs up and exchanged fist bumps among themselves.

A girl, wearing her long hair in a braid, said, "Thank you, Mr. Santorelli."

"What do we do now, Mr. Santorelli?" asked the boy who had reported the eight-legged interloper.

Vincent explained goal setting and action plans, giving examples about getting good grades or becoming the best at tether ball. He withdrew forms from his briefcase. "Please write your name and age at the top of the page. I'll help you write goals on the front of the page. Tomorrow morning, we'll turn the page over, and I'll help you write down actions."

The children picked up pencils Mrs. Wilson had left on the table and began writing. If anyone looked stuck or confused, Vincent worked with them one-on-one. He conferred separately with each of the boys and two of the girls.

The third girl, the one with her hair in a braid, wrote non-stop. She flipped the page over and pushed the pencil along—definitely not following directions. Vincent wanted to help her, but his time was up. He'd have to run to catch the bus to get to his appointment at the Mystic Woods Community. He collected the ten pages, slid them into his briefcase, and assured his coachees he'd return the next morning.

Yolanda Craig, the Life Enrichment Director at Mystic Woods, welcomed Vincent with a hug. "I talked our director, Mr. Canfield, into starting a life coaching program. You see, we can do only so many sing-along music afternoons or field trips to the alpaca farm. We need something focused on individuals, something to tap into their previous professional lives or mastery of home management to help them re-experience personal achievement."

Roger and Adele, in wheelchairs, and Marge and Shirley, with walkers, eyed Vincent as he deposited his briefcase upon the bingo table in the activities room where Yolanda suggested they work.

"So, Fancy Pants, you got a rabbit up your sleeve?" Roger said.

"Pay no attention to Roger," Marge said. "We ignore him because he's such a nasty man."

"He's narcissistic and maybe even psychotic," Shirley added.

Adele smiled and shook her head.

Vincent explained the process to his four coachees. Roger tore up the form Vincent handed him. "This is silly, Fancy Pants. You think I'm going to write down what I want so you can make sure I don't get it?"

"No, Roger, I want you to succeed. That's why . . ."

"Hush, Fancy Pants. I'm joshing with you." Roger grabbed another form.

Marge and Shirley asked for help, so Vincent pulled up a chair between them. Roger wheeled to the end of the table and scribbled across his page while cussing under his breath. Adele sat with pen poised above the page, but the pale eyes behind her glasses looked up and away. She's been transported to another time and place, thought Vincent of Adele's trance like pose.

He heard a clattering of clashing canes, walkers, and wheelchairs and turned to see the late afternoon bingo players storm the room, claiming spaces at the table beside the coachees and passing bingo cards around.

"Oh dear, Vincent, I'll hurry and write something." Adele said

Vincent scooped up the coachees' pages. "I'll see you all tomorrow, and we'll work on writing actions to achieve our goals."

"Maybe, maybe not," Roger sneered.

After grocery shopping, dinner, and the TV news, Vincent placed the pages from his briefcase on his dinette table and read them. Most boys included something like his tetherball example, substituting dodge ball, basketball, or bean tossing. One boy thought of passing his future driver's license test on the first try. The girls wrote goals about improving grades. Vincent felt satisfied with his coaching of the children until he came to the last page, the one written by the girl he didn't have time to help individually. He read:

Brandy T 12.

Dear Mr. Santorelli, I must find Grandma. My father died two years ago. My mother is in prison because of drugs and bad checks. She kept me away from Grandma. Grandma means everything to me. She showed me how to braid my hair and write thank you notes. She read to me and baked maple cookies for me. I need Grandma to see all the good grades I get and how my hair is always neat in a braid. I need to ask her about things. I cry every night because I don't know where she is. I want her to know where I am. I want to tell her I love her. Please, please, please help me.

Vincent's phone quacked just as he finished reading Brandy's words.

"Hi ho."

"Vinnie, too busy to call your mother once in a while?"

He extricated himself from the call after thirty minutes and re-read Brandy's page. The pencil marks blurred through his tired eyes and scattered and reformed on the page into "S.O.S." He blinked, shook his head, and shoved all the pages into his briefcase.

The next morning the library alcove vibrated with the children's excited buzzing. Vincent returned each child's page and suggested actions for the children's goals. Pencils clicked and children whispered and giggled among themselves.

He motioned Brandy to a pair of chairs just outside the alcove. Brandy's pale eyes reminded him of someone, but he couldn't place the person.

"Brandy, there are actions you can take to find your grand-mother," he said. "You could write a letter to her if you remember her address."

"Mr. Santorelli," Brandy said, "she isn't there anymore. I wrote a letter. It came back undelivered. I sneaked out of school and took the bus to 2021 Oak Street. The house was empty, with a sign on the gate, 'NO TRESPASSING.'"

"Does Mrs. Wilson have your grandmother's address?"

"Just the old address, the one I already have."

"Did you ask the neighbors?"

"Yes, most had just moved there and didn't know her. The woman across the street knew her but hadn't seen her in over a year."

"You should phone the prison, ask your mother if she knows."

"I'm in protective custody. I'm not allowed to phone my mother until my sixteenth birthday. But you could phone and ask her. Please, Mr. Santorelli."

"Maybe I can. I promise I'll look into it."

Brandy smiled and placed her hand over her heart.

After helping the children write actions, Vincent told them he or another associate would check their progress in a few weeks. Brandy waved good-bye as Vincent hurried out the door to catch the bus.

He reviewed the elders' pages as the bus crawled through traffic, making five stops on the way to Mystic Woods. Marge and Shir-ley had written about making better quilts and baking creations in the facility kitchen, especially maple cookies as delicious as Adele's.

They both had written their desire to "get rid of Roger." Marge had drawn an unhappy face on the page. Roger's goals were to move into hospice and live there forever. Adele had written, "I must get home to leave a note."

Vincent met with his coachees in the activities room. He suggested Marge and Shirley borrow quilting books from the library, make bake plans with the facility cook, ask Adele's help with the maple cookies, and treat Roger cordially to elicit his better nature. The two ladies remained skeptical about getting along with Roger.

"Roger, please explain your goals," Vincent said as he took a seat next to Roger.

"Sure, Fancy Pants," Roger said. "The hospice unit is upstairs."

"Roger, you can't go to hospice unless you're dying, but you want to live forever, right?"

"Right. You see, Huey, the predictor cat, lives upstairs. He visits the hospice residents all day. At night, if someone is going to die before morning, he gets on their bed, right up to their chest. Then the caregivers gather the family together. I've always wanted a cat. I love their purring. It's the most heavenly sound. My mother wouldn't let me have a cat. She preferred dogs. I married young, and my wife, Angie, was allergic to cats."

Roger looked away momentarily and sniffled before continuing.

"I had a stroke, and Angie died, so I had to move here. Stupid Canfield won't let me have a cat. If I could have a cat, I'd be happy and maybe even pleasant to be around."

"Why don't you go upstairs and visit with Huey?" Vincent said.

"Canfield banned me from hospice because I've been nasty to the residents. The relatives can't stand to see me around their dying loved ones."

"Okay, Roger, how about if you start being pleasant to everyone? When somebody eventually has to move upstairs, you'll be welcome to visit them and see Huey, too."

"You're not as dumb as you look, Fancy Pants. Let me mull that over." Roger wheeled away, humming the theme song from *Cats*.

Adele rolled up next to Vincent. "I want to go to my old house and leave a note on the gate."

"Why? Where's your old house?"

"It's a couple of miles from here. It's vacant now. My husband built the house, with a huge front porch and wisteria vines along the railing." Adele again seemed in a trance, seeing a past life filled with good times. "My husband died five years ago, and my son died two years ago. I had to leave the house when I fell and broke my hip. I couldn't manage the stairs anymore. I must leave a note on the gate."

"Adele, you could write a note and give me the address. I'll put the note on the gate for you."

Adele placed her hand over her heart and smiled, but the smile seemed pasted on her blank face. "I have stationery in my room. I'll write that note and put it in an envelope with the address." Adele wheeled down the hall.

While waiting for Adele, Vincent phoned Bonnie Wilson to find out how to contact Brandy's mother in prison, but she told him not to because of the protective custody order. Fear of failing, of letting Brandy down, crept over him. He needed more days to work on his life coaching assignments, so he phoned his friend, Lenny, who worked the swing shift at DITS. Lenny agreed to trade shifts for a few days if Vincent would start right away.

Almost four in the afternoon and Lenny's shift started at five o'clock. Vincent still waited for Adele. After ten more minutes, Yolanda came over and handed him an envelope. "Adele asked me to give this to you. She's in her room with a caregiver. She suffers from depression, so we keep an eye on her. She told me to thank you." He slipped the envelope into his briefcase and left.

On his way to work, Vincent dropped the briefcase at his apartment and grabbed a jacket from a hook by the door. Darkening clouds portended a chilly walk to work and a cold and possibly wet walk home at one in the morning. He walked a block and a half, rounded the corner, and encountered a crowd on the sidewalk, all eyes looking up into the branches of a giant maple, with its thick, long roots bulging through the tree lawn. He recognized the red-headed woman from his life coaching class and edged around others to find a place beside her.

"Hey, remember me from life coaching class?"

"Can you climb a tree?" the redhead said.

"Sure. Why?"

"See the one-eyed cat?" The redhead pointed. "He's a neighborhood stray. Everyone feeds him, but no one owns him. A dog chased him up this tree. He's meowing but won't come down."

"If he got up there, he'll come down," Vincent said. "Leave smelly food, like tuna, at the base of the trunk."

"That's not right," the redhead said. "I volunteer at an animal shelter. I know cats can get stuck in a tree. Why won't you help?"

"What do you want me to do? And why are you here? Do you live nearby?"

"I live up the street." She handed him a business card for the animal shelter. "Climb the tree and get the cat and take him to the shelter. If he continues living on the street, that dog will eventually kill him. I can find him a good home when he's at the shelter. I'd stay to help but I'm on my way to the hospital. My sister is having her baby."

"I don't have a cage or a carrier," Vincent said.

"Put him in a pillowcase and secure it closed."

"How can I get him in a pillowcase?"

"This cat is a greeter, real friendly. Just pick him up by the scruff of the neck and lower him into the pillowcase," she said, her voice trailing off as she left.

Others, having heard their conversation, left also. Perhaps they felt unneeded, thought Vincent, because he was the luckless guy assigned to rescue the cat. Running late, he decided to continue on to work and check the tree later on his way home. Perhaps the cat, having rescued himself by then, would be busy menacing rats in some alley. Nice to know the redhead lived nearby and he had an excuse to drop by the animal shelter sometime and get acquainted with her.

At work, another customer support technician clicked problem reports on a keyboard. Vincent poked his head around the cubicle partition, expecting to see Lenny's office mate, Harold. But when the desk chair spun around, he felt as if struck by lightning, or as he imagined that would feel—tingly, breathless, feet off the ground. A young black woman, embodying all the silky, shimmering, attractive women of the movies and all the everyday women, of any color or ethnicity, whose hair, skin, shape, fragrance, or combination thereof had at some time disrupted his brain waves, smiled up at him.

"Hi. I'm Candy Doppler."

He forgot his thoughts about the cat and the redhead. He stammered his name and a few pleasantries. Between answering customer calls in the next hours, he and Candy chatted. No food since breakfast, his stomach grumbled, and he hoped Candy didn't hear it. Near midnight, he felt zombie-like, craving sleep in the last hour of the shift. One-on-one with a beautiful woman before him and he could barely keep his eyes open or speak coherently.

At one in the morning, rain pelting him, jacket hood over his head, he ran in the quiet darkness of the sidewalks, wanting to get home, inside and warm, and fall into his bed for a ten-hour pillow hug. He flipped the furnace switch on in the apartment, pulled off his wet jacket, and wrestled a dilemma—eat or sleep—he needed to do both. Sleep could wait a bit longer. He threw open the cupboard door, and his eyes fell upon a can of tuna. Oh no! He remembered the cat.

Gianara Santorelli had raised Vincent and Angela to do right, and that included helping people and animals whenever they could. He thought of all the poor animals Angela had rescued. Back on the wet sidewalk, he scanned both sides of the street, hoping to see the one-eyed cat peeking out from under a parked car or sheltering under a porch awning. In his jacket pockets he carried a pillowcase, a Christmas tie his mother had given him, and a zip lock bag full of tuna in oil.

He rounded the corner and stopped. No one was out. A streetlight near the giant maple illuminated rain falling on branches and on the cat, still high in the tree, exactly where he had last seen him. He called, "Kitty, here kitty," but the rain muffled his voice and the cat didn't move. He had climbed trees as a boy, but this maple, having no low branches, was not a climbing tree.

A light came on in the window of an apartment in the building where branches of the maple reached to the second floor. Somebody was awake at two in the morning. Vincent entered the unlocked building entrance, bounded up the stairs, and knocked on the apartment door.

"Who is it?" a man's voice boomed.

"I'm trying to rescue a cat in this tree by your window," Vincent said.

"I know who you are," the man said as he opened the door. "I was on the sidewalk earlier and saw you talking to the redhead. Come on in."

The man opened the window for Vincent to lean out. Vincent

grabbed a thick branch with both hands and hoisted his body up to straddle the branch. He scooted along the branch toward the V where it met the tree trunk. Not so bad, he thought, until he heard the window shut and turned to see the apartment light go out. A few minutes later, the man exited the building, got into a car parked across the street, and drove off.

The rain stopped. The cat, on a limb on the opposite side of the tree, didn't move. Vincent dripped tuna oil on his branch to entice the cat to come over. While waiting, he thought about Candy. Candace Doppler's family had lived in Japan for ten years because of her father's business. She learned Japanese as a child. During swing shift, DITS received many service calls from Japan and therefore paid Japanese-fluent technicians highly. Candy had suggested he learn Japanese. The thought amused him. He leaned forward to rest his cheek against the wet tree trunk, and he slept for hours, even in his precarious position.

He woke to find the sun up and the one-eyed cat sitting by him on the branch. He grabbed the cat by the scruff of the neck and lowered him into his pillowcase, which he secured with his Christmas tie.

"Hey, buddy, are you a protestor or a nut case?" Vincent looked down to see a police officer standing next to the tree.

Once Vincent explained his situation, the officer radioed for a utility company crew to rescue him with their cherry picker. He walked home, cradling the cat in the pillowcase and pleased with himself for doing what had seemed impossible.

He let the cat out in the bathroom, where he added a plate of chicken Vienna sausages, a bowl of water, and a litter box improvised from shredded newspaper in a plastic dish pan. He ate oatmeal and crawled into bed at seven o'clock. The cat's meowing awakened him at eleven thirty.

Vincent headed to the bus stop with the cat in the pillowcase and Adele's note and the business card for the animal shelter in his jacket pocket. He planned to drop the cat off at the shelter and then find Adele's old house so he could leave her note on the gate.

As the bus groaned to a stop where a long line of riders waited to get on, he pulled out Adele's envelope and read the address, 2021 Oak Street. That sounded familiar. He took his seat on the bus and read her note:

To Whom It May Concern—I, Adele Tandy, lived here. I moved to assisted living. If you know my granddaughter, Brandy Tandy, where she is now or where she has been, please contact me at Mystic Woods Community.

Vincent sprang up, lifted his pillowcase from the seat beside him, and bolted for the back door of the bus. He jogged a mile to Mystic Woods, where the automatic doors parted for him as he darted to the unattended reception desk. He rang the desk bell and waited. No one came. He rang again and again. He could wait no longer and ran down the hall, where he met Adele as she wheeled toward the dining room.

"Adele, just who I wanted to see," he said. "I've a wonderful surprise."

"Oh, Vincent, do you have something in that pillowcase for me?" Her eyes widened as contents in the pillowcase moved.

"No, this is a cat," he said.

"For Roger?"

"No, no, Roger mustn't see it. He can't have a cat. He'd get in trouble with Mr. Canfield. I'm taking this cat to the shelter, but we're going somewhere else first. Where can I hide this cat until we get back?"

"The girls already made my room up. So you can put it in there. They won't be back."

Vincent eased the pillowcase under Adele's bed and closed the door.

He wheeled Adele out the automatic doors to the street to meet the bus and helped her onto the wheelchair lift device. They exited the bus at the fifth stop, and he pushed Adele another block to the county school. On the way to the front entrance, they walked along the playground fence where children at recess chased soccer balls.

"Stop, Vincent," Adele screamed.

Vincent spotted Brandy, braid bouncing side-to-side, running toward them across the field and to the fence. She sprung to the locked gate, where she pulled up and over the top. She stepped to Adele's wheelchair and threw her arms around her sobbing grandmother.

That's when Vincent noticed the surveillance camera above the gate. Next he noticed the burly security guard bearing down on him. The guard escorted the three through the front entrance and into Bonnie Wilson's office. Brandy and Adele smiled and cried while answering Mrs. Wilson's questions. Mrs. Wilson invited them to go to the patio for a lengthy visit and offered to bring them iced tea and sandwiches.

Vincent phoned Mystic Woods to inform Yolanda about Adele.

"Vincent, everyone has been worried about Adele," Yolanda said. "You should have signed her out. Oh, and do you know anything about this cat Roger has?"

"Oh, dear! I'm sorry about the cat," Vincent said. "I was on my way to the animal shelter with it."

"One of the staff looked for Adele in her room and saw a pillowcase crawling around on the floor. When she opened it, a cat ran out and into the hall. Roger scooped it up. He won't let anyone take it from him. If Mr. Canfield sees it, Roger will be evicted. Please come back and get it."

"But Adele is visiting with her granddaughter. I can't rush her."

"Come right away, Vincent. I'll send the Mystic Woods shuttle bus to bring Adele back later."

When the automatic doors at Mystic Woods opened for Vincent, a white-haired woman with a small terrier on a leash walked out.

"Are you a resident here?" he asked the woman.

"Yes, I live here."

"I thought pets weren't allowed."

"Trixie's a service dog. Doctor's orders, you know—emotional health. She's my companion dog. The facility must allow service animals. It's the law."

"Can doctors order a companion cat?"

"Sure, my doctor has several patients with a companion cat."

Vincent found Yolanda at the reception desk. "Does Roger have a doctor?" he asked.

"Yes, Dr. Argentina is his doctor. In fact, he's doctor to several of our residents. He's upstairs in the hospice unit right now." Vincent told Yolanda about Roger needing a doctor's order to keep the cat. She agreed to send Dr. Argentina to Roger's room when he finished his visit upstairs. Vincent waited with Roger.

"Vincent," Roger said, "thank you so much for what you're doing." He offered a handshake as the one-eyed cat snuggled against his neck and purred like an idling motorcycle. "You're one helluva life coach, my friend."

On the bus ride home from Mystic Woods, Vincent smiled to himself as he thought about Candy and seeing her at work again soon. His phone quacked as he was about to leave his apartment for the swing shift at DITS.

"Hi ho."

"Vincent, this is Linda Hyatt. I'm sorry, but I have to fire you." Linda told him she had learned of the incident reported by the security guard at the county school and of Vincent's failure to sign Adele out from the Mystic Woods facility.

"Vincent, you broke the cardinal rule of life coaching. You got personally involved with the coachees and tried to solve their problems yourself."

That evening at work, Vincent told Candy about his early morning cat rescue; his day with Brandy, Adele, and Roger; and his getting fired as a life coach.

"Wow, you did so much good today," Candy said. "You're a kind man. If that makes you less as a life coach, it makes you more as a man." Vincent felt himself blush.

At shift end, Candy invited him to an all night movie theater. "It's in the Emerald District," she said. "The bus stops right in front. They show foreign movies, with subtitles. We can watch a Japanese movie so you can hear the language in case you want to learn. I think *Kagemusha* is still playing."

He would go see *Godzilla* in Japanese without subtitles just to be with Candy. On their bus ride to the theater, he learned Candy lived in the popular Emerald District, with its many eateries, high-end boutiques, salons, jazz clubs, and fine jewelry stores. She owned a restored Pontiac GTO her father had given her, but she preferred riding the bus during the week to avoid parking hassles. On weekends she liked driving through the countryside.

In the next weeks, as spring dried into summer and newly leafed tree branches threw punches of pink and white blossoms, Vincent found himself thinking about Candy non-stop: her smile and her laugh, the way she dressed, how her hair smelled as fresh as honeysuckle. He fell in love with Candy and Candy with him. He traded jobs with Lenny to go on swing shift permanently, and Candy taught him how to speak Japanese well enough to pass his proficiency test and receive a promotion and pay raise.

At the close of their shifts at DITS, early mornings found them patronizing all-night spots in the Emerald District or snuggling on the couch at her place or his to watch a movie before showers, bed, and a fresh afternoon for stopping in at the library or taking in a new exhibit at the museum. On weekends, they drove to Silver Creek Park to hike and pick wildflowers. As summer surrendered to autumn and afternoon cloud bursts dowsed the trails more often than not, they switched from hiking to reading poetry, bringing a takeout basket from Banana Bandana Bakery or Quiche Creations and poetry books from the library to the park's sheltered picnic tables.

In early November, after their Friday night shift, the two watched a movie, and Candy remarked on the chill in Vincent's apartment. The building manager had said the heater needed repair. Vincent went to his closet to get a sweater for Candy, which Candy wrapped tightly around her. She heard a paper crinkle in the pocket and pulled out a page folded in quarters.

"That's my homework from life coaching class," he said and took the page from her. "Would you like to hear my five life improvement goals from six months ago?"

Candy nodded.

"One—get a better job. Two—learn something new. Three—get a girlfriend."

Candy smiled.

"Four—make three new friends, not counting the girlfriend."

"Well, that would be Roger, Adele, and Brandy," she said.

He nodded and read the last goal to himself. "I haven't achieved this one yet."

"What is it?" she said.

"Five—get married."

"So, have you written an action for that one?"

He turned the page over, jotted something, and handed the page to Candy.

She read.

"Well?" he said.

"Yes, Vincent, I'll marry you."

He drew her to him and whispered in her ear, "We'll cancel our country drive today."

"Why?"

"We'll be too busy shopping for the best diamond ring I can afford."

On Christmas Eve, Vincent and Candy joined the residents of Mystic Woods Community for an eggnog and cookies celebration.

"I named my cat, 'Jolly'," Roger said. "I'm getting so much

attention from the ladies now that I have him." Jolly sat on Roger's lap, kneading his knee and purring. "Shirley hurries each morning to get me a cup of tea before Marge can do it, but then Marge brings me a plate of cookies."

Brandy, who had been given permission to stay in Adele's room over Christmas, sat in the lobby on an ottoman in front of Adele's wheelchair. She and Adele presented Vincent with a glitter-adorned thank you card decorated with a heart border.

Brandy handed Candy a Christmas tin. "For you and Mr. Santorelli, Grandma and I made pumpkin bread."

Adele reached to Candy for a hug. "We hope to come to your wedding, if you want us, that is," she said.

"Yes, we'll feel honored to have you," Candy told her.

Needing three hours for the drive to the home of Gianara and Salvatore Santorelli for a Christmas feast, with Angela, Lanz, and other relatives and friends, Vincent and Candy bid farewell and Merry Christmas to their Mystic Woods friends and hurried through the brisk cold to get into Candy's car.

"Do your parents know we're interracial?" Candy said.

"I told Ma you are beautiful, black, sweet, and the smartest person I know."

"What did she say?"

"She told me I'd better have a wonderful wedding soon before you change your mind."

Light snow fell on the windshield. Vincent turned up the car heater.

Michael Rourke, The Ladies' Man

New York City, 1897

MICHAEL DROPPED HIS DUFFEL bag on the dusty floor. "No, no, you scrawny kid," Mrs. Arnold said. "You're not bunking in this room. Adult men, Americans, stay in this room. You belong in the basement with the Italian boys. They all look alike. But you'll stand out with them blue eyes. You best be stronger than you look so you can do the work I tell you. You can't live here free. You'll pay me with work and sweat 'til you have coin in your pocket from the bakery. Miller's gonna work you harder than me. You best be happy now 'cause you won't be too happy next week."

Michael Rourke was small but smart, having earned a university degree in accounting in Dublin at age seventeen. Even after two generations, the horror of the Great Famine still haunted families. Michael's father wanted his only son to achieve the prosperity and happiness found by others who had emigrated.

Michael worked in Miller's Bakery six days a week, making bread in the hot ovens from four until noon, filling in for Miller as cashier while Miller took lunch, then cleaning ovens and sweeping the floor until Miller dismissed him.

Upon first meeting Jack Miller, Michael showed him a priest's letter of introduction referencing Michael's accounting degree. Miller threw the letter on the floor and kicked Michael in the shin. "That's what I think about Paddy University. I know 'bout you Micks. Thank God you nearly speak English. I-talians can't wait on customers."

The boy worked hard, and Miller noticed business picking up. Women came with their young daughters to buy baked goods. The girls all stared at Michael as he tallied the mothers' orders. Michael

told Miller he could predict sales somewhat, based on regular customers' habits. Soon Miller asked Michael to plan the daily baking.
Michael noticed the glances of the young ladies and started flashing
smiles their way after the mothers had turned away from the counter. Within two months, Miller gave Michael a raise, promoted him
to full time sales, and hired another Irish lad to do all the baking,
cleaning, and sweeping.

Michael had fallen away from the Church, not attending services
since the last time in Dublin with his family. He felt like his own
man in America, and the longer he stayed away, the longer the path
back to the Church stretched. He told himself there would be plenty of time in later years to return to his Catholicism. He didn't miss
his Church, but he did miss his family. He sent a letter home so
his mother would have his address in America. The postmaster told
him not to expect a reply soon—letters took two months to cross
the Atlantic and longer during winter.

Michael's raise at the bakery gave him money to squander. His
Italian bunk mates took him to taverns where he met girls, many
of whom were American-born children of Italian immigrants. Michael didn't think about their nationality, but about their soft skin
and deep brown eyes. He even learned a few Italian phrases to im-
press the young ladies. The Italian boys introduced him to drinking,
flirting, and escorting tipsy beauties to the grassy knoll behind the
bandstand in the park. Michael celebrated his eighteenth birthday
with a multi-national group of revelers: several Italian-American
girls, two Italian boys, a Swede, and two Scottish brothers.

"War? Sure!" A headline burst from a newspaper one of the Scots
had spread on the bar top. The Scots wanted to go to war as an adventure. The party ended with them escorting drunken Michael to
the boarding house and Michael agreeing to sign up with a New
York State company of volunteer militiamen, rallying to avenge per-
ceived wrongs perpetrated by Spaniards.

Michael's company reached the bay at Santiago de Cuba at the
end of May, 1898, staying aboard ship as the US Navy executed a
blockade of the Spanish ships. In June, Michael's company disembarked and joined a camp of militiamen on the city's outskirts. As
the weeks dragged on, the would-be combatants heard more news
reports than gun reports. Enduring primitive camp conditions, the

men feared getting sick more than getting shot. Word spread of victories at Kettle Hill and San Juan Hill. By the end of July, Michael's company set sail to return home.

At midnight, Michael and his new friend, Charlie Bauer, had just completed a grim task ordered by the company's captain. They stood together on the ship's upper deck and waited for the new day to replace what had become for each the worst day of a short life. Many onboard the homeward bound vessel had taken ill. One had died on the ship as it slipped out of the bay. The captain ordered a burial at sea, requiring Michael and Charlie to wrap the body in blankets and secure it with ropes and anchors. Michael whispered the Lord's Prayer as he and Charlie hoisted the dead man overboard.

"You know, Mike, that wasn't a real war," Charlie said.

In his transition from bakery boy to Spanish-American War veteran, Michael had also transitioned to "Mike."

"How can you say the war wasn't real? We faced real dangers on foreign soil while carrying the American flag."

"Real danger, no lie, but the war wasn't started to free the Cubans. It was started to sell newspapers and give Teddy Roosevelt more clout."

"Why did you come all the way from Nebraska to fight for America if you thought the war was contrived?"

"I didn't know at the time. My father insisted I volunteer. But some of the boys from Chicago said the news reports they heard didn't square with what the *New York Journal* reported."

"I don't know 'bout that. I just want to get back to New York."

"I'll go back to Nebraska," Charlie said, "but from there I'll head to San Francisco. Fortunes are to be made on the West Coast. When you settle, mail me a letter to San Francisco, General Delivery."

On Mike's return to New York City, Mrs. Arnold handed him a letter postmarked from Dublin. Mike tore open the envelope, finding that his sister, not his mother, had written. Mike wept as he read. His father died shortly after Mike left for America, and his mother passed a few months later. Mike had realized he might never see his father, but expected someday to return and see his mother. Now he had no reason to return. His sisters would be fine. The older girls married well and looked after the younger girls.

In his last year in New York City, Mike partied in the taverns each night. Depending on the mood or dynamics of the tavern-goers, Mike might end an evening by fighting, flirting, or fleeing.

"I heard you fought in the Spanish-American War," a woman said as she slipped into the stool next to Mike. "So which are you, Spanish or American?"

"American, of course. I'm Yankee Doodle, but you can call me Mike." He had noticed the blonde when she entered the tavern. Her ample red lips and powdered white complexion impressed as she looked intently into his blue eyes. His affair with Marlena Wolfe started that night and continued for several months.

"My father says he will come after you with his gun if you don't do the right thing," Marlena declared one night. "My father and I will meet you at the courthouse steps, noon tomorrow."

Mike felt like a caged animal as Marlena told him how his life would unfold and unravel. She told him they were having a baby, and that she would be Mrs. Rourke the next day. Mike questioned she was having a baby. She slapped his face. He questioned she knew for sure it was his. She slapped him again.

The next morning Mike fled, boarding a Boston-bound train. At nineteen, he didn't feel ready to marry. If he knew for sure Marlena was with child and if he could be certain the baby was his, he would have married her. The threat of her father coming after him made it so Mike had no time to think or discuss matters with Marlena. He felt she should have told him before getting her father involved.

"Where can I find work?" he asked the first Boston bartender he met.

"Everywhere," the bartender said, "Boston has lots of work. 'Course most of you Irishmen get work in one of two places, the priesthood or the police department."

"Not me. I'm too sinful for the priesthood and too short for the police force."

The Boston Terminal Company hired Mike as an accountant. At night in his apartment, he wrestled with guilt and loneliness. Without family in America, he felt lost. He reached out, sending a letter to Charlie.

Charlie replied quickly. "Mike, I've so much good news. I married a gorgeous artist. I'm the happiest fellow in the world. I now belong to Bessie and Southern Pacific. You've got to hire on to the railroad. There's so much fortune to mine in a railroad career. I'm in sales. I sign clients to move freight along the West Coast and inland, too. Tracks are being laid everywhere. Great opportunities. Write soon."

Mike knew at once he was San Francisco-bound, not because of fortune's lure, but because, with that letter, he began to treasure Charlie as the brother he never had. Charlie was the closest thing he had to family on the continent. Charlie, just a couple years older than Mike, had spent the last year and a half well. Mike valued Charlie's friendship and sought his counsel.

Mike hired on at the Southern Pacific office in San Francisco. Dinner with the Bauers became a monthly routine. Bessie would invite an additional dinner guest, seating a proper, unmarried lady, with fine manners, next to Mike at the table. He didn't warm to any of them. After Bessie ceased her matchmaking efforts, he would ask if he could bring a friend with him to dinner. He seldom brought the same lady twice.

Prohibition curbed Mike's drinking and brawling. Bessie said the Eighteenth Amendment helped Mike grow up. Mike, then clear-eyed and clear-thinking, became introspective. "I can't figure one damn reason why I'm here in America. Where am I going? What's the purpose?" His purpose would not emerge until he moved to the City of Angels.

In 1928 the Bauers moved to Los Angeles. Charlie wrote, "We bought an automobile because no one can live in Los Angeles without one. You must see it—a De Soto Six! We got a house north of downtown. Now I drive to work. The company offices downtown are sprawling, just like all of Los Angeles. Reminds me of milk spilled on a floor, the edges going out in all directions. You must visit. Bessie says hello. Regards, Charlie."

Mike moved to Los Angeles early in 1929. He collected rents from first floor retail spaces in Southern Pacific's downtown buildings. He bought a De Soto Six, as Charlie had. Boulevards lined with palm trees rolled out to golden beaches under cloudless skies and to foothill canyons sporting wildflowers year round. On weekends Mike fanned out, searching locales he had read about. Hollywood topped the list. Mike imagined life as a movie celebrity.

Mike asked neighbor Joseph about good places to go. One Saturday morning, Mike encountered Joseph in the apartment courtyard.

"Mike, there's a bathing beauty contest in Long Beach this

afternoon. You should go," Joseph said. "You'll meet ladies there."

"I don't know. How many ladies will enter the contest, and how many men will be there trying to get a date with them? Don't like my odds, Joseph."

"Man, I thought you were smart. I'm not talkin' 'bout meeting contestants. Think about it. If a lot of men go there to meet ladies, a lot of ladies will go there to meet men. Your odds won't be bad." Joseph winked.

Mike found a seat in the bleachers as the contest began. Many in the audience had never seen the modern bathing suits—colorful wool tank tops with swimsuit legs extending to mid thigh.

Mike noticed a woman sitting alone at the end of a bleacher row. He waited to see if anyone joined her. Nobody came. The woman finally turned her head and then turned away. He continued to stare. The woman turned again, this time sticking her tongue out at Mike.

"Please excuse me, Lady. I didn't mean to stare," he said.

"Yes you did. And I caught you at it."

"You're right. I stared because your red hair reminds me of two of my sisters in Ireland, Brigit and Corey."

She didn't say anything.

"I have seven sisters," he said. When she did not respond, he turned to walk away.

"My name's Anna. What's yours?" she said.

"I'm Mike Rourke. Glad to meet you, Anna. It's almost evening. How are you getting home?" he said, concerned about the lady walking home in darkness.

"I took the Red Car here. I'll go back the same way."

"I could drive you in my De Soto. Have you ever ridden in an automobile?"

"Yes, of course," Anna said. "My brother-in-law owns a Model T."

Mike drove Anna to a house owned by her sister and brother-in-law, where Anna, a thirty-six year old spinster, lived in a back apartment. She worked as a seamstress, making clothes and doing alterations for neighbors and friends.

"Where are you from?" Mike said.

"Detroit."

"No you're not. I met boys from Detroit. They didn't talk like you. Say 'wash,' like washing clothes."

"Warsh," she said, finally smiling.

"Now say, 'I like Mike and want to know all about him.'"

She giggled. "I like Mike and want to know all *aboot* him."

"Aha. You're from Canada. I'm right, aren't I?"

"I was born in London, Ontario. When my folks passed, my brothers stayed on the farm and we girls moved to Detroit. Lizzy and I moved here *aboot* ten years ago."

Anna and Mike began a relationship. He took her out to eat most Saturdays and visited with her family, Lizzy and Bill. He took her to meet the Bauers, who were surprised and pleased he continued the relationship throughout the summer.

The mellow summer of 1929 in Los Angeles provided a great memory to cherish as the stock market crashed in the autumn, and the Great Depression followed. But Mike and Anna had more immediate concerns in the autumn of 1929.

"I'm going to have a baby," Anna said.

At forty-nine, Mike felt like a caged animal as he had at nineteen when Marlena had made the same announcement. But that was Marlena, not Anna. And now he was a man, not a boy. Mike thought, "What would Charlie do?"

"Anna, will you marry me?" Mike said, getting down on one knee as an afterthought.

Mike and Anna married. Margaret Rourke was born in April, 1930. The family moved to Tujunga, not far from Charlie and Bessie. Although the Great Depression made life hard for many neighbors, Mike continued supporting his family well with his job at Southern Pacific. Mike and Anna were generous, delivering boxes of groceries to folks having a hard time. Mike brought fabric home from the garment shops downtown, and Anna sewed clothes needed by families who couldn't afford them.

Margie befriended a Jewish girl on her first day at school. The girl's father had emigrated from London, her mother from Lithuania. Just as Mike had endured ethnic ridicule, so did this Jewish family in Tujunga. Mike felt a kinship with every man who came from somewhere else.

The Twenty-first Amendment ended prohibition and restarted Mike's drinking habit. Mike spent Saturday afternoons and most evenings at the local tavern. Anna took Margaret to the picture show matinee on Saturdays.

"Mike, you can get a divorce ya know. The movie stars get divorced. Why don't you divorce Anna and marry me?" Nellie worked at the tavern and lived in a room in back. She and Mike were having an affair.

"Sorry, can't do that. I'm Catholic. Divorce may be legal, but it's not allowed if you're Catholic."

"Catholic, you? I've known you for five years and you've never gone to church in that time. You may have been born Catholic, but you're not Catholic now."

"Once a Catholic, always a Catholic. It doesn't matter if I don't go to church."

"You're not going to Heaven. I can tell you right now."

"Oh yes I am. St. Peter will stop me at the gate because he'll smell my singed coat. But when I tell him my name, he'll wave me through. God forgives sinners named Michael."

"Then just leave Anna. Come away with me. We don't need to get married," Nellie said.

"I'm going to tell you something, Nellie. Listen. I don't love Anna. But I will not leave Margie. She is the love of my life, the purpose of my life. She needs me to protect her and guide her. I didn't become a father until late in life. I must see Margie grow up and get married."

Margaret proved to be a child of worries. "Daddy, the president said we will be in war against Germany and Japan. I'm so afraid." Margaret, at age ten with wide set green eyes and curly blond hair, sat on the floor next to the radio and listened to President Roosevelt's Fireside Chats.

"The war will not touch a hair on your head, my angel," Mike promised Margaret. Except for shortages of some goods and periodic air raid siren practices, the war had no effect on the family.

By the time Margie finished high school, she was tall and willowy, a head turner. In his last year with the railroad, Mike took her with him on days he ventured away from downtown on railroad business. Margie kept her head down, not seeing the admiring stares of young men.

"Margie, here's a dollar. Go order what you like," Mike said when he dropped Margie off in front of their favorite ice cream parlor in Santa Monica. "I need to talk to Mr. Joiner about rent contracts. His office is around the corner. I'll meet you shortly. Don't leave the shop."

When Mike finished business and looked for Margie in the ice cream parlor, he scanned the shop until seeing her at the counter with her head down, a dish of vanilla ice cream in front of her. She didn't see him.

Mike watched. A young man at the counter seat next to hers turned toward her. He said something to her, and she nodded without looking up. The man continued trying to start a conversation, getting only a head shake or nod out of Margie. He was still trying when Mike walked up and introduced himself. Relief washed across Margie's face when she saw Mike. The young man introduced himself as Paul Murphy.

"Are you a military man, Paul?" Mike said.

"Army, Private First Class, honorable discharge. I served in France during the war. Was sure glad to get home."

"Live nearby?"

"Rampart, near Wilshire, Mr. Rourke."

"Are you working now?"

"Yes, sir, I work nights in the shipping department of a supply company. Been there six months."

"Good for you, Paul." Mike handed him his business card. "I sure appreciate you boys serving our country. Telephone me. You are welcome to come for dinner anytime. My wife makes terrific beef stew."

Paul thanked Mike, said good-bye to Margie, and left to catch his bus home.

Mike took the counter seat next to Margie. "That's a fine man, and he likes you."

"No he doesn't. Nobody likes a girl who's shy. I'll never get a boyfriend or a husband."

"Don't say that, Margie. Did you see Paul trying to meet any of the other girls here? Your shyness intrigued him. Our flaws, like me being short, make us more attractive because we're more approachable."

Margie smiled. Mike always made her feel better.

Paul accepted dinner invitations to the Rourke home and became Margie's steady boyfriend, frequently taking her roller skating, bowling, and to Saturday movie matinees.

"Daddy, Paul talks as if we'll marry someday. I don't think we should. He's the only boy I've dated. How will I know if he's the right one?"

"Oh, my dear, he's the right one. Don't think you have to date others. These days, young women aren't safe in Los Angeles. You might meet the Black Dahlia murderer. The police still haven't caught that monster, maybe never will. Stick with Paul. He's safe. Marry Paul and have children while you're young. I waited too long. But at least I've been here to watch you grow up."

"Daddy, shouldn't I find a job before I get married?"

"No, Margie. You see how the classified ads are divided up. Only a few jobs, like babysitter or switchboard operator, hire women. Men can be radio repairmen, store managers, car salesmen, truck drivers, accountants, policemen—no limits. I predict someday women will have the same opportunities, but not now." Mike's smile teased something intriguing. "You know what else I predict?"

"What, Daddy?"

"Men will go to the moon someday, Margie. And women will go, too, not at first, but after the men build a base camp. Like the pioneers, men will blaze the path, and women will join them to make a colony on the moon. You wait and see."

Mike had an eager audience in Margie on the many occasions they went for ice cream and he shared his thoughts on what the future would hold. When he retired, two years after Charlie did, Mike felt optimistic about future opportunities for all.

"Mike, Bessie telephoned last night while you were out," Anna said as she poured Mike's morning coffee. "She said Charlie is in the hospital and wants you to come." Anna was tight-lipped as she delivered the message. Arriving home after the tavern closed, Mike had once again plowed down Anna's rhododendrons next to the driveway.

Bessie and her sister, Glenda, sat on a couch in the hospital waiting room. They clung to one another, sobbing. Bessie told Mike of Charlie's inoperable brain tumor, and that Charlie had only a few more days to live. Mike patted Bessie's shoulder and asked if he could go in and see Charlie. Bessie asked Mike to wait because another visitor was with him.

Mike spun his hat on his finger, paced, and waited. In a few minutes, a scowling, heavy-set man, dressed in a wrinkled gray suit, emerged from Charlie's room. The man glared at Bessie, Glenda, and Mike and bounded down the corridor. He pounded the elevator button as if he wanted to break it.

Charlie's gaunt appearance surprised Mike. His eyes were dark ringed holes, his mouth a lipless, dry slit. Mike knew he was looking at Death.

Charlie's voice belied his appearance with its clarity as he spoke. "Mike, we have been friends since the night we had to hoist that dead boy over the side of our ship. I have to tell you something."

"I'm listening, my friend."

"Mike, I'm homosexual. I never told you." Charlie's ringed eyes seem to search Mike's face for reaction.

"Wait now. You and Bessie have been happily married all these years." Mike thought Charlie must be out of his head, fogged by medication.

"Bessie is homosexual, too, a lesbian. Glenda is her lover. We've always introduced her as Bessie's sister. Our marriage is one of convenience and necessity. We each would be ruined if the truth came out. As a married couple, we have been able to hide our lifestyle. If Southern Pacific had found out, I would have been fired, blackballed for immoral conduct. Bessie, too. No gallery would have shown her art."

Mike remained silent as he regarded his dying friend.

Charlie continued, "Frank Peretti, the man who was just in here—he has been my lover for the last twelve years. He's an LAPD detective, four years from retirement. Imagine him getting caught, a homosexual cop. He wants me to change my life insurance, make him the beneficiary instead of Bessie. Says he deserves it for taking the risk. Mike, Frank doesn't need my insurance. His police pension will be substantial. I want Bessie to receive my life insurance. She's been my best friend for nearly fifty years."

"How can I help, Charlie?"

"Please just watch over Bessie for me."

"I will, Charlie. Don't worry."

"Mike, now I've told you my secret, do you feel differently about me?"

Mike pulled a handkerchief from his pocket and dabbed his eyes. He looked around the bare walls of the gray hospital room while collecting his thoughts.

"Yes, Charlie. I feel closer to you. I never knew that much about homosexuality. I still don't. But you will always be the brother I love, no matter how you lived your life. You and Bessie have always been there for me. Now I know what you've been going through, I love you both more."

Charlie died six days later.

Bessie and Glenda dined frequently at the Rourke home as the nineteen forties tumbled into the fifties, and Bessie's artwork continued adding modern designs and uniquely bold perspectives in private and public spaces throughout Los Angeles.

In the autumn of 1951, Margie and Paul married in a small ceremony at the Rourke home. As if the responsibility for watching over Margie had suddenly lifted, Mike surrendered to illness, taking several ambulance rides to the emergency room over the coming months.

"I met your daughter during visiting hours. She's a lovely young woman," Nurse Louise said.

"Yes. I raised her, and the old lady raised me," Mike quipped. Then he added, "Raising her to be the lady she is was my purpose in life."

"Shall I telephone your wife or your daughter and son-in-law?" Louise asked. She had been told by the attending physician Mike would die shortly.

Mike gazed at the window, seeing only the reflection on the glass—he in a hospital bed, Louise sitting beside him, and the clock, in reverse image, on the wall behind them.

"Don't, please. I don't want them on the road this time of night. I promise to hold on 'til morning."

As dawn broke over the City of Angels, Margie ran into Mike's room. "Daddy, don't die, please. I need you. Paul and I just found out we're having a baby. You must be here when your grandchild is born. Daddy, you must," Margie squeezed Mike's hand and laid her head on his chest. Paul and Anna stood at the foot of the bed.

"Margie, my dear, you needn't worry. I'm not going anywhere. I'll always be with you." Mike stroked Margie's curls. "I'll go shortly to meet St. Peter, but after that I will be in Heaven looking down on you and smiling, always smiling. I'll stand on the moon for you so I can wave, and you can wave back at me. What are you and Paul going to name your baby?"

"We thought 'Paul' if it's a boy and 'Mary,' after your mother, if it's a girl."

"Maybe a different name if it's a girl. I like the name, 'Elaine.' I dated a beautiful woman named Elaine. Of course that was years before I met your mother." He glanced at Anna.

Michael Rourke died in a Los Angeles hospital in the summer of 1952.

Los Angeles, 1957

Voices in the backyard awaken Elaine. She clambers out of bed and steps to the back door. Through the door glass Elaine sees two figures on the back porch. They talk in low tones and, with light shining through the kitchen window, cast long shadows across the lawn.

"Keep watching, Margie. We may see Sputnik yet. It's just going to look like a star, except it will move across the sky," Paul says.

Margie buttons her sweater against the chill autumn night air. "Russians shouldn't be sending satellites. They may get to the moon before we do. My father said men would reach the moon. He never said they would be Russians and not Americans."

Margie and Paul both jump as Elaine taps on the glass. Paul opens the door.

"Honey, you should be asleep. Did we wake you?" Margie says.

Elaine nods. "What are you doing, Mama?"

"We're looking at the sky and the stars. See them all, Elaine? Isn't the sky beautiful?"

"Where's Grandpa? You said he's on the moon. I don't see the moon, Mama."

"Tonight it's just a sliver moon. You can only see a little bit." Margie points toward a crescent moon in the clear sky. "Grandpa Mike is there. He's waving at you. Wave back, Elaine. Then we must go inside and go to sleep."

"Good night." Elaine waves to the night sky. "I love you, Grandpa Mike."

Sycamore Leaves

THE MID-WEEK, THROW-away newspaper, filled with grocery ads, landed on lawns and driveways throughout California's San Fernando Valley, including the driveway of Encino resident Frank Randall, who shared his home with daughter, Joan, and her three girls. Frank's youngest granddaughter, Abby, placed the newspaper on the kitchen table before leaving for school.

After the other house occupants left for work and school, Frank settled at the table with a second cup of coffee and unfolded the newspaper. He browsed the ads until flipping to the back page. He found, below the fold, a picture of the woman he had secretly loved for fifty years. The picture caption identified Kathleen Howard as an army veteran who had served as a field nurse during the Vietnam War. *Wuppa-wuppa-whop-whop-whop*—Frank "heard" helicopter blade slapping at any mention of Vietnam. He phoned the newspaper office and spoke to the reporter identified in the article.

"Yes, sir," the reporter said, "my editor wanted an article about a veteran to promote picnics and barbecues in the run up to Veteran's Day. Mrs. Howard has an interesting story, but the editor gave me only space enough for a picture and caption. Do you know her?"

"Yes, we served in Vietnam together. Let me ask you, the picture background looks like a hospital room. Is Kathleen ill?"

"I interviewed her at West Los Angeles VA Medical Center. Perhaps you should phone there."

When Frank phoned the hospital, the nurse who answered wouldn't connect his call to Kathleen's room but took his number so a relative could return his call. Later Frank spoke with her daughter. Kathleen, in good spirits on Monday, had told her daughter she would be out of the hospital before Veteran's Day. She was wrong.

The cancer had spread, and her hospital stay became hospice care. The former army nurse had only a short time to live.

When Joan arrived home from work, Frank asked her how long before dinner.

"Forty minutes, Dad," she said. "Do you have plans for tonight?"

"A friend of mine is in the hospital," he said. "I'll go there after dinner. I'll probably get home late. Where's Abby?"

"Grandpa, I'm here." Abby popped into the hallway.

Frank gave Abby his conspiratorial wink and pointed to the family room sliding glass door leading out to the yard. She nodded and looked at Joan, who had turned back toward the kitchen. He pulled a paper bag from the utility closet and motioned Abby outside. He checked his watch, confirming time enough for the outdoor task before dinner and time after dinner to finish the project before leaving for the hospital.

Frank explained to Abby what he hoped to find, and they selected from piles of autumn leaves strewn by wind, choosing certain leaves, not the red or yellow ones, but brown ones, and only those from the neighbor's sycamore tree. Together, bent over side-by-side, grandfather and granddaughter evaluated the brown leaves. They deposited some into Frank's paper bag and threw others back among the not chosen.

"Do you have nail polish, Abby?" he said.

"No, but Kim and Michelle have nail polish. I can ask them for theirs."

"Don't ask them. They'll just give you a lot of lip. If you know where it is, just go in their room and borrow it for me."

"They have all colors, Grandpa. What color do you want?"

"Pink, dear. That will contrast well with the brown on the leaves." Abby nodded.

Thirteen-year-old Kim and fourteen-year-old Michelle grated on Frank. Both girls obsessed over their beautifying possessions: hoop earrings, platform sandals, skinny jeans, and tees knotted in back to make them tight-fitting in front. Frank imagined it would be many years before they would discover where real beauty comes from.

By contrast, ten-year-old Abby inspired Frank's grins and laughter. Each morning Abby helped Frank lift his prosthetic leg from a box beside the nightstand, and each night she helped him put the leg back in the box. She had named the leg and labeled the box, "George Washington."

After dinner, Abby put her empty plate and utensils on the kitchen counter and disappeared down the basement steps. Joan looked at Frank. "She's helping me with something," he said. He put his plate and utensils on the counter and leaned against the refrigerator to wait for Abby.

After a few minutes, she emerged with a plain, golden cookie tin. "Honey," Joan said, "we have more decorative tins."

"No, Mom, they have Christmas figures or writing on them. I need a plain one. This is perfect."

Frank and Abby worked in Frank's room, with the door closed, for almost an hour. He laid out the brown leaves on his desk and showed Abby how to paint them with the nail polish. They took turns with the leaves and stopped at times to blow on them so they would dry quickly. Abby placed the painted and dried leaves into the cookie tin. When the two emerged, Abby returned the bottle of nail polish to Kim's vanity, and Frank, carrying the golden tin, pulled his jacket off the hook by the door leading into the garage and left.

Frank took a seat in the waiting area beside the nurses' station and placed the tin on the chair beside him. He stared at the clock on the wall—eight fifteen. He thought back to a clock on a wall in a field hospital in Vietnam, 1968. That bewildering clock had taunted him in his make-shift hospital bed. He turned away and guessed a half hour had passed, but when he turned back, the clock had advanced only two minutes. He wanted the hands to speed, to deliver an end to his ordeal. He wanted the clock hands themselves to amputate his shattered leg.

That night in 1968, Kathleen had held his hand and told him the medic would return shortly after dawn. Another minute passed. She dabbed his sweaty forehead and asked him about his family, home, pets, and girlfriend. The nineteen-year-old stuttered his answers: hard-working dad, homemaker mother, younger brother; cookie-cutter style home in Torrance, California; dog named Frito; no girlfriend. The obstinate clock by then had given up only one more minute.

This night, the door to Kathleen's hospital room opened, and a man and woman came out. Kathleen's daughter, Meredith, introduced herself and her husband to Frank.

"Please go in," she said. She dabbed her wet eyes with a tissue, and her husband put his arm around her shoulder. "I mentioned on the phone she's fearful. Who wouldn't be, I guess? She knows she has little time. Her pastor is on his way, and my brother is flying in from Chicago."

Frank stepped into the room and placed the tin on the tray table at the end of the bed. He moved to the bedside and gazed at the woman in the bed, eyes shut, wispy strands of gray hair weakly defining a receding hairline. A single wire, connected somewhere beneath a sheet, led to a monitor. He looked up to see if he could discern anything about her condition from the constantly changing display of lines and numbers.

He looked back as the woman opened her eyes, Kathleen's deep, emerald eyes. Frank thought of something his father told him two decades earlier. "Son," his father had said, "you'll reach that age, as I have now, when you can see beauty in women of all ages." Frank saw beauty in seventy-nine-year-old Kathleen.

She mouthed, "Frank."

He bent forward and stroked her cheek. Her smile washed away fifty years. She was again twenty-nine and he, nineteen and in love with the angel comforting him, his love made more poignant, not because of the age difference, but because she was engaged to marry a Midwest doctor. He would never have her.

Frank reached for the tin on the tray table and brought it near for her to see.

"Kathleen," he said, "the night before the medic amputated my leg, I feared dying and feared even more living as a disabled man. You eased my fear. You were calm, even as bombs blasted throughout the night and robbed us of peace. I asked you if you had ever been afraid. Do you remember what you told me?"

"Frank," she whispered, "yes, I remember. I told you about the sycamore leaves."

Frank opened the tin and removed several leaves for Kathleen to see, placing them on the sheet by her hand.

Kathleen stared at them and wept and then smiled. "Thank you, dear Frank," she said. "These sycamore leaves, you made them funny instead of scary. How clever and kind. I knew on that night in Vietnam you had the soul of an angel."

"Oh, Kathleen, you were my angel that night."

"Frank, you are my angel tonight."

Frank lifted her hand into his and then put his other hand on top to warm her coldness. "Kathleen, I wrote you so many letters after you moved to Chicago with your husband. I hoped you would divorce him. I finally gave up and got married, but I always loved you."

The monitor flashed red lights. A nurse burst into the room, along with Meredith and two men Frank assumed to be the brother and the pastor.

Frank bent and kissed Kathleen's forehead. She squeezed his hand and whispered, "I always loved you, too."

Joan had heard the garage door open and close after two in the morning on Thursday. Frank still slept as she and the girls left for the day around eight o'clock. When Joan arrived home, the still house seemed a compromised comfort, solitude at last but no one to talk to. After school, the girls had gone to Orange County with their father, Joan's ex-husband, for the Veterans Day weekend at his house. Frank's scribbled note on the kitchen table told her not to wait up. He had accepted a dinner invitation with old buddies in Long Beach.

Joan peeked through the door peephole when the doorbell rang. She didn't recognize the man outside but recognized the golden tin in his hand. After introductions, Joan and Pastor Louis sat down in the living room.

"Your father probably told you about Kathleen Howard. I left him a voicemail shortly after she passed. Kathleen will be buried in Chicago, next to her husband. Her daughter asked me to return this tin."

"I didn't know about Kathleen," Joan said. "I had no idea my father's friend lived close."

"Kathleen moved from Chicago when her husband died two years ago. She wanted to live near her daughter. After Frank left the hospital, Kathleen told me she wasn't afraid anymore because of the sycamore leaves, but she grew too weak to explain. Do you know their significance?"

Joan didn't know. After the pastor left, she placed the tin on the kitchen table. She opened it and picked up a leaf, brown with a pink smiley face drawn across it, and beneath it, more smiley-face leaves piled loosely. She put the leaves back in the tin and replaced the cover.

In the morning, Joan noticed the tin's absence from the table. Frank poured Joan a cup of coffee and slid an omelet onto her plate.

"Who brought the tin over?" he said.

"Pastor Louis stopped by last night. He wanted to speak with you."

"It's probably too early to call him now. I'm taking a shuttle to the airport. I'll call him later. Kathleen's funeral will be Sunday morning in Chicago."

The doorbell rang.

"I'll be back Sunday night." He gulped his coffee and left with the shuttle driver.

After the long weekend with their father, the girls returned home Sunday afternoon.

"Grandpa said the funeral had a lot of people," Abby said.

"You talked with him?"

"Yes, Mom, I called Grandpa while Daddy drove us home. I wrote down when his plane will come in tonight. I told him you and I will pick him up at the airport. That's okay with you, isn't it? I want to ask him all about his trip while you drive."

"Yes, I'll be glad to pick him up. Can you explain to me about the sycamore leaves?"

"Sure, what do you want to know?"

"Well, Kathleen's pastor said the leaves made her feel unafraid. Do you know why?"

"Yeah, Grandpa and I picked out special leaves. They had to be sycamore and had to have lobes that were a little bit curved. You know, when leaves dry out they kind of curl, like claws. But we couldn't use really dry ones because they might crumble when we drew smiley faces on them with Kim's nail polish. They had to be brown so the nail polish would show up. We made sure they were just right."

"But, Abby, what do they mean?"

"Oh, it's about long ago, the night before Grandpa got his leg cut off. Nurse Kathy, that was Kathleen then, she stayed right next to Grandpa and made sure he didn't worry about the surgery in the morning. He told me he was really upset, being only nineteen and far from home.

"Kathy told him how frightened she had been at nursing school. She got out of class after dark because it was autumn and night came early. Several girl students had been attacked by a guy with a knife, but the cops didn't catch him." Abby stopped and looked at her mother.

"That's unsettling all right," Joan said. "Go on."

"Kathy had to walk alone to her dormitory, past a lot of sycamore trees. She saw scary shadows, and the wind pushed leaves along the walkway. She looked back because she thought she heard somebody following her, but it was only the dried sycamore leaves scraping on the cement. The sycamore leaves kept scaring her each time the wind blew. She had to turn around and look in case it really was the bad guy."

Joan had counseled her girls about stranger danger, but there was so much more. Abby's story reminded her to tell the girls they should never walk alone.

"Grandpa told me the night before he lost his leg forever, Kathy made him feel unafraid. He wanted to make her feel unafraid the night before she died. That's why we put smiley faces on the sycamore leaves."

Joan's father always picked Abby to join in his projects, and Abby delighted in helping him. Every day Joan witnessed the love they shared and ached her other daughters hadn't also tapped into the man's heart. She ached even more at her own failure to do so. Somehow, Abby had pulled emotion out of him, while Joan managed only a cordial father-daughter dynamic.

Joan hugged Abby. "You and Grandpa helped Kathleen. I'm proud of you. You have a big heart."

"It was Grandpa's idea," Abby said. "I just helped."

"Grandpa has a big heart, too."

"Yes, Grandpa has a heart full of love. He told me he loves you and me and Michelle and Kim. He loves Grandma, too, even if they are divorced."

"How did that conversation come up? Why did he say that?"

"Because I asked him," Abby said.

"Abby, how come Grandpa opens up so much to you? He never tells me anything about his feelings."

"Mom, you just have to ask him. That's all it takes. He'll tell you anything you ask him."

Joan thought about Abby's words through dinner. She looked at the clock, seven thirty.

"What time should we leave for the airport?" Abby said.

"Traffic will be heavy because of people coming back from the holiday. I'm going to leave right now so there's plenty of time. Abby, I'm going by myself."

"Mom, I want to go with you."

"No, Abby, I need to talk to Grandpa one-on-one tonight. Besides, you have to get up early for school tomorrow. You'll be in bed before Grandpa and I get home."

"I have to stay up to help Grandpa put George Washington into the box."

"Sweetie, I'll help Grandpa tonight."

"Mom, you don't know how."

"I'll ask Grandpa how to do it."

Joan pulled into the LAX cell phone waiting lot forty minutes before Frank's scheduled arrival. She watched the flickering lights of arriving planes while she thought of all the things she wanted to ask. But more than anything, she wanted to tell her father how much she loved him.

Head Over Heels

"BALENCIAGA, FENDI COLIBRI, VALENTINO Garavani, Alexander Wang, Manolo Blahnik, Jimmy Choo, Prada—just some of what I have. Spoiled girls have all the best shoes." Skye nodded, as if agreeing with her own assessment. "I spent all day Sunday organizing the shoe racks in my closets. Big decision—color, heel height, designer, or price?" She threw her hands out, shrugged, and smiled. "I went with price—my most expensive shoes all at eye level. I took over my roommate's closet. Poor baby has so few. He has maybe four pairs at the most."

"Skye, did you hear me? I just said my mother's dying of cancer."

"I know. You said something about it on the phone when I told you where to meet me for lunch. This is the new 'it' restaurant. Don't you remember, Janna, I said I felt sorry?" She picked up the menu. "Did you look this over while you waited for me? You knew I'd be late. Sometimes I just can't decide which shoes to wear."

She turned sideways in her chair to show me her shiny, black, pointy-toe pumps, with four-inch stiletto heels. She flexed her feet up so I could see the designer signature red soles and grinned so wide her elongated, purple painted lips reminded me of the tubes connecting my mother to the oxygen tank on the pole in her hospital room.

"Skye, stop right there." My heart thumped in my ears, and the slick-haired waiter twirled from the table he was serving to see who spoke so loudly. A dropped fork clanked somewhere. I yanked my Kmart sling purse like a pup on a leash. It bounced against the hostess station when I rushed out to the street, bolting past those waiting to be seated.

That was the last time I saw Skye until today.

I ignored all Skye's emails and texts in the intervening two years, deciding her repeated, "so sorry," punctuated with any number of crying emoticons, emoted no truth. My best friend since tenth grade, Skye disregarded my mother's illness and turned our conversation to her own interests when I needed her to hear my heartache. Skye probably didn't even know or care my mother died three months after the day I stormed away from her.

Debbie's Diner—I had to look again at the text message. We hadn't met at our old hangout in over five years, ever since Skye had gone all uptown on me and insisted we patronize only trendy places, places where, she had said, "my shoes feel appreciated." It seemed a joke until it became unfunny—her obsession with shoes.

"Debbie's at 11?"

I texted back, "OK." Mention of the diner brought back memories. Skye had been my buddy. Feeling disloyal made me hurt. It wasn't in me to stay mad any longer.

I arrived at eleven fifteen, in no hurry because I expected to wait, expected Skye to pirouette in front of her full length mirror in many different pairs of shoes before deciding which to wear. I selected a booth near the door in this casual-dining, seat-yourself establishment so I would see her coming in.

"Hi, dear, haven't seen you in ages," Sharna, the waitress, said. "Skye is in the booth by the window. I guess you didn't see her."

I saw her, but didn't recognize her. She turned as I approached. She looked like a younger version of herself, the old Skye with the sweet smile. She jumped up, hugged me and wouldn't let go. "I'm so sorry about your mother, Janna. The Sunday after she passed I went to the church in your old neighborhood and lit a candle for her. Mrs. Conley, the neighbor you used to babysit for, was in the church and told me how distraught you had been at the funeral. I should have been there for you."

"I needed you, Skye."

She released me from her hug and pointed me into the booth while she slid in across from me. "I've missed you so much, Janna. Tell me all about the last two years. How have you been doing?"

An imposter, not Skye—Skye would never arrive first, never inquire about my life, never miss an opportunity to gush about all-things-Skye, and never wear such ugly, flat shoes—who was this woman, holding my hand and looking into my eyes as if seeking out my soul?

Sharna brought silverware and menus. Nothing about Debbie's had changed, not even the prices. Sharna returned with glasses of water, and Skye and I ordered.

I mumbled about selling my mother's house, being promoted at work, breaking up with my boyfriend. Skye kept asking me details, as if she really cared. At last I had Skye's undivided attention, but I wanted to know about her, about how and when and why she had changed.

"Skye, stop right there. Enough about me—what's happened to you?"

Our meals arrived. Skye complimented Sharna on her changed hairdo and asked about her children. I hadn't even remembered Sharna had kids. When Sharna left us I asked Skye again, "What's new in your life?"

"Janna, no worries, I'm doing fine. In a nutshell, I lost my high paying job. With an unemployment check, an additional roommate to help with the rent, and the money I got when I sold my shoes. I squeaked by until I landed a new job. I'm marketing manager for a renewable energy company. Half the pay, but it works 'cause I'm no longer blowing two to three thousand a month on designer shoes."

"You sold your shoes?"

Skye laughed. My old Skye—I could read her mind the way I did in tenth grade. Amused because I reacted only to the news about her selling her shoes, she fell into a giggle fit and dragged me along with her. I giggled until I couldn't breathe. Sharna winked at us as she hurried past with a full tray.

"Whew! We haven't laughed so hard since forever," Skye said.

Then I noticed the brown paper grocery bag beside her on the booth seat.

"Janna, I have a gift for you, my last pair of designer shoes. At the time I needed money, I got physically ill each time I parted with a pair of shoes. I received cents on the dollar—shoes that set me back thirteen or fourteen hundred dollars I had to sell for only two or two fifty." She patted the grocery bag. "Janna, I want you to have my most expensive pair of shoes. Don't take them out of the bag in front of me, and don't offer to pay for them. I'm so glad we wear the same size. I want you to have them." She looked neither physically ill nor sad to part with her last pair.

"Keep them, Skye. You can afford to now, and there's no need to give them away. I do appreciate the offer, but I've never been one to wear fancy shoes. I'll love seeing you wear them."

"I can't wear them," she said. "I had bunion surgery on my right foot. The podiatrist said I came darn close to needing the same on my left foot."

"So sorry, Skye, does your foot hurt?" I wondered about the unusual shoes she had on.

"No, I had the surgery over a year ago. These shoes are so comfortable." She turned in the booth and stuck one foot out. "They're expensive, but not like designer shoes. They work for people with foot problems, like bunions or hammer toes. Knit shoes with a wide toe box. I know they're not attractive. I'll say it so you don't have to—they look like clown shoes." She wiggled her foot and laughed.

We ate and reminisced. I hesitated to ask but had to know. "Skye, you've changed back to your old self. How? Why? Was it the job loss or having to sell your shoes?"

"No, Janna." She reached over and squeezed my hand. "The job, the shoes—they were unimportant. I lost your friendship, your love. That tipped me over and turned me around. I did a lot of soul searching and crying because I behaved badly. I'm so sorry."

I envisioned her tribe of texted emoticons. They had been real. She meant her apology.

Sharna removed our plates. Skye sipped her water. I could tell she had more on her mind. "Skye, what is it you're dying to tell me?"

"I'm in love, Janna. His name is Ryan, and we're engaged to be engaged."

"Wonderful! How did you meet him?"

"I met him at the podiatry office. He suffers from plantar fasciitis."

Old Skye had a new man. She didn't gush about him, so I asked questions and decided my best friend, with respect to her love life, had landed on her feet. We made plans to lunch again at Debbie's in three weeks, when Skye returned from a business trip.

For two days after our reunion, I didn't open the grocery bag. I left it on the floor in my closet. On the third day, I placed it on my dresser. On the fourth day, while getting ready for work, I pulled out the shoes and slipped them on—pale blush suede, T-strap pump, four-inch heels, perfect fit. I teetered around, nearly losing my balance until I remembered what Skye had told me when she started wearing skyscraper footwear. "Counterbalance is the key. Thrust your bust forward and your butt back," she had said. "The shoes make your legs look oh so long and make the muscles in your calves and thighs stand out. Wear a short skirt, and the guys can't help but notice."

In high school, shy Skye never attracted the boys in our class. Perhaps her obsession with shoes had grown from desiring male attention. With Ryan, Skye could be herself, happy in comfortable clown shoes and happy with a man who appreciated who she was, not what she wore.

Before we had parted at Debbie's Diner, Skye told me about writing a message on tiny pieces of paper, like those found in fortune cookies. She stuffed the notes into the toe point of each left shoe before she started selling off the pairs.

I sat on my bed, took off the shoes, poked my index finger into the left shoe toe point, and pulled out the little roll. It read:

Let these shoes bolster your confidence, but don't let them change who you are.

I stuffed the roll back into the shoe, put the shoes in the bag, and placed the bag in my car trunk. After work I dropped the shoes off at Dress the Part, a charitable organization providing job seekers with fashionable interview clothing they could not afford to buy.

Naomi got off the bus at the stop in front of the building, breathed deeply, crossed her fingers, and stepped through the revolving door into the impressive lobby, with its tall marble walls and massive, sparkling chandelier. Out of work since the layoff a year ago, single mom Naomi had held teenage daughter Kelly's hand and practiced walking around in their apartment in the stiletto heels. Without the tailored suit, sleek handbag, and high end shoes, Naomi wouldn't have thought about applying at World Edge Solutions, Inc.

"Glad to meet you, Naomi. I'm Laynie Pierson. Call me 'Laynie.' We receive hundreds of resumes for each open position. Your background and experience landed you in the top three for the opening in my department."

After a friendly back and forth conversation, Laynie surprised Naomi with her next question.

"Those are Valentinos, right?"

Laynie must have meant the shoes. Naomi remembered seeing a name starting with "V" inside the shoes. "Yes, right, Laynie."

"I have three pairs in my main closet, but not the ones you're wearing. That's a smart outfit—great choice, Naomi."

Laynie wore her own expensive looking shoes. Naomi hoped Laynie wouldn't ask if she knew the designer.

"One more question, Naomi. When we have a tie, like the three-way we have now, we base our decision on the finalists' answers to the all important question." Laynie poised her fingers on the keyboard on her desk, ready to capture Naomi's answer. "Ready?"

Naomi nodded.

Laynie smiled. "Where do you see yourself in one year?"

That's it, thought Naomi, the all important question? She had to think fast.

She spoke slowly, feeling her way to a safe answer. "If I'm selected for the position, I will learn all I can to promote the team and positively impact the corporate bottom line."

Laynie did not type. She shook her head. "Let's try that again. The question is about you. How would this great opportunity change you? I mean your lifestyle, your own personal brand, as they say."

Naomi felt like a beached fish floundering for air. Kelly's future rode on her answer—art supplies, music lessons, cheerleading outfits, class ring, prom dress. She tried again. "I would hope to be able to change the position."

That didn't even make sense. Thank goodness Laynie hadn't typed what she said.

"Like more pay and prestige, better title, office on one of the upper floors?" Laynie said, almost in a whisper. Was Laynie coaching her?

Naomi's head spun, and her feet hurt. Get it right, Naomi, for yourself and Kelly. She flashed back to Kelly's surprise when she read the message rolled up in the left toe point: *Let these shoes bolster your confidence, but don't let them change who you are.*

Don't let them change who you are. You can answer the question without being coached. On the bus ride to the interview, many thoughts crossed Naomi's mind. She took a moment to reflect on those thoughts, breathed deeply, and straightened in her chair.

"Laynie, if I came onboard and then after one year I crossed the busy street outside and got taken out by a bus, I would want you to revise your description of the ideal candidate when looking for my re-placement. Your new job posting would reflect the unique qualities I brought to the position and used to improve what could be achieved."

Laynie nodded. Her fingers clicked away until the interruption.

Naomi jerked. A female voice emanating from a speaker on Laynie's desk had startled her. "Laynie, that's the best answer ever given to our qualifying question, including the answers given by the other two candidates for this position. Hire Naomi. I'll text HR to prepare the offer letter so she can take it with her."

Naomi looked from the speaker to Laynie, almost certain her eyebrows formed two question marks.

"That's Eileen, the boss. She listens in on the interviews." Laynie stood, came around her desk, and offered a handshake. "Congrat-ulations, Naomi! You've got the job if you want it. Please wait here while I go up to HR and get your letter and have Eileen sign it. Back in a few."

Naomi wiggled the Valentinos under her chair. She thought about Kelly happy dancing and saying she's so proud of her mother. She thought about writing a note to Dress the Part asking them to express her appreciation to whichever kind soul stuffed the rolled up note into the toe point of her left shoe.

Star Burger

THE PLAZA SIGN PROMISED Gary Wheatcroft a liquor store nestled in the cluster of storefronts between Safeway and Rite-Aid. Gary had not been to this end of the county in seven years. He squinted through swollen eyes to read the store signs: acrylic nails, brow threading, donuts, Tai Kwando, and liquor—yep, stop for Jack Daniels on the way home, but drop off the mutt first.

He pulled into a fast food drive-thru lane, his dusty pickup truck fourth in line to order. His stomach grumbled, unfilled since the middle of the day before. He stared at bloodshot eyes in the visor mirror and then caught sight of the dog in the rear seat. If Estelle had been there, the dog would have been in her lap. Gary wiped the stained cuff of his shirt across his eyes. Damn! The kid in the drive-thru window would probably stare and smirk and tell the burger flippers about the old man bawling in his truck. He pulled Estelle's purple rimmed sunglasses from the console and whipped them on.

"Double cheeseburger and cola," he shouted into the intercom. The voice in his head, Estelle's, whispered: *Don't forget a small, plain burger—no mayo, onions, pickles, lettuce. She needs something to eat, too.* He pulled forward. They'd feed her at the pound. He didn't look at the dog or at the empty seat beside him. He parked and ate robotically and downed his cola in big gulps.

Eight miles down the highway, a small sign announced the exit for the county animal shelter. The paved road ran into gravel and then became a dust driveway leading to a low-slung cement and brick building. Gary heard barking and yapping dogs, probably in runs behind the building. He removed the sunglasses, took three deep breaths, and checked his eyes in the mirror.

Three women, all wearing t-shirts with cat lover slogans front and back, stood together ahead of him, each with cat carriers stacked beside them. While waiting, he thought of his son's advice: *Dad, do whatever you need to. Take care of yourself. Now is not the time to worry about anyone or anything else. Call if you need anything.* Kind of an empty offer because Bart lived too far away to help.

Estelle's aunt had advised otherwise: *Now is not the time to make any decisions, Gary. Things will unfold and look different as you work through your feelings.* Women always talked about feelings.

"You ladies here to pick up the hoarder's cats?" said the young man behind the counter. He wore a khaki green shelter uniform with a name badge, "Curtis," above the chest pocket.

"Yes, I spoke on the phone with your director. We'll take all twenty-eight. Sixty-seven already in our foster network—there's no end to our cat rescue." She sighed and exchanged nods and smiles with the other two women. Another uniformed shelter employee took carriers from the women and disappeared through a door behind the counter. The women went out for more carriers. Gary stepped forward.

"Turning the dog in?" Curtis poised his fingers over the computer keyboard before him. "Your contact information and the dog's gender, breed, name, and age, if you know it."

Curtis typed as Gary gave his name, address, and phone number. "You have all that stuff on the dog, don't you, from the adoption?" Gary said.

"Probably, when did you adopt the dog?"

"About seven years ago."

"No sir, we keep only two years back." Curtis stretched his fingers, as if to play a piano, and then repositioned them above the keyboard. "So, male or female, breed, name, and age."

"Female, mutt, name is 'Burger.'"

A woman, with a green vest labeled, "Volunteer," had opened another position at the counter. She glanced at Gary and the dog beside him.

Curtis leaned over the counter for a good look at Burger. "She's a strange one, maybe Airedale and spaniel. What do you think, Jennifer?" he asked the volunteer.

"No, too short for Airedale, but some kind of terrier and small poodle mix. Looks like my brother's dog, shaggy and black also, but his dog doesn't have a white mark on his head like this one."

Curtis typed and then asked, "Mr. Wheatcroft, how old is Burger?"

Another man had brought in a large dog. The volunteer completed the intake form and escorted the dog through the door to the back. She returned and leaned over the counter. "Burger, good girl, Burger," she said in a lilting voice. Burger remained head down. "Her name isn't 'Burger.' She doesn't respond to that." The woman looked from Gary to Curtis and back to Gary. "Is that really your dog?"

The woman's harsh tone startled Gary. "My wife called her, 'Star.' I call her, 'Burger'—a running joke, a long story."

"Star, good girl, Star," the volunteer cooed. The dog looked up to the counter and strained her leash to stand on her hind legs and wag her tail. "Does your wife even know you're turning her dog in?"

"My wife is dead."

"Oh, I'm sorry." Color drained from the volunteer's face. "How long ago did she pass?"

"Eighteen or twenty days ago."

The volunteer gasped. She came around the counter and patted Gary's shoulder. "I'm truly sorry. I was out of line."

Gary shrugged. Star, slow-wagging her tail, watched Jennifer, who turned to greet two teenage girls looking for their lost Shih Tzu.

Curtis finished typing, printed the form twice, and handed one copy to Gary. "Bring this with you. Waiting list is eight to twelve weeks. With your senior discount, the fee will be forty-five dollars, cash or credit card. We don't accept checks."

Gary opened his wallet on the counter.

"No, not now—pay when you bring your dog back for intake. We'll call you."

"Wait, what do you mean? Are you telling me to bring her back later? You won't take her today?"

"We're full, so we can't take in any O-T-I. You have to wait."

"O-T-I? You mean mutts? You only take purebreds?"

"No, O-T-I is *Owner Turn In*. When we have space, you can bring her back. Otherwise, you can try to find a good home on your own, place an ad, ask friends and neighbors."

"That other guy brought in a dog. She took that one." Gary nodded toward Jennifer.

"A stray, we have to take strays. That's the purpose of animal control."

"So if I tell you this dog is a stray you'll take her?"

"Not now, we know she isn't. License number and owner name popped up when I keyed in your phone number. Estelle Wheatcroft owned her. Sorry for your loss, Mr. Wheatcroft, but you're the owner, so I can't intake your dog today."

"You're no help!" Gary shouted. Curtis ignored him and motioned the woman in line behind Gary to step forward. I'm invisible, Gary thought. Jennifer checked her computer screen and told the girls no Shih Tzu had been brought in. The girls left, and Jennifer disappeared into the back. The other shelter employee and the cat ladies shuttled carriers in and out.

No one to help, what would Estelle say or do? He couldn't think what she'd say or do. He couldn't think of anything. For eighteen or twenty days his brain misfired when he tried to think of something—clicking but not catching, like a dead battery. If only he could slip through the floor and forget about everything.

Gary and Burger trudged out, both head down and still connected by leash. Gary stopped in front of a sign in the parking lot which read:

Unlawful for any person to abandon an animal on these premises—Violators subject to fine and/or imprisonment (Ordinance 98, Section XIV)

The voice behind Gary startled him. "We prosecute violators, Mr. Wheatcroft. People show up after hours and think they can just leave their pet in the parking lot. You wouldn't do that."

Gary turned to see Jennifer pointing to surveillance cameras on the building. She had changed into a uniform: crisp white shirt, black tie, brown slacks, a badge, and a belt laden with, among other things, a gun and holster. Gary recognized the insignia on the arm patch, County Sheriff's Department.

"I'm a cop when I'm not volunteering here," she said. "I don't recommend what Curtis said about placing an ad. Predators get dogs from ads to sell for inhumane purposes, or they charge a desperate owner a fee to find a good home and then dump the dog in a canyon. You don't want that."

"No, Estelle's aunt told me not to place an ad. But she can't take Burger. She's in a wheelchair and has a service dog. I asked around. Nobody wants a dog. I dunno what to do?"

"Just wait. The shelter will take your dog when you're up next on the waiting list."

"I can't wait. I can't take care of her. I can't even take care of myself." He pointed to his wrinkled and soiled shirt. "I hardly think to eat. I don't know when Burger ate. There's a food bowl in the basement, full of ants. Estelle had sticks, like chalk, for repelling ants—safe for pets. She'd draw a circle around the bowl. I can't find the sticks, and I don't know where to buy them."

"Feed stores have them. Wait here. I'll get something for Star to eat." The dog's ears perked up at the sound of the name she knew.

Jennifer disappeared behind the building and came back with two bowls, a bottle of water, and a bag of dog food. Burger dove for the food in the bowl, ate down to the last kibble, lapped the water bowl dry, sniffed again at the empty food bowl, and wagged her tail high speed. "I'd give her more, Mr. Wheatcroft, but too much to eat at once will make her vomit." Jennifer ran her hands over the dog's fur. "You need to brush out these mats. They'll irritate her skin and stress her."

"Estelle took care of all that." He turned away, holding Burger's leash in back of him. "You don't understand. I can't function. It's like there's a cloud around my head. Nothing comes out right, and look at that." He turned back and pointed to his feet. "My shoes don't match. How'd I do that?"

"Maybe I do understand, Mr. Wheatcroft. I studied psychology before I switched to criminal justice. I know sometimes grieving people can't perform day-to-day functions well because their brain can only concentrate on the grief. The problem will go away, but it takes time. Perhaps you could talk to your doctor."

Star continued sniffing all around the food bowl and licked at pebbles in the dirt. Jennifer pursed her lips and shook her head. She took a notepad and pencil from her shirt pocket. "There's another dog shelter, a private shelter. Rita and Lou trap dogs abandoned in the canyons and work with breed rescuers to re-socialize and re-home them." Jennifer peered into Gary's face, as if to confirm he was listening before she continued. "They don't usually take dogs from the public, but they'll take Star if I ask them to. Here, I wrote down the exit, Stone Canyon Road, about twelve miles further down the highway. After you drive on that road three or four miles, you'll see a blue house, no sign, no number, but it's the only house there. I'll phone and tell them you're coming."

———————

Gary jerked at the sound of the truck horn and panicked seeing his rearview mirror filled with truck grille. He pulled back into the left lane. Safer to stay left, he thought. Estelle always rolled her eyes when he cut drivers off. He zoomed past trucks in the right and watched for road signs. He turned to glance in the backseat. "How you doing, Star?" She raised her head.

He had passed a sign. Could that have been the exit? He moved into the right and watched the signs: Henley Road, Carbon Canyon Highway, Red Creek Road. He'd turn back if he didn't find the right road soon. Traffic diminished as he rolled along. Another sign loomed ahead. He squinted and slowed—Stone Creek Road. "That's it, Star!" He turned off the highway.

His truck bucked through potholes and shimmied left and right. No one should live out here, along this unpaved road, he thought. The elevation rose as he poked along, gripping the steering wheel, which gyrated with each bounce and shake. Antelope dotted a hill on the right, and a guardrail on the left promised a drop, where Gary saw only the tops of trees. Wind blew sand swirls across the road. He could imagine people abandoning dogs in this desolate place. No one would catch them doing it.

He looked into the backseat. "I know you're grieving, too." He thought of how Estelle always talked to her dog. The pastor at the funeral said when you think of your loved one, she is right by your side, and you may even feel her presence. "I still hear her in my head, Star. Do you, too?" Star rose from the backseat, crawled over the console, and plopped into the passenger seat, where Estelle always sat. She curled up, her face turned toward Gary.

Gary, she's thirsty. Get the bowl from under my seat and water from the bottle in your door pocket.

He stopped the truck, turned on the hazard lights in case another vehicle approached, and filled the water bowl half way. As Star gulped, Gary noticed a figure by the side of the road—a whitish gray, medium-sized dog standing a few yards away, motionless and staring. Swirling sand ruffled its scruffy fur. The skinny canine moved in front of the truck—not a dog, but a coyote.

Leave water for the coyote.

When Star finished drinking, Gary got out of the truck, refilled the bowl, and left it roadside, behind the truck. The coyote moved away as Gary drove around him. Gary watched the rearview mirror. The coyote headed toward the bowl.

Thank you. Estelle's brown eyes always twinkled when she thanked him, even for a simple favor.

The sunset aimed blinding rays at the windshield. He checked the clock—a quarter after five. He had planned to get home by four o'clock and slouch in his patio chair with glasses of whiskey, just as he had done for the past however many nights since the doctor came out of Estelle's hospital room and shook his head. Not a heavy drinker before Estelle died—just a glass of wine with her on the patio after dinner—Gary sought one hundred forty proof grief relief. Without Estelle next to him in bed, he clutched the pink camisole she always wore, wrapped it around his neck, and smelled her fragrance. The clock ticked his life away without her while he prayed to Jack Daniels for oblivion.

Sun glare and sand swirls blocked his view of the winding road. He could not see more than ten feet in front of the truck. *Please slow down, Gary!* He rounded a curve and felt the muscles in his face pull into a grimace. He stopped breathing. Could he avoid striking the antelope?

If a deer jumps out in front of you, steer the car toward its hindquarters. The deer will be moving forward, so you may end up not hitting it—Estelle's words from twenty years earlier, when they moved into the then rural west end of the county. He yanked the steering wheel left. The antelope bounded up a hill on the right.

Gary's ears rang with the screech of metal on metal. The guardrail buckled and split. An airbag exploded in his face. When the airbag deflated, the truck stilled moved, tumbling over the embankment, striking boulders, and bouncing off tree trunks, like a careening sphere in a pinball machine, until settling upright atop a boulder. Gary peered through the shattered windshield. The last glint of daylight played upon the hissing vapor rising from the twisted truck hood. A whiff of acrid odor alerted him to the warm blood on his face and hands. Gravity was not done with him. He unbuckled his seatbelt and pushed three times against the bent driver side door until it creaked and fell away. He crawled out and slid downhill another fifty yards, bumpety-bump over sagebrush and shale, to the canyon floor.

Face down on cool earth, a rock nudging his cheek, Gary tasted blood and heard wings flapping above. *Woo-woo-hoo-hoo, woo-woo-hoo-hoo*—he flinched—must be how owls panic their prey into running out from hiding places. Water gurgled nearby. He rolled over. A brilliant star canopy confirmed he had lain unconscious for hours. He sat up, legs out before him, one shoe on, the other not in sight. Oh well, his shoes didn't match anyway. He watched water sparkling in the creek bed ten yards away, shivered like the sagebrush quaking in the chill breeze, and wondered how much colder the canyon could get on this cloudless night.

A glint on the ground five yards away prompted Gary to check his shirt pocket for his cell phone—not there. When he stood to walk, his shoeless foot collapsed. He sank to the ground and cursed the blazing throb in his left ankle, then stood again and hopped on one foot. The recovered phone, still intact, offered no service in the canyon.

He eased back into his sitting position and glared at the mean canyon walls, too steep even for able ankles. He couldn't imagine any way to be found unless the dog rescue couple came upon the torn and pleated guardrail, looked down, and spied the mangled truck. But perhaps he had been on the wrong road, not the one leading to the blue house. Even a grief-stricken man doesn't want to fossilize in a desolate canyon, where only vultures might care. Bart might never know what happened to his father. Despite his busy life six hundred miles away, Bart still cared.

Thank you, Estelle, for raising a good man—two good men, if you count me, too.

He curled into a fetal position and thought about the night when he, at age eighteen, met sixteen-year-old Estelle.

Estelle pulled her white cardigan around her lithe body as she and two girlfriends headed for Star Burger, a popular hamburger joint on Crenshaw Boulevard in Los Angeles—no dining room and no drive-thru in 1963. Gary and Kenny Sands, both high school seniors, waited on customers at the walk-up window from six to eleven at night. Gary watched the girls leave the movie theater across the street. Kenny had seen the matinee showing of *Bye Bye Birdie* and talked about Ann-Margret non-stop. Gary, with no interest in the movie star, thought only of Estelle, the prettiest girl he had ever seen. He saw her in the hall at school every day and every day hoped and failed to think of a way to get her attention. That night at Star Burger he thought of a way.

Estelle and her friends waited in line behind two boys. Her lilting laugh rose above the chatter of her friends and tickled his ear. He handed a bag of burgers and fries to his customer, sprang open the side of his register, and put a hand up to keep the next customers, the two boys, waiting. He dawdled changing the roll until Kenny, at the other register, motioned the boys over.

Brilliant, thought Gary, the Star Burger giveaway might help him. One red star appeared on the back of every roll of cash register tape. A red star on the back of your receipt won a free meal. Gary knew the star usually came up on the third order after he changed the roll. He hoped Kenny didn't see him discard a half-used tape roll, advance the new roll, and tear off a length of blank paper. He felt his face flush. He looked down as he waved for the next customers.

When he looked up, Estelle's dark eyes, framed by flawless olive skin, rendered him so enchanted he couldn't manage the perfunctory, "What would you like to order?" He stammered, "Can I, eh, just let me know, uh, we have burgers. Do you want one?" His eyes darted to Kenny and back. "A drink, too, maybe?"

The two girls who flanked Estelle choked on peals of giggles. Estelle placed a hand on each girl's arm, the wide sleeves of her cardigan resembling angel wings. "Shall I order for all of us?" she said. "It's on me."

They nodded, still coughing up laughs Gary assumed mocked his awkward behavior. Estelle shushed them and turned back to Gary. "Three burgers with cheese, two large fries—we'll share—and three crème sodas." The girls nodded and turned to hide another giggle fit. Gary wrote the order for the burger flipper and punched the items into the register. Estelle pulled a wallet from her purse.

Gary hesitated before hitting the "Total" button. He could imagine dancing with Estelle at his senior prom, the two of them gliding in the sky, two-stepping through the Milky Way—his cousin Patty had shown him how to two-step—and boarding a horse drawn carriage on the moon for a ride back to the high school auditorium. Tuxedoed boys, gowned girls, a local band, magic in the air, and, best of all, Gary Wheatcroft the envy of all because he had the most beautiful girl in the universe on his arm.

Chug-chug-whirr, chug-chug-whirr—the register spit a ticket. Gary tore it from the register. "A dollar forty-seven, Miss."

Estelle fumbled in her wallet. Gary tried to see through the ticket as he held it toward her. Dared he turn it over to check the star? He didn't have to.

"Estelle," squealed her friend, "you have a red star on the back. See it? It's free. Yippee!" Her other friend grabbed the ticket and held up the star.

Estelle smiled. "Is that right, I don't have to pay?"

"Your meal is on Star Burger tonight. Please enjoy and come again." Gary managed the red star patter he learned on his first day working. Sweat poured down his back. His heart thumped.

"On the free meal, we're supposed to ask the customer about their dining experience." A lie, he told her a lie. Too late, he told his conscience, it had already left his mouth. "Maybe you can let me know tomorrow at school if you enjoyed the cheeseburger and fries. I've seen you at Clark High. I go there, too. My name is Gary Wheatcroft." Silence—he agonized over what she might say. He wished he had never tried being so bold. He watched her lips move and then turn up in a smile before he assimilated her reply.

"Yes, I know. I'll look for you in the hall tomorrow."

He brushed at his face until wakefulness brought him eye-to-eye with something licking the blood on his forehead. The creature circled Gary and then licked his face again.

"Star, oh my goodness, what's wrong with me? I forgot you." He sat up, pulled Star onto his lap, and used his phone's flashlight to examine her—no blood, no signs of injury. "You're okay, Star, thank goodness, but you must be hungry." Hungry and cold, he thought. He lay down and pulled Star against him. They could help keep each other warm.

Woo-woo-hoo-hoo, woo-woo-hoo-hoo. Flapping wings stirred the air. Star shrieked and bolted. Gary snagged Star's hind leg and pulled her back. "Whoa, that owl could carry you off." Star wiggled and pulled, but Gary held tight. "Stay here, Star. We need each other."

They needed to stay awake to fight hypothermia. He scratched behind Star's ears, the way Estelle often did. "Did you know 'Estelle' means 'Star'? That's what her mother told me when I came to pick her up for our first date."

Estelle's mother also told him that for every good deed, you earn a star in your crown and a double star if you help an animal. He gazed up at a million stars in Estelle's crown—probably half of them double for all the injured turtles and birds, lizards and mice, and other creatures she found, nurtured back to health, and set free, and for all the cats and dogs she brought home from the animal shelter, Star being the last.

Gary bent his head and wept into Star's fur, his shoulders shaking. Star pulled away and looked back at him nervously. He gasped and moaned as he slipped into the emotional sinkhole he had circled for twenty days. Estelle was gone—further from reach than the Milky Way and never to hold him and console him, never to roll her eyes and flash a smile, never to kiss his lips and snuggle against him.

His shaking turned to shivers. The cold canyon seemed isolated, like him, until its nocturnal hunters caught his and Star's scent in the ripple of a night breeze. Star cocked her head, whimpered, and crouched, a low rumble lodged in her throat. She could hear and smell what Gary could not. He blotted his tears with his shirttails, watched the terrified dog, and held his breath. A lone bark in the distance cracked the still night just before the canyon burst into motion and sound. Shadow forms circled close by, accompanied by a chorus of barks, howls, and growls.

Gary stood on one foot, stretched his hand out, and pointed the light beam of his phone's flashlight toward the shadows. Pairs of lit eyes bounced like fireflies in all directions around him. One pair angled closer, revealing a growling coyote, its whitish gray fur bristling on its back.

Five or more coyotes swirled in and out of the light beam and approached Gary with quick lunges and retreats. He turned in a circle, beaming the light all around. Where was Star? He hopped forward and back and side-to-side, peering as far as he could.

The coyotes' pace slowed, and as quickly as they had arrived, the menacing animals blended back into the shadows, still barking. At a distance, their vocalizations reached a crescendo. Also at a distance, Star shrieked, the way she did the day the neighbor kid ran over her paw with his bike. The coyotes barked a few more times and then fell silent, and in the silence, the sound of rushing water in the creek grew deafening. Gary threw down his phone and covered his ears. Dizziness gripped him. He stumbled, fought for his balance, and ended up sprawled on his back. He looked at the star studded canopy above and whispered, "I'm so sorry, Estelle."

_____

The female coyote, with a long jaw, squinted into Gary's face. "You're a tough old bird, Mr. Wheatcroft."

The male coyote, with deep set blue eyes and a cap of thick, black hair, gray at the temples, smiled. "Welcome back into the world, Gary. I'm Dr. Macy."

Clackety-clack, a cart rolled along a hallway. A pretty, young girl in a blue teen volunteer uniform stuck her face into the doorway. Dr. Macy winked at her. "Yes, Alexis, the patient is coming out of sedation and will probably want your dinner gruel after a bit. Come back later, okay?"

Conversations in the room merged into a din as Gary recollected foggy images and vague sounds: flashing lights, voices, a big man strapping him onto a gurney, sirens. Gary, in a hospital bed with his head and shoulders slightly elevated, observed his reflection in a window. The pitiful man stared back through dark-circled eyes, his forehead bandaged and his cheeks and chin bruised and swollen.

"You're tough but not pretty," said the long-jawed nurse. "We warmed you up slowly, over sixteen hours, and pumped you full of fluids. Dr. Macy will release you tomorrow. You'll go home with crutches to keep weight off your sprained ankle. See your doctor to change the dressing on your forehead and remove the sutures. Do you have any questions?"

Gary looked again at the miserable man reflected in the window, the man who didn't protect his wife's beloved dog. "Did anybody find my dog?" he said. "I think coyotes killed her, but I have to ask."

"I don't know, Mr. Wheatcroft. When the volunteer wheels you out tomorrow, ask her to take you to the Emergency Department nurse. If the responders saw a dog at the crash scene, the nurse may find a note about it in the incident report."

———————

The morning dragged on while Gary waited for Dr. Macy, who strode into his room after noon, quipped about the whole building being full of sick people, and released Gary from the hospital. Gary, having his wallet, keys, and phone from the crash site, wore clothing provided from a donation closet for patients needing clean clothes to wear home. Ellie, the teen volunteer charged with wheeling him to his ride, waited while he spoke with the ED nurse. He held his crutches across his lap while the nurse looked for the paramedics' report.

"No, there's nothing in the report about a dog," she said, "but there is a business card with a note." She handed it to Gary.

Jennifer, the deputy sheriff, had written on the back, "Gary, call me—important."

"Mr. Wheatcroft, your rideshare is here." Ellie pointed to the sedan waiting curbside, beyond the automatic glass doors. Gary slipped the card into his shirt pocket, thanked Ellie, and crawled into the backseat, drawing his crutches in with him. At Gary's request the driver stopped at a liquor store. He carried the purchase into the house for Gary, who hobbled in on his crutches.

Gary started slow with the whiskey, viewing early evening TV movies and swirling the liquid in the glass between sips. He turned on lights when the living room turned dark. He wished he had done better by Star.

Credits for the late-night movie rolled up the screen when he awoke in his recliner, half-emptied glass on the table beside him. He clicked the TV off with the remote, hopped with the crutches, set them aside on the bedroom chair, and collapsed on the bed he had left unmade two and a half days earlier. He felt all over the bed for Estelle's night camisole, then under the pillow, under the sheet, between the sheet and blanket. Every night since she had died, except for one night in the canyon and one night in the hospital, he held her camisole as he wept and waited for the earth to turn. Even with his bedside lamp on, he still couldn't find it. He stared at his empty hands. Estelle had slipped further from him.

The futile search killed the whiskey buzz. He left the lamp on, lay in bed, and watched the wall clock. At two thirty he heard creaks and rustling sounds in the house. He had foiled a raccoon before, as it tried to enter the kitchen through Star's doggy door. He shooed it away and never encountered another. But with the house empty for two nights, furry invaders may have struck again. He picked up a crutch he had left across the bedroom chair and hopped through the hall and into the kitchen, expecting a flurry of evasive activity when he flipped on the kitchen light, but nothing moved—no raccoons and not even a rat.

He hopped through the hall to the basement stairs and pulled the light cord, which hung just inside the basement door opening. He leaned in to look to the bottom of the stairs, where a brown, braided throw rug covered the cement floor. The dim light cast by the bare bulb illuminated something multicolored on the rug. He held the door jamb for balance and poked the light bulb with the crutch, repositioning the beam to better see the dark and light blob below. Curled up atop Estelle's pink camisole, Star whimpered and wagged her tail.

Not Star, she couldn't have walked home over twenty miles! How could she find her way? His skepticism waned as the dog that couldn't possibly be there clambered up the stairs and, upon reaching the top, licked his outstretched fingers. A three-inch wide bandage encircled the upper part of one hind leg. Somebody had dressed a wound. Then he remembered the card he dropped in his shirt pocket as he left the hospital.

"Jennifer, this is Gary Wheatcroft. I'm sorry to call at this hour."

"I get calls at all hours, but mostly from Dispatch. How is Star? Did her pain meds kick in?"

"She's on my lap right now, but what happened?"

"Star saved your life, Gary. Another hour on the canyon floor and you wouldn't have made it. A couple driving west saw Star sitting by a road exit. They made a U-turn and came back to pick her up and try to find her owner, but she wouldn't let them near. She kept running back up the road. They know Rita and Lou—phoned them in case the dog escaped from their shelter. Rita phoned me. I thought it must be Star since you hadn't shown up at their house."

"I couldn't find the blue house."

"You missed the exit and drove too far east. I drove out and followed Star to the twisted guardrail. Other deputies and the paramedics brought you up the canyon wall, and I took Star to an emergency vet. She has puncture wounds on her hind leg."

"How did she get into the house?"

"I brought her over late yesterday morning. I thought you'd be home by then. She ran into the backyard and then into the house through your pet door. She wouldn't come out."

"She stayed quiet for a long time after I got home."

"Probably because of the meds. I have more for you to give her. I'll stop by later."

Pale pink, like Estelle's camisole, the morning sky held few and only the brightest stars. Gary sat in his patio chair, and Star sat in Estelle's. "I'm sorry I called you 'Burger' for so long, just my way of reminding Estelle how clever I was the night I got her attention at Star Burger." Star glanced at Gary in between licking her paws and sniffing the bandage on her leg.

"Years after we got married, Estelle told me she already knew my name before the night I introduced myself at Star Burger. She had told her mother she wished the shy boy at school would ask her to the prom. Imagine that—she wanted me to ask her out. I was the luckiest boy and later, the luckiest man." Gary reached over and pulled Star onto his lap. He had tried to keep Estelle near to him by holding her camisole. Estelle liked her camisole, but she didn't love it. She loved Star.

"Star, I promise to take good care of you."

Thank you, Gary. Estelle's brown eyes always twinkled when she thanked him, even for a simple favor.

Acknowledgments

I THANK OPEN BOOKS and editors, David Ross and Kelly Huddleston, for their belief in my stories and for following through with expertise and dedicated effort to bring *Pretty Chrysanthemum and Other Stories* to readers. I thank writing critique group members Hillary Tiefer, Lynn Deal, Amber Lewis, Anne Conway, Rosebud Kirwin-Alvord, Natalie Hirt, Mary Zvonek, and Kathleen Compton for their support. I also thank beta readers Shannon Cullen, Sue Gilman, June McCabe, and Gwen Slater. I thank Sidra Quinn for facilitating a supportive writing community where I first dipped my toe into sharing with others words I had strung together.